1/07　　$\dfrac{2x}{3-07}$　　　　　　　　　　CR

DIRTY MAGIC

Also by Carol Hughes

Jack Black and the Ship of Thieves

DIRTY MAGIC

CAROL HUGHES

RANDOM HOUSE New York

Copyright © 2006 by Carol Hughes
Jacket and map illustrations copyright © 2006 by Jon Foster

Published in the United States by Random House Children's Books,
a division of Random House, Inc., New York.

RANDOM HOUSE and colophon are registered trademarks
of Random House, Inc.

www.randomhouse.com/kids

Educators and librarians, for a variety of teaching tools, visit us at
www.randomhouse.com/teachers

Library of Congress Cataloging-in-Publication Data
Hughes, Carol.
Dirty magic / by Carol Hughes. — 1st ed.
p. cm.
SUMMARY: After his little sister Hannah becomes mortally ill, ten-year-old
Joe follows a shadowy figure to the war-torn land of Asphodel, a mysterious
and dangerous world of dying children, where he entrusts himself to a
devious blind guide, faces ruthless killing machines, and discovers a
shocking truth about himself.
ISBN-13: 978-0-375-83187-4 (trade) — ISBN-13: 978-0-375-93187-1 (lib. bdg.) —
ISBN-13: 978-0-375-83188-1 (pbk.)
ISBN-10: 0-375-83187-8 (trade) — ISBN-10: 0-375-93187-2 (lib. bdg.) —
ISBN-10: 0-375-83188-6 (pbk.)
[1. Brothers and sisters—Fiction. 2. Death—Fiction. 3. Secrets—Fiction.
4. Inventions—Fiction. 5. Fantasy.] I. Title.
PZ7.H873116Di 2006 [Fic]—dc22 2004010087

Printed in the United States of America

10 9 8 7 6 5 4 3 2 1

First Edition

For John, Faith, and Shane.
Without you I would have no stories to tell.

Contents

DIRTY MAGIC

CHAPTER 1

Hannah

Joe pulled the thin blanket over his shoulders, but the damp from the ground seeped into his bones. He was tired of sleeping outside in the rain. He'd be happy when he'd found his sister and could leave this horrid place and go home.

He stared up at the gray sky and watched the rain fall toward him. Would it never stop? He felt as though he had been searching forever. He should have kept count of the days from the beginning. He ought to have made a record of some kind, but he'd had nothing to write on, and even if he had, the rain would have soaked it through. The rain destroyed everything here. Buildings, bridges, the city wall. The rain was even wearing away his hope, the hope that he would ever find his sister.

He pressed his head back against the cold rock. *Hannah!* he thought. That's where this had all started. Ever since Hannah had been born, everything had always been about her.

Hannah was Joe's little sister. His only sister. There were six years and two months between them. She'd often been sick when she was a baby, and even now his parents still fussed over her and spoiled her rotten.

Hannah drove Joe round the bend. She would nag him to play with her, to let her borrow his toys, his comics, his pen, and then when he let her, she would leave whatever it was out in the garden or lose it completely. But if Joe kicked up a fuss, he was always the one who got into trouble, because, as his parents always reminded him, Hannah was only four and he was ten, and ten was plenty old enough to know better.

Earlier that year Joe had gotten a loft bed for his birthday, and it had been super cool until Hannah started begging for one, too. And guess what? His parents got her one exactly like his. Just like that. It wasn't fair.

Then one day, right at the beginning of the summer holidays, everything changed forever.

The day was so hot you could make a dent in the sidewalks with the heel of your shoe. The heat had given Joe a headache. By suppertime the pain was so bad it felt as though someone was driving red-hot needles into the back of his eyes.

His mom had sent him to sit quietly on the sofa and had told Hannah not to bother him. Hannah disappeared for a while and was suspiciously quiet. When Joe saw what she'd been up to, he lost it. She'd taken one of his magazines, one of his special *Monster Machine* magazines, the ones that he collected, the ones that cost two weeks' allowance each, the ones he kept in a neat pile on the highest, most-unreachable-by-annoying-little-sisters shelf in his room. And she had scribbled all over the cover with a red wax crayon.

"What have you done?" Joe cried. Hannah clutched the magazine to her chest and tried to make a run for it, but Joe snatched it away from her. His head pounded.

"No!" he yelled when he saw how much damage she'd done to the cover. It was his favorite issue. The one with the photograph of an AMAX 647 giant bucket-wheel excavator on the cover. Red crayon now obliterated the X and the numbers on the huge machine's gantry.

"Why do I have to put up with this?" he shouted. "It's ruined! Why are you so stupid?"

Hannah leaned against him and, licking her fingers, tried to wipe off the crayon.

"See, Joe, it'll come off. Look, it's smudging." Hannah was smearing the crayon about, making it worse.

"No! Get off!" cried Joe, pushing her away. He was shaking with anger, and the pain in his head was unbearable. "You ruin everything!" he shouted as loud as he could.

Hannah's face crumpled, then she started to wail. Joe didn't care.

"I wish I was an only child!" he yelled. "Just me! No you! No Hannah! Do you get it? I wish you'd go away and never come back! I wish you were dead!"

Suddenly his father was pulling him up the stairs so fast that the hall passed by in a blur. Joe was in his bedroom almost before he knew what was happening.

"You never ever talk to your sister that way!" said his father in a dangerously quiet voice. Joe opened his mouth to give his side of the story, but his father cut him off. "I don't care what she's done," he said. "This is only a stupid magazine. People matter more than things. She's your sister and you only have one—remember that." He flung the magazine on the floor and shut the door with a bang.

Joe grabbed the magazine and climbed up onto his bed. He buried his face in the pillow and screamed as hard as he could. He sat up and would have tried to smooth out the cover of the ruined magazine, but sitting up made his headache worse. He fell back against the pillow.

Joe stared up at the models he'd arranged on the highest shelf above the bed. Each one had taken him hours to build and glue and paint. There were models of machines, of tanks, of cranes, and of cars, and he'd put them up there so Hannah's thieving little hands couldn't reach them. He'd even laid traps so he'd know if she'd been messing with them. The traps were simple. He'd strategically placed soldiers among the models; if any of them had been moved, he'd know. He stared up at the soldiers. They didn't really go with the models. They were old-fashioned ones that he'd picked up at a church sale. His dad had said that their uniforms and helmets made them look as though they were from the First World War.

Joe felt cold even though the evening sun was streaming through his bedroom window. He pulled the comforter over him, but it didn't help. He lay very still and closed his eyes, and even though it was hours before his bedtime, he fell asleep.

Joe dreamed he was running first down a dark, rain-soaked alley that twisted this way and that and then across a dark, windswept plain. He didn't know where he was running or why, only that he couldn't stop. His heart was racing, its thump, thump, thump resounding loudly in his ears.

Then he tripped and fell against marshy ground. He

was cold. A harsh wind blew the rain at a bitter angle. Low clouds rushed across the sky toward monstrous black mountains. In the distance a line of trucks was crossing the barren landscape.

Joe could hear someone crying, whimpering. It sounded like Hannah.

"Hannah?" he cried. "Hannah!" But the wind snatched the words out of his mouth and the clouds closed in around him. His own voice echoed to him through the mist. "Go away and never come back," it whined. "I wish you were DEAD!"

"No!" shouted Joe. "I didn't mean that!" He woke with a start.

It was dark, almost pitch black, and at first Joe didn't know where he was. He reached out and felt the rail around his bed. It was all right. He'd just been dreaming. He was safe in his own bed. Joe kicked off the comforter and sat up. His headache had gone, but he was still cold. The air in his room felt icy, as though the summer that had barely begun was already over.

He needed to go to the bathroom, so he swung his legs off the bed and climbed down the ladder. He put his feet on the floor but instantly snatched them up. The carpet felt damp and slightly soft like firm, cold mud. He tried again. This time it was dry and soft. He must have still been dreaming the first time.

It was dark in the hall, too, and that was strange. His mother usually kept a night-light on because Hannah was afraid of the dark. Joe tried the main light switch. Nothing happened. *The bulb must have gone,* he thought.

It was then that he noticed a strange gray light that bloomed in the hall, then faded. It was like the flickering glow from a television, and it was coming from the bathroom. Cautiously he pushed the bathroom door open.

"Mom?" Joe whispered. "Dad?"

The gray light bloomed again and Joe caught his breath. The bathroom had gone. In its place was the vast, rain-swept plain from his dream. Above him was the gray sky with its dark, rushing clouds. Joe shivered and stared down at his bare feet. He was standing on mud.

Standing alone on the plain was a single loft bed, its covers blowing wildly in the wind. Joe could hear the crying again, a pitiful, high-pitched whimpering sound, like a dog having a bad dream. It was coming from the bed. "Hannah?" Joe said. "Is that you?" He could see the little hump of her body lying curled up beneath the covers.

"MOM? DAD?" Joe shouted, turning on the spot in the hope that the walls of his house would reappear.

Then he heard the sound of a car's engine starting

up. He turned back to the bed, and to his horror saw an army jeep driving away at breakneck speed.

"Hannah?" Joe cried. "Hannah!" He ran to the bed, raced up the ladder, and pulled back the comforter.

"HANNAH!" he shouted.

But the bed was empty. Hannah was gone.

CHAPTER 2

Dawn

Joe opened his eyes and found that he was in his own bed, in his own room. It was still dark, but the familiar glow from the night-light in the hall reassured Joe that he was home. His dreams had just been dreams, nothing more than that. *Hannah's fine*, he thought. *She's probably still fast asleep.*

Joe stretched luxuriously and took a deep breath. Already the air smelled of summer. His headache from the night before had gone. He rolled over to look at his alarm clock, and that was when he noticed the red lights flashing across the ceiling.

Joe leapt out of bed, slid down the ladder, and rushed to the window. An ambulance stood in the drive with its rear doors open. Two men were lifting a stretcher into the back. Joe's mom climbed in and sat beside it.

Hannah, thought Joe. Hannah was sick again.

Joe pressed his forehead against the windowpane. The red lights flashing over the grass made everything seem unreal. Joe felt cold. Hannah was being taken away. Maybe she wouldn't come back. Wasn't that what he'd wished for? He shuddered as he stared down at the blanket-bundled form on the stretcher.

A small blue car drove up the cul-de-sac and lurched up onto the sidewalk outside the house. Joe watched his gran as she heaved herself out of the car and rushed through the garden toward the kitchen door.

"Still asleep, upstairs," Joe heard his father say. "I've called Dr. Ben. He'll meet us at the hospital."

Joe's father climbed into the back of the ambulance, the doors were shut, and a moment later the ambulance pulled out of the driveway.

The alarm clock showed it was only ten past four, far too early to be up, but Joe didn't feel tired. He shoved his feet into his sneakers, hooking a finger into the back of each heel and pulling hard so he wouldn't have to untie the laces. Then he looked down at his clothes and realized that he'd slept in them. It didn't matter; he didn't feel like changing.

Joe found his gran sitting at the kitchen table nursing a cup of tea. She looked lost in a world of her own, murmuring "Oh, dear" and "Poor little pet" under her breath. Joe said hello and gently kissed her on the cheek, then wandered out into the garden.

The sun was not yet up, but the sky was already growing light. There wasn't a cloud to be seen: it looked as though it was going to be another scorching hot day. Joe crouched on the doorstep and hugged his knees. Images from his dream flooded into his mind. Hannah's illness couldn't have anything to do with his dream, could it? *That was just a dream*, he assured himself.

"Joe?" someone called softly. "You Joe Brooks?"

Joe lifted his head and saw a strange-looking girl crouching by the garden wall. She was as pale as dust and was staring at him intently.

The girl glanced at a piece of paper in her hand, then back at him. "Are you Joe Brooks?"

Joe nodded and watched as she folded the piece of paper and stuffed it in her pocket. She must have been about his age or a little older, but she looked out of place. She was filthy and her clothes were vaguely military. Grubby puttees were bandaged about her legs, and a large canvas satchel was slung across her body like a mailman's sack. Her dark hair was long and straggly and hung in her eyes, and it was dripping wet, as though she'd been caught in the rain.

Rain, thought Joe. It had been raining in his dream. He stood up to get a better look at her, but as he did, the girl crouched lower and gestured for him to do the same. Something—a bee? a wasp?—shot past his left ear.

Joe ducked, then feeling a little silly, he looked back toward the wall. The girl had gone.

CHAPTER 3

Katherine

Joe sat on the kitchen step and watched the sun rise. Soon the walls of the whitewashed garage were dazzling and the flowers blazing garishly. Joe had almost convinced himself that the gray girl had just been a figment of his imagination when the hairs on the back of his neck began to prickle. He looked up. She was standing by the fishpond, where the sun's reflection on the water was blindingly bright. Joe shaded his eyes so he could see her more clearly.

"Who are you? What do you want?" he called.

The girl said nothing. She looked left, then right, then leapt over the pond and ran through the flower bed toward him.

Joe gaped at the flower bed, expecting to see the

wreckage of crushed flowers, but the flowers weren't there anymore. Instead he saw her boots splashing through muddy puddles. Anxiously he looked around. The garden was disappearing. Through the faint image of the garage roof he could see distant mountains, their peaks buried in low clouds—it was the landscape he had seen in his dream!

"You'll have to be quick," said the girl, carefully pronouncing each word, as though Joe didn't understand English. She was crouching right in front of him now, and her large gray eyes were serious. "Are you ready? There's no time to lose."

"Ready for what?" Joe asked. "What are you talking about?"

"Shush . . . ," warned the girl. "Don't ask so many questions. There are spies everywhere. Someone could be listening, even out here in no-man's-land." She glanced over her shoulder. "I'm your fetcher; name's Katherine. I have to take you to your guide. I had a hard enough time getting you one, and he won't wait forever. Come on!"

"No," Joe said. This was too weird. The real world didn't suddenly disappear. He had to get away. He scrambled to his feet and ran toward the transparent image of the garden gate.

"There isn't time for this," the girl called impatiently.

"You must come now; you'll need a guide." But when Joe looked back, Katherine and the gray landscape were vanishing and the world was becoming solid again. Joe ran down the street, his heart thumping in his ears. *Dad will be able to make sense of this,* he thought, heading to his father's office, but then he remembered his parents had gone with Hannah. Joe stopped at the corner of his street. He looked back at his house, then turned and hurried off toward the hospital.

Joe took a shortcut across his school's summer-empty playing field, not caring if Mr. Bertwhistle, the groundskeeper, saw him and told him off. At the far side he climbed over the school fence, then ran all the way to the high street. He turned left at the traffic lights and up the road that led to Victoria Hospital, then paused at the next set of lights, waiting for them to turn to green. As he waited, the street in front of him rippled like a heat haze, and the girl appeared beside him.

"If you don't come soon, it will be too late," she whispered urgently. "Don't you get it? They can only keep the lines open for so long."

The traffic lights changed. Ignoring Katherine's plea, Joe ran across the street.

He reached the hospital and slipped in through the swinging doors. Once inside, he followed the signs to the children's ward.

When he got there he caught sight of his parents through the windows of the intensive-care unit. Joe stood very close to the glass and peered in, barely daring to breathe. His mom and dad were sitting together on one side of the hospital bed. Joe could see the small hump of Hannah's body beneath the yellow knitted blanket. He couldn't see her face. She wasn't moving. One thin arm lay on top of the covers. At the head of the bed was a monitor and a tower of electronic machines that made rhythmic beeping noises. Beside the bed a nurse was fixing clear plastic bags to an IV stand.

Joe rested his forehead against the window. He couldn't shake the feeling that this was all his fault. He wanted to bang on the window and shout "I DIDN'T MEAN IT!" but a sudden memory from his dream stopped him. He remembered how, just before he'd looked into Hannah's empty bed, he'd seen the army jeep setting off across the plain. Had someone come and taken Hannah in the night? Joe stared at Hannah in the hospital bed. What if her body was still here, but something else, something more important, was gone?

What then? What was to be done if that was the case? Joe screwed his eyes tightly shut, and the answer came to him.

"Boo," said Katherine. Joe opened his eyes. He wasn't surprised to find her standing beside him. "There's nothing you can do here," she said, nodding toward the ICU. "You've got to come with me."

Joe nodded. "It's the only way to find Hannah, isn't it?"

"Hannah?" asked Katherine.

"My sister," said Joe, pointing to the hospital bed.

Katherine looked where he was pointing. "That's right," she said, grabbing his wrist and pulling him along with her. "You've got to come and find your sister! Now hurry up and be ready for anything. We've a fog to help us, but the other side will have seen me leave and they'll be waiting."

Katherine pulled him along the hospital corridor, darting swiftly between the shadowy forms of the nurses and orderlies, crouching low as she ran.

"Here we go!" she cried. The hospital vanished and the gray, rainy world became solid and real. Again something buzzed by, close to his head.

Katherine yanked on his arm and pulled him to the ground.

"You have to keep low," she insisted. Joe lay in the thick, churned mud that was pocked with puddles. The rain smacked against his back. All around him the landscape vanished into a thick fog. Katherine checked a small, rusty compass, then pointed the way forward and began to crawl. Joe followed her and soon could make out a long fence of coiled barbed wire disappearing into the invisible distance. Joe sniffed. There was a strong tang in the air, like rusty metal.

"Where are we?" Joe asked.

"No-man's-land," replied Katherine. "We've got to get past that wire. Then we'll be back on our own side, that's if we don't get shot first."

As though on cue, a burst of machine-gun fire blasted out above the wind.

"Oh, no," Katherine groaned. "They've definitely seen us. Stay down and crawl on your belly quick as you can." Katherine moved quickly, pulling herself forward with her elbows.

"Why are they shooting at us?" stammered Joe as the bullets cracked overhead.

"Not at *us*. At you. That's what them over there do to charges like you. They'd rather you were shot than helped by us."

When they reached the snaking coils of barbed wire, Katherine pulled the thick woolen scarf from her neck and wrapped it around her hand. She grunted as she grasped the wire and pulled it up a foot or so above the ground. "Get through quick," she puffed. "It's hard to hold this up for long."

Joe rolled beneath the wire. Katherine followed. On the other side there was still more mud to crawl across.

"Don't stop!" cried Katherine as she grabbed the sleeve of Joe's T-shirt and pulled. Joe heard the stitching rip. "You don't want to get killed here."

Joe didn't want to get killed anywhere. He crawled faster. Soon he heard voices ahead and saw dark figures running toward them. A moment later strong hands took hold of his arms and dragged him through the mud. He looked up and saw that two soldiers had hold of him.

"There's no end to these charges," grumbled one. "This is the fifth one come through this morning."

"It's good work we're doing, Henry," snapped the other. "And don't you forget it."

"What good work? What am I doing here?" asked Joe, his voice rising in panic.

"Eh up, this un's a talker," laughed the first man.

"Hurry up!" yelled a voice ahead of them. "Pick up the pace."

A few moments later Joe found himself sliding feet-first into a deep, muddy trench. He landed in a heap at the bottom. Katherine landed more elegantly beside him. Suddenly the air was filled with the sound of gunfire. Joe tipped his head back. Above him, soldiers were standing on ladders that leaned against the mud walls and firing over the front edge of the trench.

"Bit of a rough ride, lad!" shouted a burly soldier as

he pulled Joe to his feet. He turned to help Katherine up. "Good job, young lady," he said. "Well done. You got him here safe and sound."

Katherine gave the soldier a nod, then began to search in her bag for something.

The soldier tapped Joe on the shoulder. "Don't be scared," he said cheerfully. "Be glad you've come through on the right side. If they didn't kill you first, them over there would have set you to work making their horrible war machines. Now buck up—you've a long journey ahead of you, but it'll all be worth it in the end."

"Can you sign him in please, sir?" asked Katherine, pulling a pen and a piece of paper from her satchel and offering them to the soldier.

The soldier shook his head. "Can't! Sorry! New regulations. You've to get the gunner sergeant to do that. He's over there."

"Wait here!" Katherine instructed Joe. He nodded and watched as she hurried over to another soldier, who was tending to a wounded man.

Joe dug his fingernails into his palms, but he didn't wake up. He blinked at the trench, at the soldiers, at the smoky gray sky. Then came a bang so loud he thought his eardrums would burst. The blast threw him against the mud wall. When he opened his eyes Joe saw that three of the men on the ladders had fallen and now lay still on the floor of the trench. Joe was still staring at them when Katherine suddenly ran over and pushed him to the ground.

"Get down!" she yelled as another shell exploded nearby.

Great clumps of sodden earth rained down on them. One hit Joe on the back of the head and pushed his face into the ground. The cold mud oozed against his cheek.

This was definitely not a dream.

Katherine was on her feet in a flash. She grabbed the back of his mud-soaked T-shirt and pulled him up.

"We can go now that I've got you signed in," she said, waving the sodden piece of paper at him. Katherine turned and ran. "I've got to get you to your guide; then my job's done. Come on!" They ran through the narrow trench, keeping as low as they could.

The trench was crowded with soldiers hurrying in the opposite direction. Katherine darted through them. Joe found it difficult to keep up.

Suddenly something stung him so hard on the back of his left hand that he fell against the wall. Joe lifted his hand and stared at it. It was bleeding—a strange pinprick pattern of tiny red dots was rising through his skin and a nasty yellow bruise had begun to form.

Katherine ran back and grabbed Joe's hand, then dropped it.

"You're lucky that bullet didn't hit you in the head," she tutted unsympathetically.

"Bullet?" mouthed Joe.

"Here, hold this against your hand," Katherine said, handing him a dirty gray cloth. "It'll stop bleeding in a minute." Then she set off again, turning down an opening on her left. This trench was much quieter, almost deserted, and the sound of gunfire seemed a long way away.

Open doorways supported by rough wooden beams stood at intervals along the trench. Joe peered into one as he passed and saw a dark room hollowed out of the earth. Inside, soldiers lay on bunks. Some men were staring out at the mist, while others slept curled up on their cramped beds.

Katherine and Joe hadn't gone very far when a runner emerged from the mist ahead of them. He looked to be about the same age as Katherine, and he was wearing the same uniform. Katherine slowed down.

"Who's he?" whispered Joe.

"That's Martin," she replied. "He's just another fetcher." Katherine nodded at the runner as he drew near. Martin nodded back. Then a wide grin broke across his face.

"Hey, Kat! What's up?" he asked. "Hasn't your brother made you his 'prentice yet?"

"Don't call me Kat," replied Katherine.

"You on a job, Kat?"

"I'm taking this one to meet his guide," she said, jutting her chin higher. Joe noticed there was an edge to her voice. "What about you?"

"Just signed mine over." Martin's grin got wider. He passed them, then turned and began to trot backward, saluting as he went. "Hope you've got a guide, Kat. Long wait if you haven't. I was lucky one came free while I was waiting. See you later!"

Katherine stood and watched him as he bolted into the rain. She narrowed her eyes.

"No!" she whispered to herself. "He wouldn't dare!"

"Wouldn't dare what?" asked Joe.

"He'd better bloody not have done!" she cried as she set off running again. Joe did his best to keep up.

Farther along the trench a group of raggedy kids was sitting against the mud wall. From the way they were dressed, Joe guessed they were all fetchers like Katherine. Those in the main group were playing cards, while off to the side a couple of girls were doing cat's cradle with a gnarled piece of string. Beyond the fetchers, a line of ten miserable-looking children stood waiting against the wall. Joe stared at them while he paused to catch his breath. Some of them stared back warily. There were six boys and four girls, and while some looked very young, a couple of them might have been eleven or even older. Some were wearing pajamas, others wore everyday clothes, but all of them were splattered with mud and their hair was wet from the rain. One boy was wearing his school uniform—blazer, cap, and all. They reminded Joe of kids at school lined up against the playground wall, waiting to be given the signal to go somewhere.

The fetchers were loud and rowdy. They laughed and chatted and argued. Then one of them noticed Katherine and Joe and with a snicker nudged his neighbor.

"Look what's crawled out of the cheese," he hooted. The others all turned to look.

"You're too late, Kat," scoffed one.

"Martin took him," laughed another.

"Kat let her guide slip away," singsonged two girls in unison.

Katherine threw them a killing look but said nothing. She ducked into an open doorway, where a rough, hand-painted sign tacked above the door read CAFÉ ROYALE. Joe started to follow her in, but before he could enter, a stool flew through the doorway and smashed against the far wall of the trench. Katherine emerged a moment later. Her eyes were blazing.

"Harris!" she growled. "That low-bellied, scum-ridden, scurvy, worm-infested lout! Martin must have bribed him. Guides are supposed to be honorable, aren't they? Honorable, HAH!"

"You can always file a complaint," a small fetcher said with a snicker. "It'll only take a month or two to sort out the paperwork!"

The color rose scarlet in Katherine's cheeks. She turned on Joe and jabbed his arm with her finger. "This is your fault," she said. "If you'd come right away like you were supposed to, this wouldn't have happened."

The other fetchers laughed. "Nice, Kat, blame your charge. Great idea!"

Katherine said nothing. She grabbed Joe's arm and pulled him toward the door of the Café Royale.

"Oi!" shouted a fetcher by the wall. "You'll get in trouble if you're caught in there."

"Nobody asked for your opinion," replied Katherine, dropping Joe's arm. "If Harris doesn't give a fig for the rules, then why should I?" And with that she disappeared through the doorway.

CHAPTER 4

Secrets

Joe ducked his head and followed Katherine into the Café Royale. It was dark and he could only just make out Katherine moving about. The room smelled of wet earth, mildew, and boiled vegetables.

As his eyes became accustomed to the gloom, he could make out a rough, rectangular table with benches along the sides. Dirty tin plates and crumpled yellow sheets of newspaper lay scattered on top of it. Joe picked up one page and read the headline. "Meridian Counterattack Defeated. Elysian Forces Strong." Another one read, "Ambassador Secures Safe Passage for Mercy Mission."

Joe put down the newspaper and glanced around the room. Beyond the table, large metal canisters and boxes

were stacked against the wall. Squeezed between them
was a small gas stove where a pan of something sim-
mered above a low circle of blue flame. In the right-hand
corner was a tatty old armchair piled with rags. On the
floor around it were file boxes overflowing with papers.
One box had tipped over and spilled its contents across
the mud floor. Katherine was crouched down, rifling
through the mud-smeared sheets and muttering to herself.

"Where am I?" asked Joe.

"Guides' canteen," replied Katherine without looking up.

Joe sat down at the table and frowned at the wound
on the back of his hand. It wasn't bleeding anymore, but
it still hurt a lot.

"Nothing useful here!" said Katherine, dropping the
papers back on the floor and standing up. "I thought
Harris might have dropped his part of the contract.
Doesn't matter. I've got my copy, and I'll get him somehow."

Joe kept quiet and watched as she sat down at the
table and lifted one of the dirty plates.

"Still warm," she said. "Harris can't have been gone
more than an hour." She dropped the metal plate. It rattled noisily against the wood. Joe put out his hand and
stopped it.

"Where am I?" Joe asked again.

"I already told you," she replied, mimicking Joe's measured tone. "You're in the guides' canteen."

"No," said Joe carefully. He was trying not to let his fear show. "Where am I? What is this place?"

"You're safe. That's all you need to know," she said sharply. "And as soon as we find you a guide, you'll be on your way."

"On my way where?"

Katherine shrugged. "It's your guide's job to tell you that."

"He'll take me to find my sister?"

"Yeah, something like that," she said.

"Why do I need a guide?" Joe asked.

"Because you do. It's the rules. Charges have to have a guide. They always have had, at least ever since the war began."

"When was that?"

"You don't half ask a lot of questions, do you," she said, looking directly at him. Joe hadn't noticed before, but her eyes were an almost violet shade of gray. She took a deep breath. Joe waited. "The war between the Elysians and the Meridians started a long time ago, and you don't need to know any more than that. Get it?"

Katherine turned away from him, and lifting her foot onto the bench beside her, she began to fix her puttee where it had unraveled. As she bent to her task, her long dark hair fell across her face and dripped onto her knee. Katherine shook her head to flick it back, but it wasn't long enough to stay. Her face was so pale that it seemed to glow in the dim light.

"And you're Elysian, right?" Joe asked, stumbling slightly over the unfamiliar name.

Katherine snorted and shot him a look. "Obviously! You'd be either dead or a slave if they'd got to you first."

"Who are those kids out there?" he asked, pointing at the children outside, huddling in the rain.

Katherine groaned. "They're charges. They'll have been fetched through the same way as you, 'cept they probably came when they were told and didn't keep anyone waiting."

Joe ignored her scathing tone. "Why are they standing there in the rain?" he asked. "Why don't they come inside?"

"'Cause they're not allowed to. Only guides is allowed to come in here. Fetchers and their charges is supposed to wait out there."

"Wait for what?"

Katherine rolled her eyes. "For their fetchers to hand 'em over to a guide. Look, it's very simple. No one can go beyond these trenches without a guide and, of course, the proper paperwork. You know, permits and the like."

Katherine jutted her chin toward the line of children. "It's almost impossible to find a guide these days. They've probably been waiting there for weeks. The rules say I'm supposed to keep you out there, too, but what's the point in getting wet to obey rules? I'm sick of rules."

Joe fell silent. He was cold and wet. He didn't want to be here in this miserable dark mud cave or standing out there in the rain. What he really wanted was to be safe and warm at home.

"Listen," Katherine said in a gentler voice, "things'll get better once we find you a guide, honest. He'll be able to tell you everything you need to know. Mind you"— she pulled a frayed cloth purse out of her pocket and turned it upside down over the table, but nothing fell out—"I don't know how I'm supposed to pay another one." She glanced at the long line of charges out in the rain. "Or even how I'm supposed to find you one now. That lot out there are all set to pounce on the next one that shows up, and who knows whe—" Katherine sat bolt upright.

"What?" Joe began.

"Hush!" Katherine whispered. Joe listened, too, but he couldn't hear anything. He noticed that all the fetchers outside were quiet as well. Then he heard it—the distant roar of an engine. It sounded like a motorbike.

Katherine leapt around to his side of the table.

"Quick!" she hissed. "There's no time to run. Get down in the shadows. Hide."

She grabbed her satchel, then pushed Joe against the darkest part of the wall.

"What's happening?" he asked.

"Shut up! Get down and keep quiet."

Through the open door Joe could see all the fetchers scarpering in every direction, dragging their charges after them, but they'd left it too late.

The motorcycle shot past the canteen door, throwing a flurry of black mud into the room. It splattered noisily across the table. From the cover of the shadows Joe saw the rider grab one of the fleeing charges by the scruff of his neck and hoist him onto the bike. The motorcyclist swerved to a stop, and another shower of mud shot into the air. The fetcher of the boy who'd been caught stopped and, panic-faced, ran up to the motorcycle.

"He's bona fide, he is," whined the fetcher, waving a soggy sheet of paper. "I've got his papers here. He's not a spy or nothing."

The rider ignored him and dismounted, pulling off his goggles and helmet to reveal a well-scrubbed pink face and short red hair that stuck up straight from his scalp.

"Who is he?" whispered Joe as quietly as possible.

"Secret police," replied Katherine. "We're done for if he finds us in here."

Joe stared through the door and watched as the policeman set a small battered box like a miniature suitcase on the ground and opened it. Inside the box were dials and wires. The policeman took out a pair of wooden headphones and fitted them over his ears, then unraveled a long wire with a metal device like a bulldog clip attached to one end. He rolled back the boy's sleeve and examined his arm.

"He doesn't know anything, sir," said the fetcher. "He's been with me the whole time. Never talked to no one." The policeman said nothing, just shoved the fetcher away; then, turning back to the boy, he pinched the muscle on the underside of the boy's arm and attached the clip to it. He turned back to the machine in the case and twisted one of the dials to the right. The machine began to click like a Geiger counter, slowly at first, then faster and faster as the policeman turned the dial farther round.

Suddenly the boy began to scream. Katherine winced and turned her face away. Joe felt sick.

"What's he doing to him?" he asked in a whisper.

"Quiet, unless you want him to do it to you, too," warned Katherine.

The policeman turned the machine off and pulled

the clip from the boy's arm. The boy dropped to the ground. His fetcher knelt beside him.

The policeman made a note in a small black note-book, then quickly packed away the headphones and the wires and closed the case. He put his leather helmet back on his head, snapped his goggles over his eyes, and had just replaced his gloves when the boy's fetcher muttered something unintelligible under his breath. The police-man lashed out and pulled the fetcher to his feet.

"What about you, then?" he growled. "You hiding anything we should know about?"

The fetcher shook visibly. "No" was all he could manage to say. The policeman pushed him away. He kicked up the stand of his motorbike and was about to mount when his eye fell on the canteen door. For one awful moment it seemed to Joe that the policeman could see him cowering there in the shadows. Joe felt Katherine's hand grip his arm as the policeman coughed and spat, then set his motorbike back on its stand.

They couldn't see his face as he stood in the doorway blocking out the daylight. He unbuttoned his pocket and brought out a large metal flashlight that glinted in the gloom. With a loud click the policeman switched it on.

Katherine gripped Joe's arm even tighter and slid far-ther down the wall, taking him with her. "Keep your head down and don't make a sound," she whispered in the faintest voice.

The policeman shone his flashlight into the shadows. Joe watched petrified as the yellow circle of light slid over the walls. It passed over the stove, the cupboards, the shelves, and the old winged armchair piled high with rags and blankets, but the secret policeman never brought the beam low enough to reveal where they were hiding.

The policeman grunted and turned to go. As he did, a rat ran out from the shadows and shot across the table. Joe hated rats more than anything, and he let out a tiny gasp of horror. Instantly the flashlight swiveled back into the room. The circle of light swooped over the walls and stopped on the table. The policeman stepped down into the canteen, dipping his head low so he didn't bang it on the lintel. A plate clattered on the table. The light shot toward the sound and revealed the rat, which had found a plate of food and was eating noisily. The policeman narrowed his eyes and spat again. Then, after a moment or two, he left.

"What was that machine?" Joe asked when the sound of the motorbike's engine had faded. "What did he do to that boy?"

"Random search," answered Katherine.

"Search? What's he searching for?"

Katherine shrugged. "Meridian spies," she said. "The police use those machines to listen for secrets. They say they can listen right into a person's most secret thoughts. Right into their hearts. "

"That's horrible," said Joe with a shudder.

Joe got up and went to the doorway. Out in the rain the fetchers and their charges who had run away were beginning to return. They gathered round the boy who'd been hurt. He was coming to.

Joe stared at him. He looked pale and frightened. What sort of secrets had the policeman been after?

"You were lucky he didn't see you," Katherine said, sitting down at the table.

Joe moved away from the door and joined her. "Are those secret police on your side or the enemy's?" he asked.

His fetcher let out a short laugh. "Our side, of course, but that doesn't mean you want to get caught by one of them. There're a lot of them about, especially these days, so you'd better be careful."

Katherine drummed her fingers on the table. Joe sat opposite her and peered out at the trench. Beyond the group of fetchers, it was deserted.

"Couldn't you take me to wherever I'm supposed to go?"

Katherine shook her head.

"We'd never make it past the first sentry," she said. "But my brother Tom's a guide, one of the best. If he was here now, he'd take us both, you as his charge and me as his apprentice."

"Oh, so you want your precious Tom, do you?" said a harsh voice from somewhere in the shadows. Katherine and Joe both jumped about three feet in the air.

"I heard your brother had stopped guiding. I heard he's a *Skulker* now," the speaker said. Then he laughed until the laugh was overtaken by a bone-rattling cough.

CHAPTER 5

Spider

Katherine lit the oil lamp on the table with a match and lifted the lamp high above her head. Then Joe saw him, the old man huddled among the bundle of rags in the ratty old armchair.

"Do you know my brother?" asked Katherine, taking a tentative step toward the chair. "Have you seen him?"

"Seen him?" the old man wheezed. "Me, child? I haven't *seen* anyone for a very long time." The old man opened his eyes wide. Joe gasped. The old man's eyes had no pupils, no irises; they were as white all over as two hard-boiled eggs, with only the faintest tinge of milky blue to show where the irises should have been. The old man sat back in the chair and started to chuckle again.

"Spider Carey," groaned Katherine, putting the lamp back on the table. "I thought you were dead."

"Dead? Heh-heh! Not me!" said the old man. "I don't die easy." He slapped the arms of the chair and, drawing his scrawny knees up to his chest, laughed so hard that his oversize boots clonked against the front of the armchair. Again the laugh changed to a cough that rattled up from deep within the old man's wool-bound chest. Joe grabbed a cup of water from the table and hurried to the chair. He held the cup to the old man's lips and watched as the gnarled fingers clamped around the bowl of the cup.

Katherine didn't move. "He won't thank you for it," she said. "Spider Carey'd never thank nobody for nothing."

The old man drank greedily, not minding if the water spilled over his wretched clothes. Joe saw that Spider's uniform was even more filthy and tattered than Katherine's. Great tears and gashes in the fabric were held together with uneven stitches, many of which were frayed and broken. The old man's white hair was as wild and as thick as a lion's mane, and his chin was covered in patchy gray stubble that ranged untidily to his throat.

When he'd drunk his fill, Spider pushed Joe and the cup away and wiped his mouth on his sleeve. Katherine was right. There were no thank-yous. The old man stood up and dabbed his sightless, teary eyes with the edge of his cuff. Still laughing to himself, he shuffled to the counter and, feeling his way, located a jug and poured water from it into a large kettle. He set the kettle on the table while with his sleeves pulled down over his hands he lifted the stewpan off the one-ringed stove and set the kettle in its place.

It was easy to see why the old man was called Spider. With his long, rangy arms and legs, he looked like one. He was so tall and skinny that his head with its shock of white hair seemed too big for his thin body.

Spider put three mugs on the table and, opening a jam jar, spooned something that looked like coffee into them.

"Dead? Me, dead?" He chuckled and shook his head. The glass jar jiggled up and down in his hand, and tiny brown granules scattered over the table. "Who told you that?"

"I hear things. Even fetchers hear things."

"Do they now. Well, I'm far from dead," bragged Spider, puffing out his chest. "It would take more to kill Spider Carey than having been set up and left to die six years ago by an overambitious, no more than a kidling guide like your precious brother Tom."

Katherine's eyes blazed at the old man.

"My brother never set anyone up!" she cried. Her

hand flew inside her jacket, and to Joe's astonishment she pulled out a pistol and pointed it at the old man. But Spider was too quick for her, lashing out with one of his long arms and snatching the gun away. He spun it around his thumb and pointed it back in her direction. For a man with two good eyes it would have been quite a feat. For a blind man it was incredible.

"How . . . ?" gasped Joe.

"Could have heard her going for it three streets away," said Spider as he set the pistol on the table beside him. "She knows as well as anyone that fetchers ain't allowed to carry these. Consider I've done you a favor and be grateful."

"I've got to have protection," Katherine snarled.

"Then get yourself apprenticed to someone who knows how to handle things," Spider snapped back. He paused, and his expression softened. "Now, will you join me for some dandelion-root tea? Or shall I throw you out to wait in the rain where fetchers is supposed to wait?"

Katherine glared at Spider, then sat back down on the bench.

"Good. Now," said Spider, "let's talk about what's to be done with your charge. You," he continued, jerking his chin in Joe's direction, "what's your name?"

"Joe," answered Joe. "But I'm not—"

"He's none of your business!" warned Katherine, cutting Joe off. Spider ignored her.

"Joe, eh? Well, Joe, am I right in thinking you need a guide?" asked Spider, leaning forward.

"Leave him alone!" said Katherine, thumping her fist on the table so hard that the tin plates bounced and rattled.

"Fine." The smile dropped from Spider Carey's mouth. He tipped the dried-root tea from two of the cups back into the jar and screwed the top back on. "I was only offering to help, but if that's your fetcher's attitude, I don't have to put myself out. I see she's just as much an ingrate as her brother."

The kettle boiled, and as Spider turned away, Katherine seized her chance and snatched up the gun.

"You shouldn't say things like that about my brother," she said as she cocked the pistol.

Spider turned around slowly and raised his fists level with his head. "My, you're quick." A broad smile spread over his face as he opened his fingers. Three bullets were tucked behind each of his thumbs. "But you won't have much luck without these."

Katherine groaned and dropped the pistol on the table. Joe was amazed. Somehow the old man had managed to empty the gun and palm the bullets right in front of them.

Spider picked up the gun and put the bullets back in it. Then he stuck the gun in his belt and patted it. He grinned at Katherine and, reaching back, lifted the whistling kettle off the stove.

"Course, you could wait for her brother to come and guide you," he said. "Only trouble is, you'd be waiting here forever. He's in the Druckee with some of his Skulker mates probably waiting to be executed—which, if you ask me, is no more than they deserve."

"You're lying!" gasped Katherine.

"If I am, it's a lie that everyone is telling," said Spider as he held up his mug and carefully filled it to just beneath the brim. "Your friend Harris read it out to me from one of these papers here." He set the mug down on the table without spilling a drop.

Katherine frantically smoothed out the sheets of paper and scanned the headlines. On the third sheet she found a small article in the bottom left-hand corner. She read it out loud.

"Skulker Suspects Incarcerated in Druckee. Our sources in the Long City sent word Monday that the arrest and imprisonment of five men is believed to be connected to recent Skulker activity in the south of the city. The men have been named as Phillip Jones, Gregory Kendal, Thomas Heany . . ." Katherine stopped reading. "Tom!" she cried. She read on. "They are to be charged with attempting to sabotage the arches and are to be held in the Druckee until further notice."

Katherine looked at the date at the top of the page. "This paper is weeks old. Wait a minute," she said, looking at the name of the paper. "The *Quarain Herald.*" She paused and a strange expression crossed her face. "Do you think this is true?" she asked Spider.

Spider sucked in his breath and shrugged. "Could be," he said. "You're a canny one to question the veracity of what you read in that rag, but it could be true. Everyone knows the papers keep their readers on their toes by slipping in a bit of truth every now and again. I hope it's true, and with luck your brother and his mates will get what they deserve in there."

"Shut up!" croaked Katherine, dropping her head in her hands and clutching at her hair. "The Druckee?" she mumbled. "That explains why no one's heard from him in so long."

"Maybe he'll escape," Joe suggested.

Katherine's head shot up. "Don't be daft," she said sharply, making Joe wish he'd kept his mouth shut. "The Druckee's a fortress. No one's ever escaped from there."

"Oh, yes they have," said Spider quietly. "Once, a long time ago, when the Heathermen were imprisoned there—"

But Katherine wasn't listening. "I've got to get him

out," she muttered. Then her face fell. "But I can't even get to Quarain, never mind all the way to the Long City."

Spider nodded slowly to himself and raised his mug as though toasting her. "You've got to think positively, young lady," he said. "Remember there's more than one way to skin a cat."

Katherine groaned.

Joe, meanwhile, was eyeing the steaming cup and licking his dirt-encrusted lips. He longed to swill the taste of mud from his mouth.

"Please. Could I have—?" he began.

"No," snapped Katherine. "You don't want anything from him. He'd only make you pay for it one way or another."

Spider ignored her and smiled at Joe. "Cup of tea? 'Course you can, lad," he said. Spider spooned granules into one of the empty mugs, poured in hot water, gave it a stir, then put the mug down in front of Joe. Joe wrapped his hands around the cracked mug. It was good to feel warmth in his fingers again. He sipped the dandelion tea. It was hot, sweet, and disgusting. And it tasted of mud.

Spider Carey chuckled and sat down at the end of the table.

"You'll feel like new after a few sips of that," he said.

"Which is a good thing. You'll need all your strength for the long wait. You could be here for months."

Katherine half rose from her seat, but Spider reached out and laid his hand on her shoulder. "Sit down and listen," he growled, pushing her back down. "There's been no guides through here except Harris and me. And Harris was never much of a guide, more of a weasel. I'm surprised you trusted him."

"I'd sooner trust him than you any day," she said haughtily. She leaned across the table and tugged at Joe's cuff.

"Listen, Joe," she whispered, in a voice that was meant to make it clear to Spider that this was private business. "I'm going to have to leave you here and try to find another guide."

"Wait," said Joe. He nodded at Spider. "Why can't he be my guide?"

"Not a chance," retorted Katherine. "Besides, who needs a blind guide?"

Spider pointed a long, bony finger at Katherine. "Blind or not, I know my way around this land better than anyone. I may be the only guide left worth taking on."

"I'll risk it," said Joe.

"It's not up to you," replied Katherine. "It's my reputation on the line." She stood up to leave, but an extra-loud explosion on the front lines rocked the canteen and sent her sprawling to the floor. Clumps of dirt dropped from the ceiling and scattered over the room.

When the dust cleared, Katherine stood and shook the soil from her hair.

"The enemy's getting closer," she said. "Come on, we'll set up farther off. I can't leave you here."

Spider's hand darted across the table and grabbed Joe's wrist. The old man's grip was surprisingly strong.

"Stay a moment. Drink your tea."

Katherine stared hard at the old man's face, then nodded slowly. "Oh, I get it," she said with a smug smile. "You think he's your ticket to Quarain, don't you? Well, you can just forget it. Use someone else's charge. Come on, Joe, we're leaving. And consider yourself lucky. He's probably already worked out how much he'd get if he sold you to the Meridians."

"Sold me?" asked Joe, bewildered.

Spider shook his head. "Take no notice of her, lad," he said, loosening his grip and patting Joe's arm. He dipped a finger in his tea, then drew a large, jagged shape on the table. "This land," he said, tracing a finger around the map he'd drawn, "this once beautiful land is called . . . well, there are many names for it . . . Archester, Eralon Isle, Saquila, Asphodel."

Katherine snorted. "No one calls it those names anymore."

"I do," snapped Spider.

"Stop it!" said Joe, getting frustrated with the pair of them.

"Right, yes. Where was I?" Spider sniffed. "Let me think. What's the best way to say this? Well, I suppose you could say this land is a place between heaven and earth . . ."

A place between heaven and earth? Joe didn't like the sound of this.

"Or a different way to say it would be, it's a place between life and death."

Joe felt cold to his bones.

"What I'm trying to say," Spider went on, "is that this is a place where charges, those children out there, come to wait."

Joe stared through the rain at the other charges. Did that mean that somewhere in his own world those kids were lying in hospital beds, just like his sister?

"They just wait here until they get better, right?" asked Joe slowly. "They do get better? They do go home?"

"Some do," replied Spider. "Some don't."

Whatever else Spider had to say on this subject Joe didn't hear it, because quite suddenly there was a horrible, overwhelming, rushing noise in his ears that drowned out all other sounds. The room seemed very small and close and hot. Hannah could die. It shouldn't have been a shock, it wasn't as though he hadn't thought about it himself, but hearing it like that from Spider . . .

"Noooo!" Joe groaned, shaking his head. He had to find her and take her home, and he had to do it soon. If only the room would stop spinning. He tried to get up, but Katherine grabbed his shoulders and shook him.

"Joe!" she shouted. "Are you all right? Can you hear me?" She turned to Spider. "This is all your fault," she snapped as she grabbed a cup. She sniffed the water jug before she poured. Then, still shaking her head at Spider, she offered the cup to Joe.

"Well, he ought to know the truth," responded Spider, a little put out.

Joe tried to get to his feet. "I can't stay here," he said in a croaky voice. "I can't just do nothing. I've got to find Hannah."

"Yes, and you will," said Katherine in a soothing tone. "But you can't help anyone when you're in a panic. Here, drink this. You'll feel better in a minute or two."

"Who's Hannah?" Spider asked, raising his eyebrows.

"His sister," replied Katherine. "Joe's come here to find her and take her home."

"Of course," answered Spider. He sat down on a stool at the end of the table and tapped a finger against his lips. "If you've come to find your sister, then I suppose you'll be wanting to get a move on."

"Yes," said Joe, sipping the water.

"Well then," Spider said in a jolly tone, "I'm afraid you won't be able to go in search of her until your fetcher finds you a guide." A sly smile broke over Spider's face. "And you are looking at one of the best guides you'll ever see." Spider leaned back on his stool and puffed out his chest until the rough stitching in his jacket strained.

"Then why will none of them employ you?" Joe tilted his chin at the fetchers waiting outside.

"Clever boy." Spider grinned. "Maybe I've been waiting for the right charge to come along. Ha! No, to be honest with you, none of them thinks I could be a decent guide without my eyes."

"Could you?"

"Yes!"

"No," muttered Katherine under her breath.

Spider ignored her. "Even without my eyes I'm a better guide than most."

Katherine stood up and slammed her fists down on the table. "Forget it!" she growled.

"Your loss," retorted Spider. "Or rather, Joe's."

After that, they both fell silent. Joe stared at the filthy tabletop. He had to find Hannah. And if that meant having Spider as his guide, then that would suit him fine. Katherine was just being stubborn. Perhaps there was another way to get her to sign those papers.

Joe touched Spider on the arm. "If you were to guide me, would our journey take us anywhere near that prison her brother's in?"

Spider nodded slowly. "It would." He felt the table-top to where the map he had drawn with tea had not yet dried up. He traced his finger around the edge of it; then, wetting his finger again, he drew an X near the middle. "Your journey would take you here, across the Machine Lands, to the Long City. The Druckee lies at the city's heart."

"Right, the Druckee." Joe took a deep breath and turned to Katherine. "You said before that you wanted to rescue your brother, didn't you?"

Katherine narrowed her eyes. "What are you getting at?"

"What if Spider agrees to make you his apprentice, but only until you rescue your brother? What if he promises to release you then, so your brother can take you on? That would work, wouldn't it?"

Katherine didn't say anything. Joe turned to Spider. "And you'll get what you want. You'll be able to get out of here if you have me as your charge."

Spider sat back and tapped the tips of his fingers

together. "It might just work," he said. "Good thinking, Joe. Well, miss, what price are you offering? He seems like a sound lad. If the money's right, I'll take him."

"Here, you can have all my money," said Katherine, chucking her empty purse on the table. Spider found it, felt its weight, then pushed it away. He didn't say anything.

"Thought that'd shut you up," Katherine went on.

"Tell you what I'll do," said Spider. "I'll postpone payment. You can owe me the fee. It's a loan, mind, not a gift."

Katherine scowled at him. "Mean as a widow's grave," she said. "How am I supposed to get you your money?"

"Harris owes you, doesn't he? You'll find him at Camp Quarain."

"Come on," urged Joe. "Don't you want to rescue your brother? Just say yes, and we can go."

Katherine's eyes flickered to the fetchers and their charges hunkered down against the trench wall in the driving rain. Then she looked from Joe to Spider and back again.

"All right," she said, walloping her satchel down on the table and opening the flap. "But this is only till my brother takes me on."

A broad smile spread across Spider's face. "Right!" he said, rubbing his hands together. "Let's get this rubbish done with, and we can be on our way."

Katherine pulled several sheets of paper out of her satchel. All the pages were covered in finely printed type. She set them in a pile on one side of the table, then began to sign each sheet. When it was Spider's turn to sign she tried to guide his hand to the right place, but Spider pulled away.

"You're to be my apprentice, not my mollycoddler." He walked the fingers of his free hand along the edge of the paper, counting down the inches to where he was to sign. With a florid motion he scrawled his signature in big, curling letters.

Joe had never seen so much paperwork. "Why do you have to sign so many things?" he asked.

Katherine answered without looking up. "It's so the clerks in Camp Quarain can keep track of everyone that comes through. They need the statistics."

"If you ask me, it's just a way of making things more complicated than they need to be," muttered Spider as he touched the pen to his tongue to moisten the nib.

When they'd finished, Katherine handed one sheet to Spider, which he folded and slotted into his pocket. Then he searched in the shadows for a moment and pulled out a cardboard tube. He shook the tube, and a roll of paper dropped to the table. Spider unfurled it, and Joe saw it was a certificate of some sort. Spider held it flat.

"I've taken no apprentice for over six years. Your brother was the last one." He broke off and rubbed his nose. "Swore I'd never take another after what he did, but I suppose needs must." He turned to the open door. "One of you fetchers in here now!" he shouted.

There was much grumbling and shoving. Then one reluctant girl was thrust out of the line and sent stumbling into the dark canteen.

"Witness this," said Spider, carefully writing Katherine's name on the dotted line, then signing his own at the bottom. The fetcher looked from Spider to Katherine.

"You're going to be his apprentice?" she blurted in disbelief. She clapped her hand over her mouth to stifle her giggles. She signed where Spider pointed, then burst out laughing as she ran from the room.

Spider fumbled in his pocket and brought out a tattered piece of cloth. He handed it to Katherine. "Pin this over your fetcher's badge," he said. "Wear it with pride. You're my apprentice now, albeit temporarily."

Katherine took the scrap of rag and pinned it on her arm.

"Hadn't you better get your things together?" asked Katherine.

Spider Carey heaved a backpack out of the shadows and dropped it on the bench.

"Lesson number one, a good guide is always ready," he said. "Now put that on while I get us some grub to take."

Katherine looped her satchel across her body, then lifted the heavy pack onto her shoulders. It was so big that it reached higher than her ears and lower than her backside. Spider opened a large drawer beside the stove and began to cut thick bricks of what looked like a gray, damp cake.

"What's that?" asked Joe, wrinkling his nose.

"Oatmeal," Spider said with a grin. "I've always got this ready and waiting, just in case." He loaded up one of the pockets of the pack with the solid blocks of oatmeal, then fastened it up.

"Ready then?" asked Spider as he pushed a fat, well-worn notebook into the inside pocket of his ragged coat. He reached into the shadows and took a long staff from where it rested in the corner. Grubby bandages were wrapped tightly around the length of it so not an inch of wood was showing.

Spider fastened his scarf around his neck and pulled

a wide-brimmed hat down low on his head. "Have faith," he said as he passed Joe. "You're already on your way, which is a lot more than most of them have managed in all the time they've been here." Then he bowed low so he could pass under the lintel.

CHAPTER 6

North as Far as Northridge

As Katherine emerged from the doorway, the other fetchers began to jeer.

"Look at Spider Carey's new apprentice!" cried one.

"Glad to see you got the best guide as your teacher," sniggered another.

Katherine turned as she walked and smiled at the jeering fetchers. "Don't worry, any of you," she said in a singsong voice. "I'm sure there'll be another guide through here in, oh, maybe three or four months."

"Keep up!" snapped Spider through the rain.

It was fully dark when they reached the gate that led onto the main road. The sentry's eyes narrowed to tiny slits as they approached. He lifted his rifle and aimed it right at Katherine's head.

"Halt! No fetchers beyond the gate," he snapped.

"She's not a fetcher. She's my apprentice," said Spider.

"Show me her papers."

Spider produced them. The guard unfurled the roll, glanced at the name, then laughed a short, disbelieving laugh. "Carey?" he scoffed. "Thought you were dead!"

He tried to lift the rim of Spider's hat with the point of his bayonet, but Spider swatted the gun away.

"Hey!" the guard protested, but suddenly he looked small, as though Spider had snatched away all his authority.

"On you go, then," muttered the guard, handing back the papers and standing to the side.

At the bus stop a single bulb on a pole lit the rain around it. There was no one else waiting. Katherine set the pack on the ground and crouched against it. Spider waited, still and silent, at the edge of the circle of light.

After a little while, they heard the sound of an engine in the distance, and shortly after that a set of headlights could be seen on the road. Katherine got to her feet as a yellow lighted bus, crowded with soldiers, rumbled over the bumpy road toward them. She pulled the backpack onto her shoulder and stood in the light with her arm out ready to flag down the bus.

"Not this one," growled Spider.

Katherine stepped out of the light and dumped the

pack on the ground. The bus drove past and disappeared in the dark rain.

"Why didn't we get on that?" asked Katherine. "There was plenty of room."

"Enjoy meeting secret policemen, do you? " replied Spider. "Those buses are crawling with them. You've already had one close call today. Don't sulk. Our ride'll be here soon. I can already hear it coming."

Katherine pulled a face. "He's not bothered by secret policemen," she whispered to Joe. "He's just too mean to pay our fare. That's the truth of it. I bet there's no ride coming."

But she was wrong. A few moments later Spider stepped into the light and stuck out his thumb. Joe jumped as a truck roared out of the darkness.

It was an ancient, rusty vehicle with thin slits for windows and a sort of iron skirt riveted to the front for protection. Its brakes screeched as it came to a halt. The metal shutters on the driver's window snapped open and a burly man with a shock of black hair scowled down at them.

"What do you want?" asked the driver.

"I thought this was Bishop's run," said Spider.

"He disappeared two months ago or more," said the driver. "They say he went over, but who knows? Anyway, it's my run now."

"Got room for three travelers?" asked Spider.

"Where to?"

"Quarain."

The man shook his head. "This route's changed. I'm going to Northridge tonight. I'll take you as far as the old road if you like."

"That'll do," replied Spider.

Spider moved along the truck, feeling his way with the flat of his hand. He grabbed on to the siding and heaved himself up the wooden slats.

The back of the truck was high and narrow and deep. Damp sacks full of peat bricks leaned against the cab, and empty ones were strewn around the floor. Once Spider had climbed up, he held out a hand for Joe, then one for Katherine. They were barely in when Spider banged on the roof of the cab and the truck lurched forward. Joe fell in a sprawling heap against the bags, and Katherine fell on top of him.

"You'd think you were blind, the fuss you're making," Spider laughed. Steadying himself with a firm grip on the rail, he carefully lowered himself onto the truck bed. He draped several empty sacks over his legs, wrapped one around his shoulders, and settled down to sleep.

Katherine disentangled herself from the backpack, then sat down, exhausted. Joe leaned against the sacks and hugged his knees to his chest. The rich smell of the peat enveloped him. It was warm and fragrant and strangely pleasant.

"Where are we going?" he shouted to Spider above the noise of the engine.

Spider leaned forward quickly. "If you want to ask questions, you'd better learn to keep your voice down," he growled. "You never know who might be listening."

Joe nodded, then leaned in closer and whispered, "Where are we going?"

"To a place called Camp Quarain. We'll need papers if we're to get you on your way," replied Spider. He rubbed the bristles on his chin and pulled his hat low. "You'd best sleep," he said. "You'll need your strength for the walk tomorrow."

Joe sat back against the sacks. The damp from the peat seeped through his clothes while the rain soaked him from above. He was cold but not tired. Katherine wasn't sleeping either. She was sitting by the right-hand wall of the truck in the lee of the cab, with her face pressed up against a gap in the wooden slats. Joe stumbled across the truck bed and sat beside her. He put his eyes to the gap and stared out. There wasn't much to see. No houses or anything, just a dark land stretching out to the horizon where it met a slightly lighter sky.

He looked up. There were no stars in the sky, or if there were, they were somewhere high above the clouds.

The rain fell on his upturned face. He wiped it away with his hand. Something strange was happening. Far ahead of the truck, far beyond the yellow pools of light from the headlights, the sky grew brighter for a few moments, then faded to dark gray again. Joe watched, fascinated. When the gray light bloomed in the distance, it revealed the silhouetted crest of a dark and jagged range of mountains.

"I know this place," he said suddenly. "I mean, I've seen it before."

"What?" asked Katherine.

"I dreamed about it." Joe shook his head, trying to piece together the strange images. "It was raining like it is now, and I saw that light and the mountains and that's when I saw someone take my sis— OW!"

Spider's shoe clocked Joe on the back of the head. Joe spun around to find Spider's face only inches from his own. He would have said something, but Spider lifted a finger to his lips, then pointed toward the front of the truck. Joe looked forward through the slats and saw the driver's face reflected in the rusted wing mirror.

Katherine looked rattled. "What makes you think he was listening?" she asked in a low voice.

"Look." Spider pointed at a little panel on the back of the cab. Joe hadn't noticed it before, but it was a small rectangle of perforated metal that was painted the same color as the rest of the cab. In an almost imperceptible whisper Spider said, "He'll easily have heard you through that. Out here, you'd best assume that everyone is a spy and keep your mouth shut. The less any of us gets noticed, the safer we'll all be. Now do what I said and get some sleep."

CHAPTER 7

The Road to Quarain

"Wake up!" said Katherine, pushing Joe's shoulder. "We're getting out."

"Mommm, I'm not asleep," he mumbled, then with a start he sat up. It wasn't his mom waking him. He wasn't at home. He was outside somewhere, and it was raining. The strong, earthy smell of freshly cut peat was everywhere. He looked up and saw Katherine standing over him.

"Hurry up," she said impatiently as she climbed over the rail and dropped down the other side.

Joe wiped the rain from his face and blearily stood up. "I'm coming," he replied with a yawn. It was cold, and it was early. Day was just dawning. The clouds had lifted a little, and Joe could see the mountains to the north, brooding and ominous in the distance.

Joe climbed over the rail, jumped down, and landed heavily on the ground. His shoes squelched in the mud. As he walked over to where Spider was waiting, he could sense the truck driver watching him. Spider took Joe by the shoulders and turned him away from the truck.

"Stand over there, lad," said Spider under his breath. "And don't look back. We don't want him to get a good look at your face, do we? Don't want anyone taking too much of an interest in our little party."

Spider turned and in a louder voice hailed the driver. "Thanks much!" he called.

Spider prodded his staff into the mud and set off along the empty road. "Come along, miss," he shouted back over his shoulder. "Get that pack on your back and look sharp!"

Joe helped Katherine hoist the backpack onto her shoulders. "Thanks," she mumbled. "Let's get out of here. That driver gives me the creeps."

The truck had stayed where it was, its engine idling.

As Katherine and Joe set off after Spider, the truck's engine revved noisily before the vehicle rumbled off in the direction it had been heading.

Katherine turned and watched it go. "Crazy, isn't it?"

she said. "We have to go all the way to Quarain just so we can get the passes to come back here, then travel north to where that truck is going today."

"What's Quarain like?" asked Joe.

Katherine's eyes lit up. "Tom says it's an amazing place, crowded beyond belief, but amazing. It's the operations center for all of Elysian-controlled territory. You have to go there to get passes and chits and information. I can't wait to see it."

After trudging along the muddy road for some time, they reached a small wood. The road split in two here, one branch skirting along the outer edge of the forest, the other leading straight into the thick of it. The first road was broad, and from the number of tire ruts, well used. The second was narrow, with weeds growing along the middle of it.

Spider took the second road.

Katherine groaned and hitched up the pack. "It's all right for him to pick the more difficult way," she muttered under her breath. "He doesn't have to carry this lot. His shoulders aren't fit to break."

"Them that don't want to carry their master's goods don't have to be apprentices," called Spider over his shoulder.

Katherine pulled a face.

"I'll take it for a while if you want," offered Joe.

"No," replied Katherine, jutting her chin out. "I can manage."

It was quiet in the wood. The trees were black and bare. Only a few dead leaves remained caught like rubbish in the uppermost branches. But even without leaves the trees formed a dense enough canopy overhead to hold off some of the rain.

Before long the ground began to slope upward and the path all but disappeared in the tangled undergrowth. Spider scrambled up between the trees, and though he couldn't see the branches, he dodged them without any difficulty, while Joe and Katherine slipped and struggled on the muddy slope. Before long their knees were slick with muck and their faces smeared with sweat.

At last they reached the upper edge of the forest. Joe stretched and arched his back. He hadn't thought he'd be grateful to be out in the rain again, but he was. There were no more trees ahead of them now, just a wide, empty hill that sloped slowly toward the sky.

Katherine yanked Spider's pack off her shoulders and dropped it to the ground. With a cry of relief she flung herself down full-length on the soft, wet grass and lay staring up at the rain.

Spider walked on a little way and stopped. The rain ran in silver streams off the brim of his hat as he prodded the ground with his staff. He sniffed the air, then pointed to the top of the slope.

"Not so far now," he said. "You'll see Quarain from there."

Joe peered at the slope. It didn't look too far to the top, but it was hard to tell. The only landmark was a tiny bush about halfway up. Joe stared at it and realized with astonishment that it wasn't a bush at all—it was a full-size tree. It would take them hours to get to the top.

Spider let them rest, but only for a moment. Soon he was striding up the slope, once more admonishing them for lagging behind. Joe hurried to keep up, but Katherine, slowed by the weight of the pack, trudged far behind.

As they neared the top of the slope, Spider crouched down as though he didn't want to be seen from the other side. Joe was amazed that Spider could tell how close to the top they were.

"The ground's less marshy the higher up we get," said Spider. "And the wind blows fresher."

"But how did you know what I was going to ask?" asked Joe.

Spider smiled. "I could tell from the way your steps slowed. Sometimes if you listen carefully to the way somebody walks, you can tell what's on their mind."

Joe stopped in his tracks and stared at the old man. Spider laughed and kept on walking.

At the top of the slope, Spider dropped to his knees and, keeping low, crawled the last few yards. He motioned for Joe to do the same. Joe got to the ground, and as he did he looked back at Katherine. She was a long way behind. Joe started to get up to go back and help her, but Spider caught his sleeve.

"Leave her be, lad," he said. "If she wants to sulk, she can do it on her own."

Joe peered over the crest of the hill but could see nothing. The town or the camp or whatever it was was hidden from view by a dense fog.

"Is my sister in Camp Quarain?" asked Joe.

Spider sniffed. "No," he said. "Quarain's barely the beginning of your journey. You've a long way to go. We've got to get you to the Long City. That sharp-tongued miss never let me finish telling you where you are, did she." Spider cocked his head and listened. "She'll be a while yet." He pulled the tattered notebook from his inside pocket and removed the band that held it together. He felt carefully through the pages, and when he reached a map, Spider turned the book toward Joe.

He felt along the picture and pointed to a row of triangular peaks. "Here in the north are the black mountains. You saw them last night. They are sheer and treacherous, made of a magnetic rock that sends a compass haywire. You don't want to go there."

"Why not?"

"Some say the mountains are full of sounds that will drive a man mad; some say they're full of dragons. Who knows? No one who's gone there has ever come back to tell us.

"Now this here," he continued, pointing to a dark strip just below the mountains, "this is the Long Lake. It's a wide lake, and as you'll guess from the name, it's long, too. But it's not deep. It's no more than four feet at its deepest point—used to be perfect for swimming in, did that lake. But since the war began, chemicals and toxins have leached out of the mountains. It's very beautiful, I've heard. In daylight it shines with colors not seen anywhere but there."

"But it's poisonous?" asked Joe.

"Deadly," replied Spider. "The toxins corrode everything. Nothing, not even the sturdiest ironclad ship, could cross those waters. Its hull would disintegrate in seconds."

Spider moved his finger farther down the map. "Northridge is where you'll be going once you get the right paperwork. From there, if we get a place on the convoy, you'll travel along this road, through the Machine Lands, to the Long City. Elysia tries to get all the charges there so they are ready when it's their time to pass through."

Joe felt his mouth go dry. "Pass through?" he croaked.

Spider nodded. "Back to your world or on to another."

Joe could hardly make himself ask. "H-h-how do they . . . ?"

Spider ran his finger over the page and stopped at the very center of the city. Just above his nail was a symbol that looked like a castle, and inside it were three tiny arches.

"That's the way the charges go when it's time," said Spider. "These are the arches. When a charge is ready, they'll pass through one of these and on to wherever they have to go. That's why we move them into the Long City as soon as we can. They need to be near those arches when it's their time."

Spider turned and called to Katherine. "Keep your head down as you get to the top," he warned. "We've a thick fog, but it could clear at any moment."

Katherine staggered up the last few yards of the slope, then threw her pack and herself down on the ground beside Joe.

"Do we get to rest now?" she panted.

"You've got till dark" was Spider's response. "I think it's best not to waltz into Quarain in daylight. There's plenty of folk I'd rather didn't see me too easily."

"Owe them money, do you?" said Katherine snidely

as she lay back on the grass and closed her eyes. Spider sniffed but didn't respond.

Joe peered at the map. "Where are we now?" he asked.

Spider pointed to a mark in the southeastern quarter. "We're here, just outside Camp Quarain. East of this line belongs to us and the rest to the enemy. Except here." He pointed to the peninsula at the bottom of the map. "This is no-man's-land, where you came through."

"So the enemy controls the Long City and all this land around it," said Joe, running his finger over the map.

Spider sniffed but said nothing. It was Katherine who answered.

"Not yet they don't," she said. "Though it's not from want of trying. The city's been under siege since the war began twenty years ago, but so far the walls have kept the city safe."

"Twenty years?" Joe was aghast. "You mean you've been fighting for twenty years?"

"We've tried to end it peacefully," Katherine said. "Hundreds of times. Elysia sends her ambassador to talk to them about peace, but the reports that come back are always the same. Merid will not hear of a truce. She wants complete surrender and nothing else."

"In the old days," said Spider quietly, "before the war, when the Heathermen were still—"

"Hush!" warned Katherine. She dropped her voice to a whisper. "You could be hung just for saying their name, and I could be hung just for hearing it. Don't talk about them. They were traitors. They started the war. They—"

"That story makes no sense," retorted Spider. "Never has."

Katherine looked shocked. "Then my brother was right," she said in disgust. "You are a Meridian sympathizer."

"In times of war," replied Spider, "I sympathize with everyone."

Katherine humphed and flung herself back against the grass.

"What started it?" Joe asked Spider. "The war—how did it begin?"

"Before the war," Spider began, "this land was ruled, or you could say looked after, by three sisters. Three noble sisters. Elysia was the eldest, then came Merid and then Cornell. They looked after this island and all the children who passed through. We called them children then, not charges. They weren't called charges till the war began.

"The sisters were our rulers, but they were more than that. They were all born teachers. Even if you were a grown-up, they made you want to listen and keep on learning and never stop. And their stories . . . oh, my." Spider let out a little laugh. "Their stories could go on for days and days. And they were the most amazing stories you had ever heard." Spider laughed again, but a moment later his smile vanished and he hung his head. "Then," he said, "then Cornell died and everything changed."

"Why don't you tell the truth?" asked Katherine. "Everyone knows Cornell was murdered by Merid with the help of her"—she lowered her voice—"Heathe . . . mmumph."

Spider clamped his hand across her mouth. "Everyone *assumes* that that's what happened, Miss Clever Clogs," he said. "Nobody, NOBODY knows for sure."

Katherine squealed and fiercely wriggled free. "Yes they do," she retaliated. Katherine's gray eyes were bright, and the words gushed out of her like water through a broken dam. "Everyone knows Merid was jealous of her sisters and paid her Heathermen to kill Cornell. They would have killed Elysia, too, but Elysia found out about the plot and fled to the east of the island with those loyal to her.

"And then Merid sent her terrible war machines across the plain to destroy us, to wipe the Elysians out, but even those weapons couldn't get rid of us. We were smaller in number, but we fought back."

Katherine curled her hands into tight fists. "We dug the trenches to keep the machines out, and we set up systems so we could keep on bringing the charges through to our side and not let them be captured or killed by the others. You know it's true," she said, glaring at Spider. "You can't deny it. The Heathermen were the most evil, disloyal, and treacherous vermin ever to draw breath. They started this long and horrible and wasteful war! They ruined everything."

Katherine wiped away the hot tears that had, despite her best efforts, wet her cheeks. Spider was quiet for a while, staring sightlessly out into the rain, and when he spoke, his voice was soft and his words slow.

"There are many versions of this story," Spider began. "Katherine just told you one of the most popular. But just because it's popular doesn't mean it's true. Let's look at the facts for a moment."

Katherine made a noise as though she were about to interrupt, but Spider held up his hand. "You've had your turn. Now be fair. Let me have mine."

Katherine sat back, sulky but quiet.

Spider went on in a clear, gentle voice. "Katherine is right," he said. "Cornell, the youngest sister, was killed. She was the best loved of the three. But there was no rivalry. I still believe her sisters adored her as much as everyone else did. Neither of them would ever have wanted any harm to come to her.

"Cornell was clever. Cleverer than her sisters, cleverer than all of the professors and inventors in the Long City. They all looked to her for advice on their theories and ideas and inventions. You see, that's who the Heathermen were. They were simply a society of professors and inventors. They were called the Heathermen because outside the city on the great plain, where the broom and the heather grew, was where they would take long walks to discuss new inventions or just to think through some new project.

"The Heathermen spent nearly all their time thinking up new inventions to entertain and amuse the children who were in their care. They did their best to make sure that the children weren't too homesick or unhappy." Spider paused and frowned. "People nowadays think the Heathermen were murderers and warmongers. Preposterous!" Spider's jaw twitched, then he shook his head. "But people will believe what they want to believe, and there's nothing I can do about that.

"Long before the war," he continued, "Cornell built a library in the Long City. It was constructed close to the arches, and when it was finished, three tall towers reached into the sky, each housing an incredible collection of books and manuscripts and models and artifacts. One of the professors worked out that it would take a hundred and fifty years to read just the first page of all the books in that library."

Spider lifted his scraggy chin and smiled at the darkening sky. "The library wasn't stuffy or fusty or stale. It was a vibrant place full of new ideas and innovations. From morning to night the corridors buzzed with debate and argument. It was an amazing, magical place. And even though there were hundreds—no, thousands— of extremely precious, even ancient books in there, the library was for everyone to use. It was always open. It was paradise.

"I have thought about this a great deal," said Spider. "Why would these learned men and women give up everything they held dear to destroy someone they loved and respected? Even if I could believe that Merid would turn against her sisters, it still makes no sense to me that the Heathermen would help her. No sense at all."

"That's all rubbish," Katherine declared, throwing her hands up in the air.

Spider instantly retaliated, and the argument between Katherine and Spider raged on. Joe stopped listening. The wound on his hand stung sharply. He'd have to be careful. He had to remember he could get hurt in this land. He didn't want to get killed in someone else's war, at least not before he'd found Hannah.

"I bet you're a spy," cried Katherine, "come up here to sell us off for secrets."

"You should put that imagination of yours to work in some more productive way," retorted Spider.

"I can't believe it," groaned Katherine. "I knew I shouldn't have signed Joe over to you. Where's it got us? Nowhere. Some soggy hillside in the middle of nowhere."

"If I haven't brought you to Quarain, then I haven't brought you anywhere at all."

"Quarain?" she scoffed. "Where?"

"There!" Spider pointed over the top of the hillside. Just at that moment, as though nature were responding to his command, the mists parted, and Katherine's face lit up.

"Quarain!" she gasped.

Perhaps no more than a quarter of a mile from where they lay, Joe saw a long, flat island in the middle of a muddy plain. Every inch of it was covered with a sprawling, unruly mass of makeshift tents and rickety buildings. Some seemed to hang off the edge of the island, built as they were on stilts that stuck out of the mud. From each shack or tent thin ribbons of smoke curled up into the air and joined the dark cloud that drifted away from the island.

To get there, they would have to climb down the hill and cross the plain. Joe cast his eye over it. The crossing didn't look too difficult. The wide expanses of rippled brown sand and darker strips of soft mud were splotched here and there with patches of coarse yellow grass. A dirt road wound like a drunken beetle's track across the sands. Here and there channels of silver water reflected the sky as they wound toward the faraway strip of gray-green sea at the edge of the world.

"Ah, Quarain," said Spider with a sigh. "I'd give my teeth to see that fine place once more."

Joe didn't see so much that was fine about it. It looked like a shambles to him.

"Sounds like there's a market on," said Spider.

"A market?" said Katherine in an awestruck voice. "My brother told me about those. He said they were amazing. Oh, and look, Joe, look at that big house up there. That belongs to Elysia. Isn't it lovely?"

Joe looked where she was pointing. A dilapidated mansion stood on the hill at the center of the island, rising high above the sea of tents. It was built of dark, almost black, stone and looked as though one part of it had split away and crumbled down the hill.

"Lovely," said Joe, not wanting to say what he really thought.

Somewhere beyond the thick banks of clouds the sun must have set, for the color of the sea was changing from green to slate gray, then to a deep, murky blue, and the clouds grew dark.

"Tide's about to turn," said Spider with a sniff. He got to his feet. "That won't give us much time. Come on, up you get, look sharp."

CHAPTER 8

The Market

Spider hurried down the hill with long, sure strides. Joe and Katherine kept up as best they could, but it was more difficult for them in the near dark than it was for Spider. Their eyes played tricks. His, though useless, were at least honest.

About halfway down Spider stopped and waited for them to catch up.

"We'll have to be especially careful in Quarain," he said as they joined him. "If that truck driver reported Joe, then they'll know we're coming. They'll be watching for us."

"That driver was going on to Northridge," Katherine protested. "We saw him go."

Spider shook his head. "He could easily have turned around. They make half their money reporting things they've overheard."

The old man loped down the remainder of the hill.

"We'll have to hurry!" shouted Spider when they reached the winding road to the camp. "The water's coming!"

Joe stared at the strip of sea beneath the horizon. Spider was right. The narrow line of water was growing wider at an alarming rate. Joe could already hear the roar of the waves.

"It's a riptide!" shouted Spider. "You'd better run if you don't want your journey to end before it's started!"

They ran. Spider in the lead, then Katherine, then Joe. The heavy pack on Katherine's back seemed to no longer bother her. Her feet flew along the mud road. Joe tried to keep up, but the sea was faster.

He soon felt the first shallow wave lap at the backs of his ankles. The next wave was up to his knees, and the next to his waist. Joe struggled against the powerful undertow. He knew if he fell, that would be it. Ahead, Spider and Katherine had already reached the steep bank.

"Spider!" cried Joe.

"Keep yelling, Joe!" shouted Spider. "I can't tell where you are if I can't hear you!"

"I'm here!" cried Joe. "HERE!"

Spider leaned out across the water and extended his staff toward Joe. Joe lurched forward and caught hold of it as the foaming waters closed over his head.

Joe held tight to the staff, and as he came up for air he noticed that the bandages that covered it had started to unravel and were floating around him in the water like tentacles. The wood was engraved with what looked like letters, but Joe had no time to look more closely. The next wave caught him by surprise as it swept him forward.

"NOW!" Spider shouted. Joe felt a mighty pull on the staff, and the next moment he found himself lying on the muddy slope, panting for breath.

"Nearly lost you then," said Spider. "Now get up there. We've got to get above the tide line or we'll all be goners. Come on."

The riptide chased them to the top of the slope, only letting them go as they crawled onto the rough road in front of the ramshackle, stilt-legged houses. Joe rolled onto his back and lay gasping for air. He turned his face and saw the water lapping at the road's edge. Moments before, the stilts beneath the houses had been visible. Now they were completely submerged.

Spider sat at the edge of the road and tended to the loose bandages on his staff. He unwound them partway, then he began to rewind them. Joe marveled at the methodical neatness of the blind man's work. The bandages were dirty and tatty, but Spider left no part of the staff uncovered. Joe peered at the wood, trying to see the markings he'd noticed, but Spider worked too quickly. When the staff was covered, Spider stood and held out his arm to help first Katherine, and then Joe, to their feet.

Joe could hear music and shouting. It was coming from the market that wound its way up the center of the island.

Spider tapped him on the shoulder. "You stay close to me. You too, Katherine. Now that the tide's in, we're stuck here till morning. We've a lot to do if we want to be off early. I don't want to waste any time looking for you if you get lost. Understand?"

Katherine pulled a face. "You've got to be joking," she scoffed. "Do you really think we'll be leaving tomorrow? It's impossible. How are you going to get his papers in such a short time? Tom told me it can take weeks just to get an interview!"

"I've got my ways," said Spider. "Are you coming? Or would you rather wait here and not see anything at all?"

"We're coming," replied Katherine, answering for both of them.

"Good," said Spider. "Now, Joe, take my arm. My feet

won't remember the camp as well as they do the sands. A lot will have changed since I was last here. Katherine, walk in front, but stay close, mind."

Spider tugged his hat down over his eyes and bowed his head. Joe took hold of his arm and was surprised by how much smaller and older Spider suddenly seemed. He now walked with a hobble and leaned more heavily on his bandaged staff.

As they squeezed past the parked buses and trucks, Joe noticed how ancient the vehicles were. Most of them were little more than wrecks that had been patched together, slabs of iron riveted over yawning rusty holes, skeins of wire holding ill-fitting doors in place.

They left the buses behind and climbed toward the market. The way was lit by tattered paper lanterns that swung on wires above the path. When they reached the first stalls they were swallowed up by the slow river of the shuffling crowd.

"Who are all these people?" asked Joe.

"Most everyone on Elysia's side of the island comes to Quarain on market day," replied Spider. "That's if they're allowed to travel. It's probably the only bit of fun any of them get these days. There's the farmers— they come to sell their wares, do a bit of trading, and catch up on the news. Soldiers—those who can get leave. Guides like me, who've come for papers and the like. Then there're the bureaucrats, the officials, the bloodsuckers, and the time-wasters. There're the lay-abouts and a whole bunch of charlatans and snake-oil sellers. There'll be spies, too. These days spying is a booming business."

"You probably know a lot about that, don't you," said Katherine. Spider deftly caught her ankle with the end of his staff, and she stumbled.

"Sorry," he said in a not very apologetic tone.

It was more like a carnival than a market—a place of music and wood smoke. The stalls were bathed in a golden light from the paper lamps. There were stalls with muddy root vegetables piled high on wooden boards. People picked through them while fat, ruddy-faced women stood hands on hips, watching to see that none of their wares accidentally slipped under coats or into pockets.

Baskets full of nuts and berries filled the smaller stalls, and pyramids of wormy apples stood hemmed in by narrow boxes of herbs. Crabs, their pincers wired together, wriggled in crates next to barrels full of stink-ing sardines and dried fish. Meat speared on long skewers smoked and spat across braziers full of red-hot coals, while butchers with sharp cleavers split bones and wrapped bloody chops in paper. Dogs waited and drooled, tongues lolling, beneath the tables.

Katherine stopped and turned to Joe. "Isn't it wonderful?" she said. Her eyes were glowing with excitement.

Spider banged his staff against her foot. "No time to stop and stare," he muttered. "There'll be a fork in the road up ahead. We'll be going to the left."

Katherine protested. "But the house is up to the right."

"It'll take too long to get through the crowd," replied Spider testily. "My way'll be quicker. Come on."

When the road split in two, they turned left as Spider had wanted. As Katherine had said, this road appeared to be taking them in the wrong direction. The market was less crowded along this path. The food stalls petered out and were replaced by stalls selling junk. String, wire, old nails, screws, misshapen pieces of rusted metal, hooves, cardboard scraps, driftwood, bent spoons, and broken scissors were laid out on greasy tarpaulins on the ground. At one stall they passed, a woman was haggling fiercely with the vendor over a coil of twisted wire.

Some stalls were piled high with greasy engine parts, ranging from the smallest nut to the largest blunt-toothed cog. Dislocated pistons, unattached valves, and glass-fronted gauges with broken dials were placed beside worn tires and broken windshields. Nothing, it seemed, was wasted. *This*, thought Joe, *must be why the trucks and buses looked so cobbled together. They're all made from scrap.*

Halfway up the hill, there was one stall that wasn't really a stall at all. It was more like a heap of junk spread over the ground. Four braziers burned, one at each corner of the stall, lighting the pile of enormous rusted rods, pistons, and wheels that were for sale. Three men stood deep in conversation at the far side.

Spider stopped and turned his ear in their direction.

"So he *didn't* go to Northridge," murmured Spider. "No surprise there."

Joe looked more closely at the men and with a start recognized the truck driver who had given them a lift from the front. The truck driver spotted Spider and smiled. He said something, then pointed. The other men turned, and Joe shrank behind Spider.

The two men were both wearing long, dark leather coats. Each carried a small brown suitcase and a pair of motorcycle goggles. The first man was tall and had thin white hair and a yellow mustache. The stub of a black cheroot stuck out of the corner of his mouth, and he had to squint to see through the smoke. As he stared at Joe he rolled the cheroot slowly from one side of his mouth to the other. The second man was a bullish-looking fellow, broad and muscular. His black hair was short and greasy and his eyebrows were thick and ran in an unbroken line across his forehead. His cheeks were pockmarked, and a jagged scar on the left side of his mouth had given him a permanent grotesque smile.

"Secret police," said Katherine. "Two of them."

The policemen started across the stall toward Joe, but the truck driver took hold of their arms. The policemen looked furious and said something. Then one of them reached deep into his pocket.

"Tell me what they look like," said Spider.

"One's tall with white hair," answered Joe in the quietest voice. He was afraid that the men might hear him.

"Don't know him," murmured Spider. "The other?"

"He's got a scar running up one side of his face."

"That's Radworth! Did they see you?"

"I think so."

"Then we'd best try and lose them in the crowd." Spider scratched the end of his nose and turned in a full circle as though trying to decide which way to go. "Come on," he said, setting off back toward the more crowded part of the market. He kept his finger to his nose.

Radworth and the other policeman had paid off the

truck driver and were closing in on them when a woman carrying a large basket of apples suddenly stepped in their path. The three collided, and the apples spilled everywhere. The woman cried out and began to berate the policemen for being so clumsy. Others joined in, and although Radworth and the other man tried to push past, the crowd closed in and held them back.

Joe was just thinking how lucky they'd been that the apple lady had been in the policemen's way when he looked up and saw the merest hint of a smile pass over Spider's face.

"Lead us back to the main market, Katherine," said Spider. "We'll have to go that way now."

The path grew more crowded as they reached the heart of the market. At the very center the road opened out into a rough square where three fiddlers stood on a makeshift stage and played energetically over the heads of the crowd. Here, the awnings and canopies of the stalls were painted with pictures of dancers and acrobats. In the flickering lamplight the dancers seemed to come alive. Katherine hurried forward and stood on tiptoe to see them.

"Don't stop!" growled Spider in a low voice as he pushed her forward through the crowd. "Let's get through here."

But it was easier said than done. The crowd was so

dense that they could only move forward with small, shuffling steps. People pressed in on all sides.

Suddenly Spider's hand flew to his chest.

"Get out of it!" he snarled in a voice as hard as granite. A scruffy little man had his hand in Spider's inside pocket and had half pulled out his notebook. Spider took hold of the man's other wrist and deftly twisted his arm up behind his back.

"Owww!" the man squealed. He looked up, and his eyes widened in disbelief. "Carey!" he stammered. "I thought you was dead."

"You know me better than that, Wyn," said Spider. His voice was low but steely. "Now put it back, there's a good man."

"All right, but let me go." Wyn released his grip on the notebook. Spider quickly stuffed it back in his pocket, then twisted the little man's arm harder.

"Owww! Spider," squealed Wyn. "No need for that. I wouldn't have done it if I'd known it was you. Please . . . let go."

"Katherine, lead the way through the stalls!" said Spider as he pushed Wyn after her. Away from the road, Spider shoved Wyn to the ground.

"What else have you got in here then?" he asked. He crouched and searched through Wyn's pockets. Joe and Katherine watched as Spider pulled out an amazing array of packets and parcels. "Still the thief you always were, I see."

"Get off," whined Wyn. "It's my charity work, honest. All I was doing was trading. You know, bits of meat for the lads at the front, a pack of cards, a bar of chocolate, some bread that don't have worms in it. Nothing harmful. No guns or anything. Honest, Spider. You know me. I never know nothing important."

"Still," said Spider, pulling Wyn to his feet, "I bet there's one thing you can tell me. Where's Cloves?"

Wyn's mouth dropped open, then he smiled. "Why do you need Cloves?" he asked with suspicious sweetness. "What you up to, Spider?"

"I'm guiding, that's all," replied Spider.

Wyn's small, piggy eyes shot to Katherine and Joe. "Guiding, eh? I see you've got a charge, but who's the girl?" he asked.

"My apprentice," replied Spider.

Wyn laughed. "Never thought you'd take on another, not after what you went through with the last one. Nasty specimen he was, or so I heard."

Katherine took a step toward Wyn, but Spider put out his hand.

"Leave it," he growled. Then he turned back to Wyn. "Take me to Cloves," he said, "and quick. Joe, Katherine, stay close by."

Wyn gathered up his muddy parcels and jammed them back in his pockets.

"I don't know how I got mixed up in this," he grumbled under his breath. "This wasn't supposed to be my life. I'm a peace-loving man."

"Get moving," warned Spider. Not waiting for another sharp shove in the back, Wyn set off.

Katherine caught up with Spider and tugged on his sleeve. "What are you doing?" she whispered. "He's a racketeer, a thief. If anyone sees us with him and tells the clerks, they won't let us have passes. We'll never get through to the front."

"We need him to get us to Cloves," Spider replied. "A lot has changed since I was last here."

"Who's Cloves?" asked Katherine.

"A seer," answered Spider. "One of the best. He'll tell us what's what."

Katherine stopped dead in her tracks. Joe bumped into her back. "What's wrong?" he asked. "Why are you stopping?"

"Unbelievable!" gasped Katherine. "He's taking us to a fortune-teller. A blabberer! What good will that do?" She gnawed her lip and waited for a moment, letting Spider and Wyn get farther in front. She cupped her hands and whispered in Joe's ear. "I'll find a way to take you to the Long City myself. Then, once we've rescued my brother, I promise you he'll take you wherever you've got to go from there."

"To find my sister?" urged Joe.

"Yes!"

"Keep up, you two," growled Spider.

Wyn led them away from the bright lights of the market and through the maze of tattered tents where families sat huddled around smoking fires. Everyone stared at Joe and Katherine as they passed. There was something odd about the families, but it wasn't until they'd rejoined the market road that Joe figured out there were babies and young toddlers but no children older than that. No one his age or Katherine's. A woman caught hold of Katherine's wrist.

"'Ere, love, d'you know Sari Shorrocks?" the woman asked, desperation in her voice. "She's a fetcher, like you. Have you seen her? I just want to know she's all right."

Katherine shook her head. "Don't know her. Sorry," she said.

As they walked on, other families asked Katherine the same thing, over and over.

The way Wyn led them was no shortcut. They went far in one direction, then looped back so they rejoined the main market road by the foot of the great, dark house.

There were fewer people on this stretch of the road

and only a handful of market stalls—five, maybe six at the most. These stalls were poorly lit and smelled rank.

Katherine wrinkled her nose in disgust. "These are the blabberers," she muttered to Joe. "They call themselves seers! Fortune-tellers. Waste of time. No one really believes in their rubbish anymore."

Joe peered at them. Behind each stall sat a muttering, hunched figure, dealing cards on a table in front and beckoning to passersby.

Wyn took them to the second-to-last stall. It looked even dirtier and more disheveled than the rest. An enormously fat man wearing a copious hood sat in the stall, muttering and chanting and rocking back and forth. In his huge hands he deftly shuffled a pack of damp cards that had brightly colored figures on both sides. As Wyn and the others approached, the great hands briskly laid them out on the table. The fat man didn't look up.

"Spider," he said softly.

"Hello, Cloves," replied Spider. "It's been a long time."

"They were all saying you were dead."

"But you knew different, didn't you," replied Spider.

"Of course." The hooded figure looked up briefly, and Joe saw the flash of a smile. "That is my art. Come, we'll talk in the back. Stow your stuff under the table. You'd better pay me, so it all looks legit."

Spider took Katherine's pistol from his belt and handed it to Cloves.

"Hey!" cried Katherine. "That's not yours!"

"If you want to get to your brother, it is," Spider snapped. "Now, put my pack under there."

Katherine fell into a smoldering silence. She dropped the pack on the ground; then, lifting up the oilcloth that covered the table, roughly shoved the pack out of sight.

"Be careful," growled Spider.

Cloves took the gun and examined it closely.

"Very pretty," he said, running his plump palm over the handle. "Meridian-made, if I'm not mistaken. Let's go through, and I'll tell you what I know." He stood up with great difficulty, then shuffled through the opening in the dirty tent. Spider, Katherine, Joe, and Wyn followed him.

In the middle of the tent floor a miserable fire sputtered and spat, sending acrid smoke swirling up and out through a ragged hole in the canvas roof. Rain dripped through the hole, making the embers hiss as it fell on them. The air was foul and close and smelled of mushrooms and damp socks. Joe wrinkled his nose.

Cloves slowly lowered himself onto a large, worn cushion at the far side of the fire and gestured for the others to sit wherever they could. He crossed his legs underneath him, then reached up and pulled back his hood to reveal a perfectly round and perfectly bald head. His eyes were gray and bright and they twinkled in the massive moon of his face. He folded his hands over his great belly and smiled at his visitors.

"You want to know how things stand?" began Cloves, speaking directly to Spider. "There's much to tell, but if you'll excuse me, my supper is long overdue."

"Of course, please go ahead," said Spider. Cloves nodded and Wyn set a blackened frying pan across the fire, then pulled a raw, gristly pork chop out of his sock and carefully wiped the mud off it with his sleeve.

"Will you have a share of my meal?" Cloves asked. Joe shook his head and so did Katherine, but they were both worried that Spider, who hadn't seen where the meat had been carried, might accept for them.

"That would be kind," said Spider, "but we wouldn't dream of depriving you. We came for information, not food." Spider bowed slightly.

"Then we can talk while Wyn cooks," said Cloves.

Spider cleared his throat. "How many are waiting at the house for passes?"

"Just about all the guides who've been allowed back are there, at least all those that haven't got sick of the bureaucracy and gone off to be Skulkers like this girl's brother."

"What do you know about my brother?" asked Katherine.

Spider shushed her, and Cloves went on. "There's another one of Orlemann's mercy mission convoys supposed to leave from Northridge in a day or two."

Spider's face tightened. "Orlemann?"

Wyn, who up until now had been absorbed in his task, lifted his head and stared at Spider. The little man's eyes narrowed, and the briefest of smiles crossed his face.

Cloves went on. "The clerks say there are no more passes to be had. From what I hear the waiting room at the house is full to bursting."

"We'll get passes," said Spider. "We have to get this boy to Northridge and get him on that mercy mission convoy."

Wyn spat in the pan, waited until the gob of spit had hissed and bubbled away to nothing, then slapped the fatty chop down to sizzle on the hot iron.

Cloves leaned toward Spider. "You know about the machines the secret police have been using?"

Spider nodded.

"Brutal things they are, but what can we do? The police have more power than they ought. And who's to stop them? Charges are sent off with guides who are hardly fit to lead the way. And as for the convoys, once they leave Northridge . . ." Cloves shrugged and held his palms up. "Who can you trust? No one really knows if they even make it to the arches."

"But you know?" said Spider.

Cloves laughed bitterly. "No; not even *I* know that."

The chop sizzled in the pan. Wyn prodded it with a fork and a bubble of fat burst, spitting boiling oil onto the back of his hand. He licked it off, then looked at Joe, crinkling up his eyes until they were just dark slits in his greasy face.

"Elysia's still putting all her faith in Orlemann, then?" asked Spider.

"She is. But she's growing impatient with his methods. Perhaps if . . . you never know . . . a word might change things."

Spider nodded. "Are many left?"

"Some, in the city. If you want, I still have my birds. I can send word on ahead."

"Maybe later." Spider paused for a moment. He seemed to grow suddenly aware that Katherine, Joe, and Wyn were still in the tent with them. He shifted in his

seat. "Little jugs have big ears," he said. "Katherine?"
Spider fished in his purse, then took out two copper coins
and a scrap of paper. He handed them to Katherine. "Go
to the market and buy me what's on this list."

Katherine stared at the coins in her hand. "There's
not enough here to buy a quarter of—"

"You'll have to make it stretch, won't you."

"What about Joe?" she asked.

"He stays here. Off with you, then, miss." Reluctantly
Katherine stood up to go. As she passed Cloves,
he caught hold of her leg and handed her back her
pistol.

"Here," he said. "You might need this." Katherine
took hold of it, but Cloves kept hold of the barrel of the
gun and stared into her eyes. "Be careful when you find
your brother. He may not be the way you remember
him."

Katherine took the pistol without a word and left the
tent.

"Your charge can shelter under the table outside,"
said Cloves, nodding at Joe. "It'll be dry enough. Wyn,
show him the way."

Wyn smiled at Joe and slid the chop from the pan
onto a tin plate, then handed it to Cloves. The fat man
lifted the plate level with his chin, tipped the plate, and

let the chop slide in its own grease toward his mouth. In two, maybe three bites it was gone.

As Cloves gulped and chewed, he waggled his fingers at Wyn to get a move on.

Wyn pulled Joe to his feet. "Come on then, my lovely," he said in a chipper voice. "Let's be having you."

CHAPTER 9

If You Ever Need a Friend

Joe stood outside the tent and watched as Katherine disappeared down the road to the market.

"Hang on, I'll just make a little room under here," said Wyn, disappearing beneath the heavy tablecloth.

Joe stood in the rain and listened to the low, mumbling voices in the tent behind him.

"What are the chances?" he heard Spider ask.

"Slim," replied Cloves. "But there's many who think the time is approaching."

"I don't know, Cloves," murmured Spider. "There's something I still can't grasp. . . ."

Then the voices dropped even lower, and try as he might, Joe could only catch the odd word or snatch of a sentence. ". . . shadows in the city . . . since Cornell's death . . . over the mountains . . . Skulkers." But none of it made sense, and the words soon blurred together.

"What you doing up there? Spying?" demanded Wyn, thrusting his head out from under the table. Joe was rattled. He'd forgotten all about Wyn.

"I'm not spying," retorted Joe, trying to sound tough. "You were the one who told me to wait up here, remember?"

"All right, all right, keep your shirt on!" said Wyn. "But you better get down here. You don't want to get caught. No one likes a spy, you know." He tugged on Joe's ankle.

"I wasn't spying, I was . . ." Joe stopped himself. Technically, he supposed, he was spying, or at least eavesdropping. Wyn chuckled as Joe crawled under the table. Joe backed into the corner and hugged his knees to his chest.

In the yellow light of an oil lamp Joe could see that Wyn had undone the clasps and fastenings of Spider's backpack and was busy rifling through the contents. Wyn looked up at Joe and grinned.

"Well, you're the chatty lad? The dreamer?" he said. He sniffed at a piece of the hardened oatmeal, pulled a face in disgust, put it back, and turned his attention to the scraps of rag and paper that the main part of the

pack appeared to be stuffed with. "What is all this rubbish?" muttered Wyn. "Oh, I can't be bothered! Spider
Carey's a strange one. Look at this, one sock. What use
is one sock to anyone with two feet? I ask you."

Joe didn't say anything.

"So, you're keeping mum now, are you?" Wyn chuckled softly as he repacked the rags and the paper and the
sock in Spider's pack. "Well, keeping your mouth shut
won't help when the secret police get their hands on
you." Joe blanched at the mention of the secret police.
Wyn laughed again. "I blame your guide. He should
have warned you to keep your mouth shut. Word travels
fast round here, 'specially when there's a market on. Half
the camp'll know you're here now."

Joe felt sick. It was close and muggy under the table,
and Wyn's pungent onion breath wafted over him like a
thick, warm fog. Joe didn't like Wyn. There was something oily and treacherous about him.

"Oh, don't worry," said Wyn, giving Joe's knee a
friendly shake with his grimy hand. Joe flinched. "I won't
give you away. Cross my heart. In fact, I'm glad I
bumped into you."

Wyn looked expectantly at Joe. When Joe didn't ask
him why, Wyn went on as though he had.

"Because I think you and I can help each other. I'm
not going to be stuck in Quarain forever. I've got plans,

and I've got friends in high places who will help me with those plans. And I'm a generous man. If I felt like it, I could help you." Wyn smiled.

"Help me what?" asked Joe. "Help me find my sister?"

"Yes, of course," Wyn said eagerly. "I know a great deal about things like that, much more than Spider Carey, believe me. Oh, find your sister, yes, that's exactly the sort of problem I could help you with, and perhaps in return you could help me with one or two little matters."

"Like what?"

"Oooh, nothing at all, really. Hardly anything. In fact, maybe I shouldn't ask . . . you'll probably find your sister by yourself . . . though it may take you a while. . . . I just hope it won't be too late."

"What do you want me to do?"

Wyn grinned broadly and leaned forward so Joe was unable to avoid the oniony breath.

"You see, it's that book of Carey's," said Wyn. He paused. "When I accidentally had my hand on it, I happened to see something that leads me to think it would be of great interest to an extremely important friend of mine. An *extremely* important friend. And if I was able to procure said book and show it to my friend, I think my friend would be most grateful. Of course, I don't want to tell anybody about what I saw until I'm absolutely certain, don't want to look foolish, you know. To be absolutely certain I need to have that book. What do you say? Will you get it for me?"

Joe shook his head. "No," he said. "I'm not a thief."

The smile on Wyn's face dissolved quick as a snowflake in boiling water. He grabbed Joe by the collar and yanked him close. "All right, so you don't want to help me, but you listen well. Be careful who you trust. Spider Carey's no friend to you. He'd slit your throat for the price of a newspaper."

Wyn's greasy face glistened in the light. He released Joe and pushed him back into his corner. He returned to Spider's pack, muttering about ingratitude.

Wyn had just started to undo the buckle on a side pocket of the pack when Katherine crawled beneath the tablecloth. A blast of cool, rain-scented air blew under the table.

"I couldn't find half the stuff he wanted," she said as she dropped an armful of small packages on the ground. "And the half I could find, I had to beg or steal because I didn't have enough money to . . . oh!" Katherine stopped short. "What's he doing here?" she asked rudely, making no attempt to disguise the way she felt about Wyn.

"I live here!" snapped Wyn. "You're a guest in my house, if you don't mind."

"Well, that's not yours," she said as she reached past him and snatched up a flashlight from the ground. "It's mine. You've been rooting around in Spider's backpack, have you? Find anything else good?" She rudely reached across him, grabbed the backpack, and put her flashlight back in the pocket he'd taken it from.

Wyn shrugged. "Manners!" he said haughtily. "I'll be on my way then. I know when I'm not wanted. Excuse me!"

He pushed past Katherine and lifted the tablecloth beside Joe. As he passed Joe he whispered, "No hard feelings, lad. Remember, if you ever need a friend, you know my price." With that he ducked his head under the tablecloth and left.

Joe was relieved. Katherine lifted the tablecloth and wafted it about, to freshen the stale air. "Pheweee!" she said. "How could you stand it in here?" Katherine wafted the cloth more violently, then sat down and pulled the backpack toward her. "I can't believe you let him go through this," she admonished Joe.

"I couldn't stop him," he answered.

"He better not have taken anything," she said. "I'll be the one to pay for it if he did." Katherine opened the pack, rummaged through the rags, then began to cram her purchases into any available space. "Looks all right," she said as she fastened the last strap. "If he took something, I don't know what it could be. Right, I'm ready for a nap." She settled herself against the pack and had just closed her eyes when there were three loud raps on the wooden tabletop above them.

"Come along, hop to it," commanded Spider. "We're moving out."

Joe crawled out from beneath the table. It was still raining, and it was still cold. The rain splattered on Joe's bare head and ran down the inside of his collar.

"Where's the other one?" asked Spider. Joe pointed to the table. Spider rapped on the table again.

"I'm coming!" snarled Katherine as she emerged, dragging the pack behind her. "Where now?" she asked as she stood up and hoisted the pack on her shoulders.

"To the house," said Spider. "We've got passes to get before morning. I want us on the first bus out of here." Then with long strides he led the way up the muddy slope to the grim-faced house.

"Passes by the morning? I'm apprenticed to a madman," wailed Katherine as she and Joe started up the hill after Spider.

CHAPTER 10

The Big House

The big house was all but a ruin. The ground beneath it had been eroded by the rain, and half the building was supported on towers of stacked trestles. Stout beams were buttressed up against the walls to stop them from collapsing, and a wall of sandbags had been erected all the way around the building.

A dark crack ran the full height of the front wall, opening wider at the top, as though threatening at any moment to split the house in two. Water ran down the walls, pooling at the bottom and running into the already sopping ground. The foundations of the building were being destroyed by the rain. Even the steep flight of stone steps that led to the front door had cracked as it had subsided into the mud.

The upper part of the house was an empty shell.
Most of the roof was gone, leaving a skeleton of blackened rafters. The windows along the top floor were dark
and broken.

Lights burned in the windows of the lower floor, but
stacks of boxes placed behind the glass acted as shutters
and prevented anyone from seeing in.

As Joe started up the stairs, Spider grabbed his arm
and held him back. "Be careful in there, lad," he whispered. "Don't talk too much—in fact, try not to talk at
all. Don't want everyone knowing our business."

Joe nodded in agreement and proceeded up the
stairs. When they reached the front door Spider banged
on it twice with his staff. While they waited for an
answer, Joe looked back toward the market and watched
the bright lights dissolve in the rain like colored inks in
water. The rain dripped into his eyes. After a moment a
small hatch opened and someone shone a flashlight in
their faces. The light clicked off and a hand was thrust
through the hatch.

"Papers!" demanded a gruff voice.

Spider snapped his fingers, and Katherine dug into
her satchel and pulled out the sheaf of forms that they
had signed in the canteen. Spider took them from her
and thrust them into the hand. "Wait!" instructed the
voice. Then the hatch was slammed shut.

They were kept waiting for almost five minutes, and Joe had begun to wonder if they would ever get into the house when the great door swung open and a young man in a dark suit and stiff white collar beckoned them inside.

Beyond the door was a small square vestibule with a mosaic on the floor and wooden panels on the walls. In the corner was a tall, narrow desk with a high stool behind it.

The clerk opened a little door that was cleverly concealed in the paneling to his left. "Wait here!" he instructed them. Then, bending low, he disappeared through the doorway like a rabbit disappearing into its hole.

Joe looked around the vestibule. It was separated from the rest of the house by a pair of tall doors. They reminded Joe of ones he'd seen in the town hall at home, dark wood with engraved glass panels in the center. But these doors were a wreck. Hardboard had been tacked up over the glass panel on one side, and the engraved panel on the other was badly cracked and part of it was missing. It was still possible to make out the engraving of a dancing woman in a Roman-style gown carrying a basket overflowing with fruit and flowers. It was beautiful, and Joe thought it was a shame that it was broken.

There was one advantage to the doors' dilapidated

state. The missing glass made it possible to see into the room beyond. Joe stared through and saw a large, noisy hall. It had a high, arched ceiling and a tiled floor, which meant that all the noise echoed in a dreadful cacophony of sound. But the noise all came from one half of the hall. A long wooden counter split the room in two. On one side the room was jam-packed with guides and charges. On the other, dark-suited clerks with tired, pinched faces moved about between desks arranged in neat lines. Some of the clerks stood at the counter, dealing with the disgruntled crowd on the opposite side.

"There are so many ahead of us," complained Katherine. "By tomorrow. Huh! This'll take weeks."

"Shush," warned Spider.

Joe's eyes opened wide. "Do you mean," he asked, staring through the glassless door, "that all those guides and their charges are waiting for passes?"

"Why else would they be here?" replied Katherine.

The guides who were not arguing with the clerks at the counter sat crammed together on hard wooden benches. Some slept, while others played cards. The charges sat or stood about forlornly. Some slept under the benches; others huddled against the wall. Those who were awake looked tired, and even those who were sleeping looked miserable.

The door in the paneled wall of the vestibule

suddenly opened, and the young clerk reemerged. He
threw a stern, piercing look at Joe, then abruptly stood at
attention and held the door open as an older man, a
more senior clerk, entered the vestibule. The older man
waited while the young clerk placed Spider's papers on
the desk, bowed smartly, and disappeared through the
door in the wall.

The senior clerk crossed to the desk and mounted
the stool. He took out his spectacles, placed them on
his nose, then carefully arranged Spider's papers on top
of the lectern. Finally the senior clerk folded his hands
on the desk and surveyed Spider, Joe, and Katherine over
the tops of his spectacles.

"What is your business here?" he asked, picking up a
pen and beginning to write in a logbook.

"We need three passes to Northridge," said Spider.
"And a place on the next convoy."

The clerk looked up and his mouth twitched. "Very
amusing," he said in a very unamused voice. He handed
the papers back to Spider, then scrawled something on a
small pink pad and ripped off the top sheet with a flour-
ish. "Here's your number," he said, holding out the paper.
"You'll be called to the counter when it's your turn."

Katherine took the pink chit from the clerk. The
number 189 was written on it. Joe and Katherine looked
through the broken glass panel into the hall. A sign at

the back showed the clerks were serving number 3. She turned back to protest, but the senior clerk had disappeared through the door in the paneling.

"Weeks?" she muttered as she pushed open the doors and entered the hall. "I was wrong. We'll be here for months."

Joe helped Spider through the door. "Lead me to the nearest corner, and we'll set up there."

"But it's packed," complained Katherine. "There's no room."

"Have a little faith, will you?" said Spider under his breath. "Just point me in the right direction and I'll make the room."

Joe turned Spider toward the corner, and he set off through the crowd. Joe watched in amazement as people moved aside as Spider approached. The guides didn't even look at him. When Spider reached the corner he tapped the bottom of the wall gently with his stick, turned around, and leaned against the plaster.

"Stand here beside me," he said as Katherine and Joe joined him in the corner. "Now have a look around. Is anyone paying any attention to us?"

Joe scanned the room. "Not that I can see," he whispered.

"There's one clerk . . . ," began Katherine. "He . . . no, he's looked away now."

"Good," said Spider. "We won't have to wait too long. Katherine, you're going to go and see Elysia."

"Me?" Katherine gasped. "How do you expect me to do that? Tom told me no one has seen her in years. It's impossible to get in."

"I already told you that your wonderful brother might not know everything."

"But—"

"Shush," said Spider. "I doubt if any of the clerks will let us pass. So"—a smile flitted at the edges of his mouth—"we'll have to find another way, won't we."

He pulled out his tattered notebook and carefully felt through the worn pages. Joe remembered Wyn's offer. He wondered what was so special about this book. Spider pulled out an old, wrinkled envelope and shut the book.

Spider bent his head over the envelope and blew on it gently. A slit along the top opened, and Spider carefully reached inside with two fingers. Slowly and gently, he pulled them out. Joe could see that Spider had something small caught between his fingertips, but before he could see what it was, Spider hid it in his left palm and closed his fist around it. With his free hand he quickly closed the envelope, then slipped it back inside the book.

"Katherine, hold out your hand," murmured Spider.

Spider opened his hand over hers, and a minute sprig of some sort of dried plant dropped into her palm.

Katherine gasped. "Heather!" she said, fortunately remembering to keep her voice low. Joe stared at the tiny sprig. It was brown, not purple, like heather should be, but it was obviously very old. Katherine was glaring at Spider as though he were truly insane. "Do you want me to get k—"

"Careful," Spider warned, rolling her fingers into a fist around the heather. "If you want to get to your brother, you'll take this to Elysia." Spider cocked an ear toward the counter. "She's here somewhere in the house," he said. "I can hear her voice, soft though it is. My ears are well trained. She's two, perhaps three rooms away."

Joe tried to listen past the noise of the assembled guides, but it was impossible. How could anyone hear anything beyond the hubbub in the room?

Katherine pulled a face. "Why can't you send Joe?" she begged. "I'm dead if they catch me with this."

"You're my apprentice," snapped Spider in a quiet, steely voice. "Joe will stay here with me. I need him to be my eyes. Now, if I remember correctly, there's a door beyond the counter—along the far wall, perhaps."

While he spoke, Spider fastened the elastic around his notebook and slipped it back in his pocket.

Katherine groaned. "How am I supposed to get to the door?"

"Listen. I'm going to teach you an old thieves' trick," said Spider. "Every thief knows that there is a moment when they can become invisible in even the most crowded room. Such a moment should be easy to spot here. Everyone is distracted or asleep. It is simply a matter of knowing when the time is right. Find that moment and you can pass through that door and not one person will see you, I promise.

"When I've finished talking I want you to take a breath and listen to the room. You'll have to wait for the moment. When you sense it, walk directly to the door. Don't hesitate. Once you're through, find Elysia. Give her that sprig of heather. Tell her Spider needs three passes to Northridge and places on the next convoy. Joe and I will meet you by Cloves's stall. Do you understand?"

"Yes, but—" whispered Katherine.

"Don't worry, you can do it."

Katherine bit her lip, then nodded. She turned around and surveyed the room.

Spider pulled on Joe's shoulder and whispered, "Once she sets off I want you to watch her and tell me everything you see. Only don't look at her directly, or you'll be the one to give her away. Do you understand?"

"No!" Joe whispered.

"It sounds like there's a clock above the main door," said Spider. "Is there?"

"Yes," Joe replied.

"Good. Give it your full attention."

Joe did as he was told. "Now," whispered Spider, "without looking away from that clock I want you to tell me what else is happening in the room. What is happening over by the counter?"

Joe stared hard at the white dial and concentrated. "There's a soldier with an eye patch talking to one of the clerks," he said.

"Good," said Spider. "Now what about by the door? Keep your eyes on the clock."

"The clerk who let us in is cleaning his glasses."

"Excellent," said Spider. "Now, I want you to keep looking at that clock when Katherine sets off across the room. If you watch her obliquely you will preserve her invisibility. Do you understand?"

"I think so," replied Joe.

"Good. When Katherine goes, tell me everything you see."

Joe stood beside Spider and watched the clock. The minutes dragged as Katherine waited beside them. Joe's eyes were beginning to smart when someone banged hard on the front door. A few seconds later the vestibule door flew open. Joe let his eyes flicker away from the clock as the red-haired policeman he had first seen at the guides' canteen pushed his way into the hall.

"Mr. Doyle," simpered the desk clerk, scurrying along beside the secret policeman. "What a pleasure. What can I do for—"

Doyle glared at him, and the clerk shrank back. Doyle started across the crowded room, pulling each kid to his feet and studying him closely. Joe pressed himself against the wall.

The guides made it plain they didn't like what was going on. "Leave us alone!" one man stood up and shouted. "You make it so a man can't do his work!"

Doyle shoved him back in his seat. "Sit down and stay down," he growled.

To Joe's amazement it was at this moment that Katherine pushed herself away from the wall and started toward the counter. Joe's eyes shot to the clock.

"She's going," Joe whispered to Spider.

"Good girl," murmured Spider. "She's right on the money."

Looking directly at the clock, Joe watched Katherine make her way across the room. Then the vestibule door opened again. This time the policeman with the scar, Radworth, entered.

Everyone was watching Doyle and Radworth. No

one noticed Katherine as she slipped through the crowd
and ducked beneath the counter.

"She's made it to the other side of the counter," Joe
whispered as Katherine popped up on the far side.

Even the clerks were distracted by Doyle's search.
They had gathered at the far side of the counter to
watch. Joe kept his eyes on the clock and tried not
to worry about what would happen when Doyle got to
him.

"She's nearly at the door," he said, forcing himself to
concentrate on Katherine's progress.

But as Katherine's hand reached for the door handle,
she suddenly stopped.

"Don't stop, Katherine!" urged Joe under his breath.
"Go on! Go on!"

"What's she doing?" asked Spider.

"She's just standing by the door," replied Joe.
"Something's caught her attention, but I can't make out
what."

"Find out! Look at her directly," said Spider.

Joe pushed himself up the wall a little way and saw
that Katherine was scowling at a pile of papers on a
nearby desk. She picked up the top one and began reading it intently. Even from across the room, Joe could see
that her cheeks had begun to glow an angry red.

Katherine lifted her head and scanned the crowd of

guides and charges. Eyes blazing, she threw something to the floor. Was it the heather? Then, still grasping the piece of paper in her right hand, she leapt onto the nearest desk.

"Hoi! What do you think you're doing?" cried one of the clerks. "You're not allowed back here!"

"Hell's teeth!" growled Spider.

A group of clerks closed in around Katherine. But she was too quick for them. She leapt from one desk to the next and so on until she was standing on the counter. Then she found who she was looking for, and her face shone with a fierce anger.

"Harris! You rat!" she yelled, pointing into the crowd. "Give me my money back!"

A small, ruddy-faced guide in the center of the room turned and looked at Katherine. Joe figured it was the guide she had paid and who had been supposed to wait for her when she went to fetch Joe. The guide stared at Katherine, obviously at a loss to place her. Then, when he did, he turned to his friends and burst out laughing.

It was a mistake. Katherine flung herself off the counter and landed, fists flailing, on the guide's shoulders. The other guides jostled to get a better look at the fight, while the two policemen plowed through the crowd toward it.

Spider tugged harder on Joe's arm. "Where's the heather?" he asked.

"I think she threw it down," answered Joe. "On the floor."

"You've got to get it and take it to Elysia," said Spider urgently. "Do it quick. Now! While all this is going on!"

Spider gave him a push, and the next thing Joe knew he was hurrying across the crowded hall. No one noticed as he reached the counter and ducked beneath it. He ran low between the clerks' desks and deftly scooped the sprig of heather off the floor.

Behind him he could hear Katherine still arguing. "Wait!" she cried. "It's all legit. I have a contract. Look!"

Joe turned the handle and opened the door in front of him. A moment later he was in a long corridor. Joe let out a great sigh of relief. He'd done it! But as he turned to close the door behind him, his stomach lurched.

Radworth was staring straight at him from across the waiting room. Joe froze, and the grotesque, scarred smile grew wider as the policeman slowly lifted the countertop and passed through.

CHAPTER II

Elysia

Joe quickly closed the door and turned around. The corridor was lined with doors, but there was no time to search for an empty room. Between the doors cardboard boxes had been stacked into tall towers. Thinking fast, Joe ran to the third door down the corridor and opened it an inch. Then he raced back to the first stack of boxes and slipped in behind them. He was gingerly pulling the boxes back toward him when, with a loud click, the handle turned and the door opened.

Joe shrank back as Radworth hurried past and headed toward the door Joe had opened. Joe held his breath. It looked as though his plan had worked, that Radworth thought he had gone that way, but just as Radworth reached for the handle, another door farther down the corridor opened and two young clerks weighed down with boxes staggered into view.

"These are even heavier than the last lot," moaned the first clerk. "Why the new regulations say we have to keep four copies of everything, I don't know."

"Careful," warned the other. "Don't want anyone thinking you're disloyal, do you? The powers that be have their reasons, that's all I know."

Both lads stopped and grew pale when they saw Radworth. Silently they set the boxes down and, with a cursory bow to Radworth, hurried back the way they had come.

Radworth turned back to the door Joe had opened and glanced up at the polished brass sign. "Chief Clerk's Office," it said. Radworth's scowl deepened. He was about to enter when yet another door, this one at the farthest end of the corridor, opened and a tall clerk with smooth gray hair and a long face emerged.

The clerk raised his eyebrows when he saw Radworth. He was about to speak when a voice called through the open door after him.

"Mr. Beck?" It was a woman's voice.

The clerk held up his finger, instructing Radworth to

wait, then turned and bowed to the unseen woman in
the room beyond.

"Ma'am?" he said politely.

"These statistics are unacceptable. Make sure you tell
the ambassador I wish to speak to him about them." The
voice trailed away as though the speaker had grown too
weak to draw breath.

The clerk bowed again. "Of course, ma'am. I'll see to
it at once."

He closed the door, then hurried to Radworth.

"Mr. Radworth," whispered the clerk with a thin
smile.

"Is there a problem?" asked Radworth, nodding
toward the door.

"Oh no, indeed no," said the clerk. "She finds the
latest figures distressing, as do we all. It seems the
Meridians have been snatching more charges as they've
come through, and you know what that means. Still, we
do our best to save them, and it will all be worth it in the
end, will it not?" Beck smiled, then leaned forward.
"Between you and me, I think she's getting worse. It'll
certainly be for the better when Ambassador Orlemann
has secured the armistice." He rocked back on his heels
and smiled at the policeman. "Now, Mr. Radworth, what
can I do for you?"

If Joe could have shrunk right into the wall, he would have. Radworth would surely give him away. But to his surprise the policeman didn't even mention that he was searching for anyone.

"The ambassador asked me to meet him here," he said, looking at his watch. "I find I'm a little early."

The clerk smiled. "Then may I suggest tea or possibly something a little stronger in my room?" He held open the door Radworth had been about to enter and ushered the policeman inside.

Joe stayed where he was for a moment, barely daring to believe his luck. Perhaps he'd been mistaken. Perhaps Radworth hadn't seen him after all.

Slowly he pushed the boxes away so he would have enough room to slip out. It was as he was pushing them that he really looked at them for the first time and noticed that they were all numbered and labeled. He read the one closest to him.

"Box No. 7771. Contents—1/Paperwork for the fifty-three charges transported to Long City on Mercy Mission No. 71. 2/Paperwork for the sixty-seven charges lost to enemy machines on Mercy Mission No. 70. All files closed."

Joe frowned. Charges lost? Did that mean killed? Charges like Hannah? What happened to them in the real world if they were killed here? Joe wondered. There wasn't time to think about it. He could be caught at any moment. Clutching the tiny sprig of heather in his hand, Joe slipped out from behind the boxes and quickly, quietly, crept along the corridor to the door from which the woman's voice had come.

When he reached the door he discovered that Mr. Beck had not closed it completely. Joe pushed it open and slid inside.

The room he entered might once have been elegant, but it was now a shambles. Scraps of ornate wallpaper clung to the stained and mildewed walls. In the center of the ceiling were the remains of a large plaster rose. A broken, unlit chandelier hung beneath it. Tattered swaths of brocade curtains still framed the bay window, and in the center of one wall there was an imposing marble fireplace with a cracked and broken lintel. A fire flickered in the grate, and the light from the flames leapt up and down the walls.

The floor was bare, and many of the boards were warped and cracked along their length. Joe glanced around the dimly lit room. There was a broad desk with two chairs, a shaded desk lamp, a narrow bed against the far wall, and close beside him, a small square table covered with a tatty lace cloth. And everywhere there were boxes, the same sort of filing boxes that he had hidden behind in the corridor. Towers of them stood in the bay window. They were stacked along the wall and in the corners and on top of the little table. The desk was covered with papers and surrounded by open boxes that were overflowing with forms.

Joe stood in a shadow behind the door, wondering where the woman whose voice he'd heard had gone. Then she emerged from behind a stack of boxes by the window. Joe stared at her.

She didn't look at all the way he'd expected her to look, but he knew without a doubt that this was Elysia. She was a petite woman with slanting black eyes and tiny hands. Her black hair was streaked with gray, and she wore it piled on top of her head and secured by two large tortoiseshell combs. Her cheeks were pale and her chin was sharp and pointed. Like everyone else Joe had seen, her clothes were military in style. She wore a long black jacket with a belt at the waist and four button-down pockets. Beneath this was a black skirt that stopped just short of her ankles, as if to emphasize the heavy boots on her feet. A layer of gray dust covered the fabric of her uniform, adding to the somber effect. The only break in this funereal outfit was a torn white handkerchief that was tucked into her belt. Around her neck a pair of spectacles hung on a beaded jet necklace. She lifted these to her eyes and studied the thick sheaf of papers in her hand.

Elysia crossed the room. She stopped by the over-loaded desk and stood very still, staring into the embers of the fire, lost in thought. All at once she shuddered and looked down at the documents in her hands.

"So many papers," she said. "So many lives, such waste."

With a cry she threw the papers down, then lunged forward and swept all the forms and chits and passes off the desk in front of her. The avalanche of papers slid noisily to the floor and lay there in a heap. Elysia blinked at the empty desk, then with a groan sank into her chair and dropped her head onto her arms.

"Elysia?" Joe asked in a voice that was barely more than a whisper.

The woman's head shot up, and she stared at him.

"Who are you? How did you get in here?" she demanded. Her eyes flitted nervously to the door, then back to Joe.

"Are you Elysia?" Joe asked again.

She nodded.

"I was told to bring you this." Joe gently laid the sprig of heather in the bright circle of light on the desk.

Elysia's face grew even paler. She picked up the

heather and stared at it intently. "Araik Ben?" she said
under her breath. "It's not possible." Joe saw her eyes fill
with tears. Elysia blinked them away. "How did you
come by this?" she asked. "What do you know of the
Heathermen?"

Joe could have kicked himself. Heather—
Heathermen, of course! Why hadn't he connected it to
them before?

"I can't help you. You must leave—" She stopped
abruptly, and her eyes shot to the door.

Joe heard brisk footsteps in the corridor. Elysia hurried to the door and closed it softly, then darted to the fire
and threw the heather into the flames. She rubbed her
palms together as though to make sure none of the tiny
leaves had stuck to her skin. But as the heather burned it
gave off a strong, distinctive odor that permeated the
room. Elysia grabbed a handful of papers from the pile on
the floor and used them to waft away the smoke.

The footsteps drew nearer. Elysia threw the papers
into the fire, and they instantly caught light. The smell
of burning paper masked the smell of the heather. Elysia
stabbed at the fire with a poker to disturb the ashes.

"You have to help," Joe began. "Spider needs—" but
he was cut off by a sharp rap on the door.

"That'll be my ambassador," Elysia muttered to herself. She took hold of Joe's shoulder. "What shall I do

with you? He mustn't see you. Ah, there, quick, hide there . . . yes . . . down there."

She steered Joe toward the small table against the wall and held up the lace cloth. Joe darted beneath the table. Elysia dropped the cloth back in place, shook it to make sure that Joe was hidden, and hurried back to the desk.

There was a second knock.

"Come in!" said Elysia, composing herself. "Ah, Mr. Orlemann. I've been expecting you."

Orlemann? thought Joe. That was one of the names he'd heard in Cloves's tent. Joe watched through the holes in the tablecloth as the ambassador swept in.

Ambassador Orlemann was not a tall man, but he carried himself in a very upright manner. He was portly, and his round, almost cherubic face gleamed with sweat, causing him to constantly dab at his forehead with a large handkerchief. He was out of breath, and this made him seem rather nervous, as though he would jump at the slightest noise.

"Ma'am." The ambassador bowed low. His clothes were immaculate. The stiff white collar of his shirt shone against his dark velvet suit. Around his throat he wore an elegantly knotted silk tie, and looped across his chest was a heavy gold watch chain.

"I came to see," he said with a twitching, ingratiating smile, "if you have any further instructions for me before I leave." He stopped and, wrinkling his nose, sniffed. "Is something burning, ma'am?" he asked, his eyes growing round in alarm.

"Burning?" queried Elysia.

"Yes, burning. That smell . . ." The ambassador looked anxiously at the boxes in the corner and dabbed at his forehead.

"It's the fire," said Elysia calmly. "I was just burning some papers."

The ambassador's eyes grew even rounder. "Papers, ma'am? Documents?" His cheeks reddened, and his face filled with horror. The ambassador struggled for words. "B-b-but, ma'am, does the chief clerk know?"

"Mr. Beck? Of course, " she said coolly. "He instructed me to do it. 'All duplicates,' he assured me. 'Superfluous waste.'" She turned her attention to the desk, lifted her glasses onto her nose, and began sorting through the papers there. "Would I have done it without his say-so?"

"Oh, no, I don't suppose you would," said the ambassador. "Please forgive me for saying anything. It's just that you know how everyone here works so very, very hard to keep everything in order for you. If just one piece goes missing, the whole system will be thrown into absolute chaos."

"I know," sighed Elysia. "But when peace is restored—"

"That *is* what we are all working toward." The ambassador bowed briefly. "Ma'am, your sister has asked again for abdication as the terms for the armistice."

"So your bulletin said. But is she asking for mine or advocating her own?"

"Both, ma'am." Orlemann smiled unctuously. "I was led to believe that one would bring about the other, that if you stepped down, so would she. Though I imagine you are suspecting treachery."

"Do not presume to know my thoughts," said Elysia.

"No, of course not, ma'am, I was only thinking that it would be natural to suspect the Lady Merid's motives, but let us not forget that she claims to be as anxious for the return of peace as yourself."

"If my abdication could guarantee hers and ensure an end to all this fighting, I would step down this instant. But how, after all the terrible things she has done, can I trust her?"

Orlemann pursed his lips. "My officers have not found any more spies among the charges recently," he said. "This suggests to me that your sister is serious in her intent."

Elysia looked horrified. "Are you still testing those poor children with those barbarous machines? I thought we had an agreement."

"Alas, ma'am, we must continue in our efforts. How else can we make sure that none of her spies are among them? Though our evidence suggests that she is beginning to keep her word. The convoys have not been attacked since her assurance that she would allow them to pass through the Machine Lands unharmed."

"Yes, but if she knew they were carrying charges she would not hesitate to destroy them." Elysia dropped her head in her hands. "How can I trust my sister? Her treachery has run so deep."

"Ma'am," said Orlemann, gingerly taking a step toward the table and speaking softly, "we all want peace. Perhaps the time is drawing near when your sister is ready to see reason. Her willingness to abdicate power to a government is, I believe, a step in the right direction."

Elysia nodded. "Yes, a return to peace, a return to the way things were, is the most important thing. Please inform my sister on your next mission to her lands that I will consider her suggestion most carefully. That will be all."

Elysia settled back in her seat and stared into the fire. As she turned away from the ambassador, his expression changed. Joe saw a look of cold and malicious intensity flash across the ambassador's face. A moment later, it was gone.

"Very good, ma'am," said Orlemann. "If the convoy is to set off for the Long City at the appointed time, I must leave as soon as the tide turns. Your sister's armies might change their minds and fire on the convoy if we do not leave from Northridge at the hour agreed upon. Good night." The ambassador bowed and swept out of the room.

When he had gone, Elysia stood and began to pace. Joe crept out from beneath the table and coughed softly.

Elysia jumped and spun around to face him. She grabbed him by the shoulders.

"And you, who are you?" she asked, staring deep into his eyes. Joe was about to answer, but she went on. "Have you an honest heart? I used to think I could see honesty in a man's eyes, but I no longer believe that. You brought me something I never wanted to see again. I should summon the guards, should turn you over to them . . . but . . ."

She let go of Joe's shoulders and sighed. "It's been a long time since I saw one of your sort," she said. "Tell me, what is it you need?"

"Spider said we need three passes to Northridge and places on the convoy."

"Spider, is it? Very well," said Elysia. She took a large pad of vellum writing paper out of a drawer and laid it on the desk. Joe could see that there were forms printed on the paper and that perforated lines separated one form from the next. Elysia signed three of the forms.

"These will get you to where you want to go," she said, tearing the chits neatly from the pad. She put the pad away, then took out a small purse, which she handed to Joe along with the three passes.

"Be careful and—" Elysia stopped. There were more footsteps in the corridor. She hurried to the window and struggled to lift the lower sash. Joe helped her, and between them they managed to lift it high enough so he could slip out. Joe stared down into the darkness. He couldn't see the ground. It could have been one yard below or it could have been fifty.

"It's not far," said Elysia. "Hurry, you must go."

Joe climbed out and lowered himself over the sill. Without another word Elysia closed the window after him. There was no way back now. Joe clung to the window ledge and willed himself to let go, but his fingers wouldn't obey. He remembered the steps that led up to the front of the house and the way the house was buttressed at one side. Joe stared down into the abyss and felt very lost.

Suddenly someone wrapped their arms around Joe's legs. Joe shrieked in the darkness and kicked with all his might.

"Keep still and shut up," growled a man's voice. "I've got you. Now let go."

Joe let go, and his rescuer helped him to the ground safely, but when Joe looked up to say thank you, he saw Radworth's grotesque, scarred face above him. In the dim red glow from the distant market lights, it seemed to Joe that he had been caught by the devil himself.

CHAPTER 12

Another Front

Radworth clapped his hand over Joe's mouth. The policeman's fingers stank of oil and gasoline. Joe squirmed and tried to get away, but Radworth had other ideas.

"Ho no. You're not going anywhere, me lad," he said, grinning down at him, but before Radworth could even reach for his case a loud crack rang out and a look of shock passed over Radworth's face. "Ow!" he exclaimed. Then he started to topple forward.

"Joe, move!" cried Katherine. Joe jumped out of the way as Radworth crashed to the ground like a felled tree. Katherine dropped the large piece of pipe she was holding, then wiped her hands down her front and prodded the unconscious policeman with her toe. The policeman groaned.

"He won't be out for long," she said. "I couldn't hit him as hard as I wanted. Wrong angle. Come on," she added as she grabbed Joe's arm. "We've got to get out of here."

They hurried to the front of the house and, once they gained the path, ran toward the market.

"Where's Spider?" panted Joe.

Katherine grinned. "Don't you worry about him," she said. "He's still up at the house. I left him there to do his 'listening.' Did you get the passes?" Joe nodded.

Katherine grinned. "Good. Give them to me," she whispered. Joe handed over the passes and the purse. Katherine's eyes stretched wide. "You got money, too?" she asked as she slipped them into her satchel. "You are a clever one. Now, what do you say we ditch Spider and use these for ourselves? I'll find a way to get us to the Long City."

"But you've never been there before," said Joe.

"How do you know he has?" she snapped. "How do you know anything about him?"

"He said . . ." From the look on Katherine's face Joe thought it best to change the subject. "What about that other guide? Harris? Won't he take me now?"

Katherine laughed. "Him? No. The clerks said his contract was no longer valid. It doesn't matter. Good riddance, I say, especially as they made him return the fee so at least I've got the money. It doesn't hurt to have that. We'll have a nice, tidy sum when I add it to what Elysia gave you."

As Joe and Katherine approached the blabberers' stalls, the seers' mutterings grew louder. Joe felt uneasy. Would Cloves spot them, perhaps catch and keep them for Spider? And what about Wyn? Joe didn't want to bump into him again. But as they drew nearer, Joe's worries melted away. There was no light in Cloves's tent. It looked abandoned. Joe wiped the rain from his eyes and peered beneath the now-uncovered table. There was no sign of Wyn.

They were almost at the market when they heard a loud and unnatural yowl behind them. It sounded like a dog in pain, and it came from the shadows beneath the dark house.

"What was that?" gasped Joe.

Katherine stared back at the house. "Radworth's awake," she said. She set off at a run toward the market. "Come on!" she cried.

When they reached the main market street they pushed their way into the crowd. "Slow down now,"

Katherine warned. "We don't want to attract too much attention. Others may have heard that cry. We need to get to the buses if we're to get a ride to the front."

The path through the market was even more crowded than it had been before. Jugglers and fire-eaters and a troop of performing dogs had joined in the festivities. Joe almost stepped on a Pekingese. The dog barked angrily and snapped at his ankles until its owner scooped it up and put it back into the act.

Katherine nudged Joe. "This way," she said as she hurried down the hill toward the buses parked at the edge of the camp.

Katherine led Joe between two trucks. They could see the buses up ahead.

"Nearly there," Katherine said, but just as she said that she tripped and fell clumsily to the ground. A second later something hard caught against Joe's shins and he, too, stumbled and fell. Someone grabbed them both by the backs of their collars and hoisted them to their feet.

Radworth! Joe thought. But it wasn't Radworth. It was Spider, and the old man was livid.

"Where the blazes did you think you were going?" he growled.

"We were looking for you," lied Katherine hastily.

"Liar!" snapped Spider. "Give me those passes and

the money, too. And here, take my backpack." Spider thrust the heavy pack toward Katherine. "I thought you were up to something when you snuck off in the waiting room. Did you really think I wouldn't hear you tiptoeing away?"

Katherine fished the purse and the passes out of her satchel and threw them at Spider. Spider snatched them out of the air. "Now listen. We made a bargain, you and me, and if you can't keep your word on that, you'll never make a decent guide, nor anything else for that matter. You're my apprentice until I sign you over to your brother, so no more of these tricks. Understand?"

"Yes" was Katherine's resentful reply. She turned and was about to step out from between the two trucks when Spider pulled her back.

"Wait," he whispered. "Don't be too hasty."

"But the buses to Northridge are just there," replied Katherine.

Joe watched Spider's face. The old man was listening to something, and he didn't look pleased. "It's no good," he said. "Cloves was right; we'll have to find another way. Come on, the tide'll be receding by now. We'll go back to the road."

Katherine groaned. "Why?" she whined. "Why can't we just get on—"

"See for yourself," retorted Spider.

Katherine and Joe peered carefully around the corner. The buses to Northridge stood a little way ahead, and they were already half full. Guides and their charges were standing in a line by a long table where two secret policemen were checking their passes. Once the passes were stamped, the charges were directed to another table where, to Joe's absolute horror, two more secret policemen sat with their listening machines set in front of them. They were attaching the clips to two of the charges, a boy about Joe's age and a girl who looked a little younger.

"Cloves told me they've started testing all the charges who come through here."

"All of them?" gasped Katherine, tears springing to her eyes. "But they can't. Why would they?"

"I don't know," replied Spider. "Maybe they think it saves time. Wait a minute . . . what's *he* doing there?"

Joe didn't know who Spider meant until he saw Wyn standing by the second bus, talking to one of the secret policemen. Spider stood still for a moment, listening hard, but then one of the policemen at the table twisted the dial on his machine. The little girl began to scream.

"Let's go," said Spider. Joe and Katherine didn't wait to be told twice. Katherine took the lead and hurried back between the parked vehicles, wending her way toward the sea road.

When they reached the edge of the field, Spider stopped. "Hold on," he said. "Is there anyone about?"

Katherine and Joe peered up and down the lane that led from the field to the sea road. "Can't see anyone," said Katherine. "There are trucks starting up back in the field—I can see their lights beyond the trees—but the road's still empty."

"Good," said Spider. "It won't be that way for long, now that the tide's going out. We'll have to take the first chance we get. Here it comes. We'll have to run. Ready? Follow me."

With only his staff to guide him, Spider began to run along the side of the road. Katherine and Joe followed. Behind them a solitary canvas-topped army truck rumbled out of the parking field and careened down the road toward them. The truck soon overtook them on the lane. Spider ran faster, catching up with the truck as it slowed to turn onto the main sea road.

Spider grabbed hold of the tailgate and shouted something. In the blink of an eye, several pairs of hands reached down and pulled him aboard. Spider disappeared into the back of the canvas-covered truck. A moment later the flaps of the canvas doors were rolled back, and Spider and several khaki-clad soldiers were reaching out for Katherine and Joe.

"Come on!" cried Spider. Even with the heavy pack

on her back, Katherine ran ahead of Joe. As soon as she was close enough, she leapt at the truck. Spider caught her by her arms and with the help of the soldiers hauled her up into the truck.

"Come on, Joe!" yelled Spider as the truck sped off. Somehow Joe managed to grab hold of the tailgate and hang on.

"That's it, up you come," said Spider as he and the soldiers pulled Joe up into the truck. Joe landed on his back among a pile of lumpy kit bags.

"Much obliged," Spider told them. Then he turned to Katherine and Joe. "You'll have to hunker down here by the tailgate. There's not much room, but it's dry, and if we keep out of sight, we won't be bothered by the secret police. If we're lucky they'll think we're still in Quarain. That should buy us some time."

"But," asked Joe, "won't . . . won't the soldiers, these soldiers, won't they give us away?"

Spider shook his head. "Not many in the army care for the police."

Joe and Katherine sat with their backs against the kit bags. There was barely room to move. Katherine glared ruefully at Spider, who had managed to secure himself a seat on the end of one of the benches. Spider was hunkered over, furtively scribbling something on a scrap of paper. Joe twisted around as much as he was able and looked at the soldiers in the truck. Some of them didn't look that much older than Katherine.

Katherine leaned her head against Spider's backpack beside her and closed her eyes. She was soon asleep. Joe was amazed. How could she sleep when it was so noisy? Joe listened to the thrum of the truck's engine and the hammering of the rain on the canvas roof. At least he felt glad about one thing—he was on his way to find his sister at last.

They had been traveling for two or three hours when Joe, squinting through a small hole in the canvas, noticed that the trucks behind them were pulling over to the side of the road. A fast-moving line of dark vehicles was speeding along the road and overtaking each truck.

Joe watched as the fast-moving convoy came up behind them. One long black armored car, a sort of limousine, was flanked by four motorcycles. The lead motorcycles honked their horns. The truck slowed and obediently lumbered over to the side of the road as the other trucks had done.

The front two motorcycles shot past. Then came the car. It was fast and sleek. Its body was dark like iron, and its long, thin windows mirrored the gray sky, making it impossible to see inside. On top of the car a soldier sat in a gun turret, swiveling the gun, as though an attack might come from any direction at any moment. In a flash the car and the last two motorcycles sped by. The truck rocked precariously as it pulled back out onto the road.

"What's happening out there?" Spider asked.

Joe quickly told Spider all he'd seen. "Who was that?" he asked the old man.

Spider bowed his head and brought his mouth close to Joe's ear. "The ambassador," he said as quietly as he could.

"Orlemann," said Joe.

Spider shushed him. "What do you know of him?" he asked.

"Nothing," whispered Joe. "He was there with Elysia when I got the passes, that's all."

"Did he see you?" Spider's voice shook.

"No," replied Joe.

"You certain?"

"Yes, I'm sure of it."

"Good." Spider took a deep breath. "You stay away from him, d'you hear?"

"Why? Who is he? What does he do?"

Katherine opened one eye. "He's Elysia's ambassador. He goes off once every two months or so to talk peace with the Meridians. Then he comes back and says they 'int ready to listen yet. Waste of time. Ow!"

Katherine ruefully rubbed her backside where Spider

had kicked it. "All right, I'll keep my mouth shut," she said.

"We need to eat," said Spider. "Pass me my pack." Katherine did as she was told. Spider dug in his backpack, brought out a brick of oatmeal, and broke it in three. He ate one and gave the other two to Joe and Katherine. Katherine ate hers quickly, but even though he was starving, Joe could barely swallow his. It was like trying to eat a cold, damp sock.

By the time he'd finished his piece, Katherine and Spider were both asleep. Joe was just starting to nod off himself when the truck turned a corner and skidded to a halt. The soldiers woke up, stretching and yawning noisily.

Someone banged along the side of the truck. "Everybody out!" barked a man's voice.

Two soldiers jumped over Joe's head and leapt down. They shot back the bolts on the tailgate and dropped it open.

"Let's be having you. No dillydallying, please," barked the voice again.

When all the soldiers had gone, Spider sniffed. "All right," he said. "Let's go."

Katherine jumped down from the truck, pulling Spider's pack after her. Joe followed and then Spider, refusing their help, jumped down beside them. Katherine hoisted the pack onto her shoulders and staggered beneath the weight.

Joe looked around. They were in the trenches again. A notice was tacked up on the mud wall beside them. It was a mocked-up street sign. "Lovers' Lane," it read. Joe guessed it was supposed to be a joke, but it didn't seem very funny.

Another guide and his charge, a boy, were disembarking from the next truck. The boy was very young, and he looked scared. He had dark circles under his eyes, but the rest of his face was chalky.

The boy's guide sidled up to Spider. "Carey," he murmured, looking the other way.

"Kilpatrick," Spider said back. The other guide grunted in reply, then bent down to fix the straps on his pack.

"You going over . . . ?" asked Kilpatrick cryptically.

"Not unless I have to," replied Spider.

"I got no choice," said Kilpatrick. "It's bad news risking it without a pass, but you gotta try, 'int you? It's the only way to make sure . . . you know." He stood and hoisted his pack onto his shoulders. "G'luck then!" he muttered.

"You too," replied Spider, turning his head away.

Kilpatrick and his charge headed in the opposite

direction to the soldiers. Joe stared after them. Wherever Hannah was, he wondered if she was as scared as that poor kid had looked. Joe shuddered and pushed the thought away.

"Look lively," said Spider, tapping Joe on the shoulder. A truck loaded with rusting machine parts was backing out of a trench. Joe leaned up against the wall to avoid being flattened and found himself entangled in a clothesline that was strung with dead rats.

"Last night's catch," said a soldier beside Joe, jerking his thumb at the macabre display.

"Maybe you'll get 'em in a stew later on," added his mate. "Yummy, yummy!"

Joe swallowed hard. The truck passed, and Spider pulled Joe away from the wall.

"Come on," Spider said. "Let's see if these passes are of any use to us. There should be an officer somewhere. We'll need to report to him."

"I see one," said Katherine. "Over there."

The officer was sitting under a canvas awning. There was a surprisingly short line of people waiting to see him—guides with their charges for the most part. Joe led Spider toward the line.

Joe looked around. They were standing at the side of a broad, avenue-like trench that led to a high gate made of coiled wire. But it was what he could see in the open area before the gate that held Joe's attention.

The limousine and the motorcycles that had passed them on the road stood in this space, but these were not what intrigued him. These vehicles were dwarfed by a large, heavily armored truck. Standing a good thirty or forty feet high, it was far larger than the army trucks. Soldiers were loading the upper part of this truck with sacks of grain and flour, medical supplies, and crates of what looked like vegetables. A narrow door in the underbelly of the vehicle stood open, and a few clerks and military people buzzed about it. The secret policemen stood guarding the charges, who were all grouped together a little way from the truck. Something struck Joe as odd about the charges, but he didn't know what. And he didn't have time to think about it because in the next instant he saw Wyn standing with the two secret policemen. Joe shrank back.

Wyn must be traveling with the convoy, he thought. *But why?*

Spider nudged Joe in the ribs. They had reached the front of the line. Spider handed Elysia's passes to the officer. The man's eyes bugged out when he saw them. He turned the papers over, held them at an angle, then looked up and peered at Spider. The officer stood up abruptly and accidentally knocked his head against the awning. Rainwater that had collected there spilled out and drenched him. The officer swore fiercely and sat down again. He frowned at Spider as though it were his fault, then called to another officer, who joined him at the table. The first officer showed the second the passes, and both men scrutinized the signature on each, peering at it intently, then holding it up to the light.

"Where did you get these?" asked the second officer suspiciously.

"Quarain," replied Spider.

The officers spoke quietly to each other. Then the first officer said, "Looks genuine enough, but it's rare to see her signature. We'll have to have these verified by our superior."

"Show them to him, then," said Spider. "But be quick."

The officer pulled a face. "Can't be that quick. He's not here at the moment. Should be back at the end of the week, though."

Spider leaned on the table. "We need a place on that bus," he said forcefully.

"'We'?" laughed the officer. "You must be new to guiding, Granddad. Not even these passes, if they are genuine, would get *you* on that bus. There's no guides allowed into the city. Don't you know that? Rules say you hand your charge over here. That's the way it works."

Joe's eyes opened wide. Of course, that was what was strange about the group of charges. They were all on their own. There were no guides with them.

"Is that so?" said Spider. "Well, why don't you take him, then."

The officer shook his head. "Not until we get these passes checked. You'd better find yourself somewhere to wait." The officer slotted the passes into a thin green folder and filed them in a dispatch box beside him. "I'll keep these," he said in a reasonable tone. "We have to check them very carefully. There're too many trying to get their charges through on forged papers. We have to watch out for spies and the like. Now, I advise you to wait somewhere else. It'll get pretty hairy around here soon. The ambassador's convoy is to go through the wire, and we're sending the scavenging squad through first as a distraction."

"Why do you need a distraction?" asked Spider. "Isn't Merid supposed to disarm her machines while the convoy crosses the plain?"

The officer gave him a long look, then leaned over the desk.

"Supposed to, yes, but . . . ," he began. "The last

convoy through here was almost completely wiped out. She fired as soon as they were on the plain. Thank goodness she didn't know we were smuggling charges in the belly of that truck. If she'd known that, she wouldn't have called off her machines, would she? I think she was just trying to show she wouldn't stand for any messing with the schedule—the convoy was a little late setting off, you see. The ambassador's car took a direct hit, killing the driver. It was only by the sheerest good luck that the ambassador survived." The officer drew himself up and shuffled some papers. "Now, I suggest you take yourselves to the farthest part of the trenches till the smoke clears. Come and see me in a week or so and we'll see what we can do."

Spider nodded at the officer. Then, moving away from the table, he crossed to the other side of the trench. Katherine and Joe followed.

At first the way was crowded with people—soldiers, officers, guides, medics, and clerks all heading in one direction or another. Farther on, Joe saw a long line of guides beside a table where a clerk presided over a high stack of paperwork. Once the guides finished signing and countersigning, the clerk counted out ten banknotes for each.

Joe was puzzled. "If there are so many guides here,"

he said, thinking out loud, "why was there such a short-age when we were at the guides' canteen?"

Spider laughed. "I've been asking myself that very question—it's most likely they can't move from here without the right paperwork. Bureaucrats run the show in these trenches, just like they do everywhere else. But you know what"—Spider lowered his voice—"I bet if someone wanted this lot somewhere else, the paperwork would sort itself out and quick, no question."

"Do you mean someone has planned it this way?" asked Katherine.

Spider shrugged.

They turned east at the next intersecting trench and were greeted by the sound of noisy chatter. The way ahead was crowded with guides. Most of them were standing around in small groups, talking or leaning against the trench walls, smoking. Katherine, Joe, and Spider pushed through. Three large grills stood along part of the wall, and sausages by the dozen sizzled on them. Joe stopped as a man carried a vast platter of food past him and in through a doorway in the mud wall. Joe's mouth watered as he peered through the doorway and into the noisy room beyond. It looked like a tavern inside. In the glow of the amber-colored lanterns Joe could see guides lounging around tables, nursing glasses of beer. Every so often gales of laughter filled the air.

Spider winced. "Maybe it's not just the paperwork that keeps 'em here," he mused. "The soldiers may survive on rat stew, but the guides do very well for themselves. Fine food and beer and good company—why would anybody want to leave?" Joe glanced up at Spider. He looked angry. The old man increased his pace, and Joe and Katherine had to run to keep up with him.

Before long they found themselves walking through a series of abandoned trenches.

Suddenly Spider stopped. Joe crashed into his back, and Katherine crashed into his elbow. Both of them fell in the mud. Spider swung around and pulled them to their feet. Then he crouched in front of them.

"This," he said in low voice, "has been a very interesting morning thanks to you, Joe."

"Thanks to me?" asked Joe.

Spider smiled. "If it hadn't been for you I'd never have been able to leave the guides' canteen, where you found me. I'm very grateful to you, Joe. You've helped me enormously."

Katherine was eyeing Spider suspiciously. "You sound as though you're leaving."

Spider stood and took his pack from her shoulders. "I am. I'm going to the city—overland."

All the color drained out of Katherine's face.

"You can't!" she gasped.

"I can and I must and I will!" declared Spider.

"What about the passes?" she asked, her voice quavering a little. "The officer said that—"

"Forget about the passes," said Spider. "They won't get you or me on that convoy, and that won't help any of us."

"But we can't go overland!" she cried. "What about the machines?"

"You don't have to come." Spider harrumphed. "Though I'll miss your company."

"Don't give me that," retorted Katherine, grabbing one of the loose straps on Spider's pack and holding on tight. She narrowed her eyes and stared hard at the old man. "You weren't even planning on taking us, were you."

The muscles in Spider's jaw twitched. "No, I wasn't," he said, setting the pack back on the ground. "I can't," he said. "On my own, there's a chance, but with you two along—we'd all be killed before we got a hundred yards. You stay here and try to get Joe on the next convoy through."

Now Joe was angry. "No," he said. "You can't just use me to get where you want to go and then dump me. You have to take me with you. I have to—"

"Hush, Joe!" said Katherine. She turned to Spider. "Spider, listen very carefully. You take Joe and me with you, or the second you get on that plain, I'll start throwing everything I can your way and that'll get the machines over pretty darn quick."

"You wouldn't!" said Spider.

"Wouldn't I?" answered Katherine. "Why don't you try me?"

At that Spider burst out laughing and slapped Katherine on the back. Katherine looked confused.

"You are a little minx," laughed Spider. "Do you really want to come with me that much?"

"Yes," said Katherine.

"And you're not afraid of the machines?"

"No," answered Katherine defiantly.

"And you, Joe?" asked Spider, turning to Joe. "You're willing to risk it?"

"I am," replied Joe, though he wasn't quite sure exactly what he was risking.

"Well," said Spider, crouching again, "I'll take you, but on one condition only." His face grew serious. "You must promise—*promise*—to do what I say. No arguments. Understood?"

"Yes," replied Joe and Katherine together.

"All right, come with me," Spider threw his backpack at Katherine and set off once more along the trench, humming under his breath. Katherine watched Spider as she struggled to get the heavy pack on her shoulders.

"Ever had the feeling you've been had, Joe?" she asked.

"What do you mean?"

"Him. He's a crafty beggar. I think he only said we couldn't go with him so we'd fight to make him take us. I bet he intended us to go all along."

Spider hooted with laughter. Katherine emitted a low growl.

Two hundred yards farther along the trench they reached the blackened stump of a long-dead tree. Spider stopped and sat on the wet ground. At the end of the trench, a mound of digging equipment stood abandoned. The rain sounded sweetly melodic as it fell against the tangle of rusted iron and steel. It was a pleasant sound until Spider began to whistle a series of long, lonesome notes. To make it even worse, a crow alighted on top of the equipment and cawed intermittently. Joe put his fingers in his ears.

Still whistling, Spider reached into his pack, which Katherine had put on the ground. He pulled a corner off one of the porridge bricks, then stood up and walked to the end of the trench.

As Spider approached, the crow flapped its wings and cawed ever louder. Spider held out his hand and offered the porridge to the bad-tempered bird. The crow hopped onto Spider's outstretched arm, snatched the porridge, and let the old man stroke its neck while it ate. A moment later Spider threw his arm up, and with one last ugly caw the crow took flight. Joe watched as it flew toward the low clouds and vanished into the mists.

Spider returned to where Joe and Katherine stood. He sat.

"Now, Joe," he said, patting the wet ground beside him, "sit here and tell me everything you heard in Elysia's room. What was the ambassador's report?"

Joe told Spider all he had overheard and all he had seen. Spider listened without saying a word. When Joe had finished, he nodded to himself.

"Abdication, is it?" he muttered under his breath. "Abdication on both sides. And I wonder who will head the new government when it is appointed and what sort of power they will have."

Spider was quiet for a few moments. Then finally he said, "We'll wait till the convoy sets off. The army's distraction will serve us as well as them, and if we time it right, we'll get a good start. After that we'll use the derelicts for cover. It's not too difficult. We can move from one to the next without getting caught."

Spider cocked his head to one side. "I hear the ambassador's car and the mercy mission bus starting up. Ah, there go the motorcycles. The distraction must be about to start, which means we'd best be on our way, too." Spider went to the wall of the trench, then cupped his hands to form a step. "Come on, up you go! But don't go forward until I give you the word. Right?"

"Right," said Joe. He put his foot on Spider's hands and was hoisted up the mud wall. He pulled himself onto the higher ground, then rolled out of the way. Katherine was next, followed by Spider.

Joe lay on his belly and looked around. The ground was sodden, but not quite as muddy as it had been in the trench. It was covered with the same sparse yellow grass he'd seen before. The plain stretched away to the west, disappearing after a quarter of a mile or so into a bank of fog. Another trench and a thick mass of barbed wire lay ahead, but beyond the tangle of wire he could make out the hazy outlines of rusted and burned-out war machines abandoned in the mud. Tanks and trucks were toppled over on their sides, some sunk up to their axles, even their gun turrets, in the treacherous mud. All were orange with rust.

"Won't we get fired at by the other side?" asked Joe.

"Keep your voice down," replied Katherine in a barely audible whisper. "There won't be any actual Meridians on the plain; they don't have soldiers in trenches here. You're looking at the Machine Lands."

The rain drummed on his back, but Joe hardly

noticed it. The fog was lifting, and now the craggy mountains to the north loomed purple. They looked frightening and inhospitable. Joe remembered what Spider had said. Some people thought there were dragons in the mountains.

"Look," gasped Katherine, nudging Joe. She was pointing westward, where the fog had dissolved to reveal a honey-colored wall far away across the plain.

"That's where we're headed," she whispered. "That's the wall that reaches around the Long City. I hope we can make it."

"Remember," Spider cautioned them, "stay close by."

Joe squinted across the plain. It was a long way to the wall. Far to the south it looked as though there was a high gate cut into the stone. It shone gunmetal gray in the dull light.

"Look!" said Katherine, grabbing his arm and pointing.

A hundred yards from where they lay, a group of soldiers climbed out of the trenches, crossed the ground, then scurried down into a second trench. A few moments later they climbed out of the far side of it, then skillfully wriggled their way beneath the mass of barbed wire. Once they were through, they ran to the nearest derelict machine and immediately set to work, quickly and efficiently taking it apart. They stripped it clean of pipes and cogs and engine parts, using wrenches and claw hammers to pry sections away. The screeching, discordant noise they made was horrendous. Other soldiers were running back to the trenches, carrying pieces of metal between them. They hurled each piece over the wire and down into the second trench. Then they ran back for more.

Spider tapped Katherine's shoulder and began to crawl to the edge of the second trench. Katherine followed and then Joe. When they reached the edge of this trench Joe was shocked by how much deeper it was than the other one and how much steeper the sides had been cut.

"It's the only way to keep the machines out of our land," said Katherine. "They can't get over these trenches."

"Less talk, more movement," said Spider, poking Katherine in the ribs. "Down you go."

The second trench had a wall of long plank supports along its sides to prevent the mud from collapsing. To Joe's relief he found that wooden rungs had been nailed in a line from the top to the bottom on both sides. There was one of these "ladders" close by. Katherine led the way.

In moments the three of them were at the bottom of the deep trench, searching for a line of rungs that would take them up the other side.

"Over here!" cried Katherine, and without waiting to hear what Spider had to say, she was away down the trench.

"That'll take us too near to the distraction team," called Spider, but it was no use. Katherine was halfway to the top, and Joe had followed her. Spider set off toward them, feeling his way along the cold mud wall.

When Joe reached the top of the trench he could see that Spider had been right. They were at least fifty yards nearer to where the soldiers were stripping the derelict machine. The barbs on the wire in front of them looked terrifyingly sharp.

"Let's go!" said Spider.

"We'll have to cut through the wires first," said Katherine as she took a pair of wire cutters out of her satchel and fitted their jaws around the first wire. She squeezed the handles of the cutters together, and the wire snapped with a sharp click.

Spider grabbed her wrist. "We can't afford to make noise like that," he growled.

"No machine's going to hear this above that racket," she whispered, jerking her head toward the soldiers at the derelict. "Besides, how else are we going to get through?"

Spider frowned, then roughly pushed her hand away. "Go ahead then, but be quick about it. And for heaven's sakes, try and do it quietly."

Spider winced at each loud crack as Katherine snipped through the rest of the tangled wires. When she had finally cut the last wire, Spider wiped beads of sweat from his forehead and nodded.

"All right, we'll take it nice and slow," he said, inching forward and pushing the cut wire out of the way.

"But the plain's deserted," said Joe as he crawled out behind Spider. "We'll easily—"

"Shush," warned Spider, pushing Joe flat against the ground. "There's a Goliath coming. Keep dead still if you want to stay alive. They track by motion and sound, and this one's coming a little too close for comfort."

Suddenly Joe heard what Spider was talking about. It was the faint whir of an engine. The soldiers heard it, too.

"GOLIATH!" one of them shouted.

The other men stopped and listened, then began to work faster, tearing the engine apart with their bare hands and running back toward the trench with whatever they could carry.

"Here it comes," said Spider. "Keep still."

Joe saw a small, dun-colored machine trundling over the sodden grass. It was laughably small, a miniature tank, no bigger than a go-cart. The Goliath's iron sides were rusty, and it moved erratically on narrow caterpillar treads. It had a turret on top that swiveled, enabling its stumpy gun to point in all directions. Joe wondered what was so terrible about this "Goliath." It didn't look big enough to do much damage.

Suddenly a whistle blew. "She's going through!" shouted someone in the trenches. The soldiers on the plain grabbed what they could and raced back toward the wire, banging and clattering the parts they'd collected as they went.

At that moment the ambassador's limousine, the four motorcycles, and the enormous truck shot through the gate, over the swing bridge, and out across the plain. The gun on the Goliath spun toward the convoy. The soldiers banged louder, and the gun swiveled back to them.

The Goliath shot a twenty-five-yard arc of fire from its short gun. Katherine hid her eyes as running soldiers were engulfed by flames. Clouds of black, acrid smoke rolled into the sky; when they'd cleared there was no sign of the soldiers; there were only black scorch marks in the grass.

The Goliath trundled after the soldiers who had escaped, but it stopped by the second deep trench and the tangle of wire.

Katherine gasped and pointed toward the derelict. Three soldiers stood there petrified, staring at the Goliath.

"Oh, move," hissed Katherine. "Your mates can't fire until you're all back."

"Shush," warned Spider. Too late. Though she'd barely whispered, the Goliath had heard Katherine's voice. Swiveling its gun in their direction, it trundled toward them.

Suddenly an almighty racket started in the trenches. The soldiers were banging pots and pans and waving poles with dummies strung on the ends to distract the Goliath. It worked. The machine turned swiftly and raced back to the wire. It stopped and sprayed its flaming arc toward the trench. Its flames burned nothing but the grass.

"Those men by the derelict'll make a run for it soon," said Spider, his voice barely louder than his breath. "That's when we'll make our move. Is there another derelict close by?"

"About fifty yards away, straight ahead," whispered Katherine.

"Good girl," he answered. "That'll be our next stop."

As Spider had predicted, the soldiers by the dismantled derelict made a break for it. As soon as they did, the
Goliath swiveled and spewed another arc of brilliant
flame.

Joe had no time to see whether the men made it to
safety because Spider grabbed his wrist and pulled him
across the plain.

The fumes from the smoke almost choked them, but
they made it to the next derelict, a rusted hull of a tank
that lay on its side, half buried in the mud.

Spider felt along the base of the machine.

"Here, quick," he hissed. "Get underneath." Joe and
Katherine crawled into a space between the metal and
the earth. Spider wriggled in beside them. The three of
them lay still and quiet, trying to recover their breath.

The smoke from the burning grass was clearing. The
Goliath stood silent and proud in front of a large fan of
scorched earth. There was no sign of the soldiers who
had set off from the raided derelict.

The guns in the trench blasted angrily at the
Goliath. Joe stuck his fingers in his ears as bullets ricocheted off the Goliath's iron sides. The machine spun its
gun in all directions. Then, as though satisfied that it
had done its duty, it took up a silent post by the derelict
that the soldiers had been raiding. The soldiers in the
trench stopped firing.

Far in the distance, Joe could see that the convoy had almost reached the city.

"What now?" asked Katherine quietly.

"If we go slow," replied Spider in a barely audible whisper, "we can probably crawl to the next derelict, but take care. If that Goliath moves, stop dead in your tracks and keep absolutely still and quiet. And remember, that won't be the only one we'll meet today."

CHAPTER 13

Fairy Footsteps

There was a game called fairy footsteps that Joe remembered playing when he was very young. The person who was it stood facing a wall while everyone else had to try to creep up and touch them. But it could turn around without warning, and if they did and saw you moving, you'd be out. If you so much as wobbled, you'd be out. It was one of Hannah's favorite games, and she was always trying to get Joe to play it with her. But he never would. Now he was playing it whether he wanted to or not. This time he was playing for his life.

At Spider's signal the three of them crept out from underneath the tank and slowly stood. Katherine and Joe kept their eyes fixed on the Goliath, still standing guard by the raided derelict.

Then, like a player in fairy footsteps, Joe stealthily began to move across the wet grass.

They were almost clear of the derelict when Spider accidentally caught his staff against the underside of the tank. It resounded like a bell, and the Goliath's turret swiftly spun toward them. Lightning fast, Spider grabbed a rock and low-balled it past the Goliath. The automaton picked up on the movement of the rock, and a great arc of flame followed its trajectory.

They were perhaps three paces out into the open when the Goliath stopped incinerating the place where the rock had fallen and spun its gun back toward them.

"Hold it," growled Spider.

At least it isn't heat-seeking, thought Joe. *We'll be all right as long as we stay still and quiet.* But he was scared. His heart was thumping so loudly in his chest that he was worried the Goliath might hear it.

Five very slow minutes passed. It felt much longer. Joe's arms and legs soon began to ache with the strain of holding so still.

Katherine's eyes met Joe's. She looked frightened. Suddenly a loud, metallic creak came from the direction of the trenches. The Goliath swung its turret around. As another creak tore through the silence, the Goliath adjusted the angle of its gun, then sped off in the direction of the sound.

"What is it?" whispered Joe.

"Whatever it is, it's lucky for us," said Spider. "Come on, run! Katherine, lead us to the next derelict."

When they reached the shelter of the next abandoned machine, an overturned truck, they hunkered down beneath it. Keeping his head low, Joe looked back toward the trenches and saw what was making the horrible creaking sound. The derelict the soldiers had been stripping was swaying precariously, and the metal was groaning under the pressure. The soldiers must have removed the machine's underpinnings. As Joe watched, two more Goliaths approached from the other side. All three machines fired on the derelict. When they stopped, the burned-out carcass of the machine toppled and fell.

"What now?" asked Katherine.

"We rest," replied Spider as he very slowly and carefully took off his coat and rolled it up. "Take care not to move in your sleep, just in case one of them comes near."

With that he lay his head upon the roll of his coat and settled down for a nap. Within moments the old man was breathing in such a regular pattern that neither Joe nor Katherine could doubt that he was fast asleep.

"Great!" muttered Katherine, staring out at the plain. "Now he's got us stranded out here. How are we supposed to go to sleep? I don't know about you, but I don't think I can sleep without moving. I'm going to have to stay awake."

Joe wasn't listening. He was staring at the roll of Spider's coat, which was close to his head. Spider's face was turned away, and the notebook was right there, jutting out of the breast pocket. The book that Wyn had tried to steal. The book Spider had protected so fiercely. *Why does Wyn want it so badly?* Joe wondered.

Very slowly, Joe slid it out of the pocket.

"What are you doing?" asked Katherine.

Joe jumped guiltily. He'd forgotten she was there. "I just wanted to see what was so secret about this," he said.

Katherine shifted closer. "Let's have a look then," she said.

As quietly as he could, Joe pulled the elastic band that held the book together clear of the binding. Being careful not to let any of the loose pages fall out, he opened the book and angled it toward the fading daylight. The first page was covered in complicated drawings and diagrams of what looked like fun fair rides— roller coasters, scramblers, and carousels. The drawings were surrounded by notes and arrows. Joe tried to decipher the writing, but it was written in such a small, cramped hand that he couldn't make it out. He turned the pages and soon saw that the whole book was

crammed full of drawings—of people, of animals, of
insects, of buildings, of bridges. There were drawings
of faces, and a page full of just eyes and expressions.
There were landscapes and abstract doodles. Many were
drawings of fantastic machines that Joe had never seen
before. Every page of the book was so covered in sketches
that there wasn't even the tiniest place where the paper
was bare.

"Why would a blind man carry a book full of pictures?" whispered Katherine. "What use are they to
him?"

"But he can 'see' some of them," replied Joe. "Here."
Joe took Katherine's hand and guided her fingers over
the paper.

"It's all bumpy," she whispered.

"A lot of these have pinpricks along their lines," Joe
said. "It's like Braille. Spider must be able to read the
pictures."

Katherine took the book gently from Joe and leafed
through the pages. "These are beautiful," she whispered
as she gazed at a page covered with horses. "Look at
this—and this—oh, and this." Katherine turned another
page, and as she did, one loose leaf slipped out and fell
to the ground. Joe picked it up.

The page was folded in quarters, and while Katherine

went on gazing at Spider's book, Joe opened the loose
page. He could see immediately that it must have come
from some other book. The paper was thicker; it was
more like fabric than paper. In the upper left-hand corner of the page was a tiny painting. It reminded Joe of
the illuminated letters he'd once seen in a history book.
The colors shone in the grim light. Below the painting
the page was covered in neat writing, but the text was in
a language Joe couldn't understand. He turned the paper
over. The other side was completely covered in hand-
writing, but it was impossible to decipher. To Joe's mind
it looked more like scribble. Another strange thing about
the page was the way the paper was creased, not just
from where it had been folded in four, but it also looked
as though it had once been set in some other, more complicated pattern of folds. It was like a finished origami
animal that had been undone and smoothed out. The
animal had gone, but the creases remained. Joe started to
try to refold it to find out what it might have been.

Suddenly Spider snatched the book from Katherine's
hands.

"No one has the right to nose about in another man's
memories," he said. He felt through the book, then held
out his hand. "And the rest," he added. Joe handed him
back the loose sheet. Spider closed the book, replaced
the elastic, then put it back in his inside pocket. "You

wouldn't like it if someone went poking through your things, would you?"

Joe knew from experience that he wouldn't. "I'm sorry," he mumbled.

"So you should be," said Spider grumpily. "Now get some sleep, the pair of you. We've a long way to go, and you'll be needing all your strength."

But Joe couldn't sleep. He lay on his back, staring up through a rusted hole in the truck above him and watching as the sky grew dark. The rain fell fast but not heavily, and Joe didn't mind it falling on his face. On one side of him Spider slept; on the other, Katherine lay on her stomach, snoring softly.

As the sky darkened, a storm came on, but it wasn't like any storm that Joe could remember. There was no thunder, and the rain neither stopped nor increased. It was only the lightning that made Joe think there was a storm at all. Every so often a strange pearly light would flare, illuminating the whole cloud-filled sky the way sheet lightning does on summer nights. But this didn't fade as fast as lightning.

It was the same light Joe had seen in his dream the night that Hannah had fallen ill. The same light he had seen when he'd been riding in the back of the peat truck that first night in this strange land. The light grew brighter, lingered, then faded gradually back to darkness.

Then it came again. It happened every few minutes, and Joe watched it maybe twenty or thirty times before he fell asleep and began to dream.

In his dream he saw Hannah's hospital room, Hannah in bed, his parents sitting one on either side of her, his mother looking sad, the machines with their flashing lights and noisy beeps. As he approached the bed, he knew he had to tell his parents that it was all his fault that Hannah was sick. He had to tell them he was sorry and that he was doing everything he could to make it right. But the words wouldn't come out, and his parents didn't even notice he was there. He tried to shout, he tried to get them to understand, but as he cried, a hand closed over his mouth.

"Shhhhh!" Spider hissed in his ear. Joe's eyes snapped open. The sky through the rusted hole was a dirty early-morning gray. Joe blinked up at the rain.

"Lean over and wake her ladyship," said Spider, "but don't let her make any noise."

Joe touched Katherine's shoulder. "I'm awake," she said quietly. Then very slowly she turned around.

"Where's the backpack?" whispered Spider. Katherine pushed the pack toward him, and Spider's hands found the straps and the buckles and buttons and unfastened them. Carefully, he lifted out rolls of rags and bits of string and cardboard; then, reaching way down into the bottom of the pack, he pulled out five small rusted metal boxes that were fastened to short planks of wood. He set them in a line on the ground, then began to assemble them. Joe remembered how Wyn had rifled through the backpack when it had been stashed beneath the table. He probably hadn't gotten down to the bottom, through Spider's cleverly arranged layers of rubbish.

Spider's nimble fingers flew from one box to the next. First he gently lifted the lids off each. Then, hooking a finger down into the box, he brought out a loop of metal wire, and after closing the lid, fixed this to the top of the box. The wire was bent and rusty and it squeaked as it was screwed into place. Spider winced, then spat on the place where the wire joined the box. The spit stopped it from squeaking. When the wire was in place, Spider took two long, grubby ribbons and tied them one on either side of the metal loop.

"Haven't used any of these for a while," whispered Spider when all five little boxes were lined up and adorned with their loops and ribbons. "Hope they work."

"What are they?" asked Joe. The boxes looked like something an eight-year-old would make in a woodworking class.

"I call 'em distracters," replied Spider. "My own

invention. If they work, they'll be very attractive to the Goliaths, very attractive."

Spider then took a strange-looking contraption out of the backpack. It was a sort of instrument panel, or so Joe supposed, though it had only two crude switches on it. It was about two inches wide by perhaps six inches long and was made of the same rough planking as the base of the boxes. There was a long leather strap dangling from the top of it, and Spider lifted it over his head so the panel hung down on his chest. Once it was there he attached a long, thin strip of wire to one corner of the panel and bent it so it was pointing toward the sky.

"Not, perhaps, the most stylish equipment," he said as he fingered the rough wood, "but effective, we hope." Spider shuffled out from under the tank. "Joe, hand me one of those boxes. You take two and Katherine can manage the others, once she has the pack in place."

Katherine wriggled into the backpack straps and pulled it onto her back. "Least it's not as heavy now," she said as she picked up two of the boxes. "These must have made up most of the weight."

Joe lifted his two boxes and realized what she meant. They were a lot heavier than they looked. They felt as though they were made of lead.

He struggled out from under the tank to find the

plain as vast and gray, as rain-soaked and empty as it had looked the day before. Spider gently set his box on the bumper of the derelict truck, turned a key on its side, and left it there.

"Come on," he said.

They traveled so slowly and quietly that it was a long while until they encountered another machine. Spider heard it first and held up his hand. The automaton was another Goliath, though Joe noticed that this one was larger than the first and some of its armaments were differently arranged. *Perhaps it's an earlier model,* he thought. It was a strange thing to think under the circumstances, the circumstances being that if he made one false move he would be blasted with a plume of flame.

The Goliath stopped about twenty-five yards away. Joe could feel his heart pounding loudly inside his chest.

Out of the corner of his eye Joe noticed that Spider was moving very slowly, so slowly that at first Joe couldn't be sure he was moving at all. He was lifting his left hand. Joe realized he was trying to reach the buttons on the panel.

Finally Spider reached one of the buttons and pressed it. From behind them came a horrid squealing. It sounded like an animal in agony. And it was getting louder and louder. The Goliath lifted its gun and shot forward on its caterpillar treads. It was heading straight toward them!

"Wait," warned Spider under his breath as the Goliath sped toward them. "Move too soon, and you're dead. It's got a blind spot close up. I'll tell you when it's safe."

When the Goliath was less than two yards from where they stood, Spider shoved Joe hard and, grabbing Katherine, pulled her out of the way. The Goliath blasted past them as they fell in a sprawl on the mud.

Joe turned and watched the Goliath go. He could see the little box on top of the upturned truck. The loop of metal was spinning crazily, and the ribbons were flying in the air. The spinning loop was making the horrendous noise as it grated in its socket. The boxes weren't very sophisticated, but they did the job.

Spider chuckled softly beside him. "Now let's see how it stands up to an attack," he said. As though to oblige in the demonstration, the Goliath shot its great stream of flame, engulfing the little box and most of the truck. When the smoke cleared, the squeaking sound was still there, though the ribbons had gone. This confused the mechanical workings of the automaton, and it moved forward and tried firing again. Again, once the smoke had cleared the little box was still operating, though perhaps not as well as it had before. The Goliath moved closer.

Spider smiled. "Now," he said. "Stick your fingers in your ears and keep your heads down, you two. It's likely to get blowy." Then he pressed the second button on his panel.

Nothing happened.

Katherine looked at Spider. "Is that it?" she whispered.

Spider looked disappointed. He pressed the button again. Again nothing. Katherine rolled her eyes. Spider pressed the button again and held it down.

This time the little box exploded with such tremendous force that the Goliath was blown to pieces. Great shards of metal flew over Joe's head and landed several feet behind him.

Joe looked at the two boxes in his hands. These, too, must be packed with explosives. He would make sure to handle them with more care in the future.

Spider chuckled and set off toward the great wall in the distance. Joe and Katherine followed him, the sound of the explosion still ringing in their ears.

"Won't that just have attracted more of those machines?" asked Joe after they'd gone a little way.

"Let's hope so," replied Spider. "And let's hope it

keeps them busy while we make our way forward. At least now we can fight back." He took a box from Joe and set it as he walked. "We'll have to be sparing with them, though, save 'em for when we need 'em most."

By the end of the day there were only two of the little distracter boxes left. Joe felt as though he had walked forever and was exhausted when Spider finally decided it was time to stop. They were less than a quarter of a mile from the wall, which, Joe hoped, would mean only a short journey tomorrow.

Night was beginning to fall, and as the clouded sky grew darker, they took refuge under another derelict. This time it was a truck, rolled over on its side. Its undercar had a great hole torn in it, and what was left of the rest of the vehicle was charred black.

Spider felt the crater-like hole in the underside of the truck. "It's as good a place as any to rest up for the night."

"But we're so close," said Katherine. "Can't we just carry on? We've got two boxes left."

"Goliaths aren't our only worry now that we're getting closer to the wall," said Spider. "There're plenty worse things to fear than a bit of a scorching. Now, squeeze yourselves down there and keep still. I'll be back in a minute."

Katherine hunkered down in the space between the

crater and the truck and rested against the backpack. Joe sat beside her and stared out through the narrow gap they had just crawled through. Spider moved to the last derelict before the wall. He prodded at the ground with his staff. Then his head shot up, and with quick steps he returned to the truck.

He rolled into the dark space beneath the truck. "We can't go straight to the wall from here," he said, recovering his breath. "Must have come farther north than I thought. We'll have to go south for a ways, then across."

"Why?" asked Katherine.

"Because for one thing the part of the wall we need is farther along, and for another there's a strip of quicksand running parallel to it that'll swallow you up fast as anything."

That shut Katherine up. By now it was fully dark outside, and Joe saw the flashes he had seen in the sky the previous night.

"What's that light?" Joe asked Spider.

Spider jerked to attention. "Light? What light?" he asked urgently. "Describe it to me."

Joe did so, and Spider relaxed and leaned back with a chuckle. "You had me worried for a moment. The lights in the sky to the north? The superstitious ones say it's the dragons in the mountains snorting silver flames. Me? I don't know. Maybe it's something to do with the magnetic rock. You shouldn't worry about . . ." Spider fell silent, and his face grew grave. "Get back into the shadows," he warned.

"Goliath?" whispered Joe.

"Worse. It sounds like a Zamrami," he said in a cold voice. "Make yourself as small as possible and hide your eyes. Whatever you do, don't look at it. You understand me? Do not look at it!"

Joe scrabbled into the shadows and cowered beside Katherine.

"What did he say was coming?" asked Joe.

"Zamrami," she whispered. "They're worse than the Goliaths."

"Shush!" warned Spider. Then he clamped his hands over their eyes to make sure they did what he told them to do.

Again, the three of them held as still as death, barely breathing, not moving at all. Joe could hear the automaton approaching. Its treads squelched through the muddy grass, then stopped. There was a loud grating noise that Joe guessed was the gun turret of the automaton swiveling round. Then there was a loud clunk, and suddenly the darkness became full of bright white light. Even through his closed eyelids it was so bright that it seemed as though a hundred thousand lamps had been switched on all at once. Joe felt the pressure of Spider's hand tighten across his eyes, but even the small amount of light that seeped in around the edges of Spider's fingers was almost blinding.

The turret squeaked as it turned again, and then suddenly the light went out. Joe, Katherine, and Spider held still while the machine pulled away. When the sound of the engine had faded to nothing more than a distant hum, Spider let go of Joe and Katherine. Joe stared out at the darkness. He could still see the floating green image that the light had left on his retina.

"What was that?" asked Joe.

"That was what cost me my eyes," replied Spider. "It would have taken yours, too, if you'd looked at it."

Joe went to sleep that night dreaming of machines with lights so bright they could take your eyes away. He dreamed he saw them in Hannah's hospital room. Every time he tried to get near the bed, the lights would flash and drive him away.

The next day they reached the last derelict before the wall. The wall was fifty yards in front of them, and it seemed impossibly high. The dull yellow stones vanished into the mist. Along the base of the wall huge rectangles of rust-red iron had been riveted to the stones. Higher up, ominous brown smears stained the honey-colored stone.

Spider pointed to the ground with his staff. "See

the quicksand?" he asked. Joe could see no difference between the ground where Spider was pointing and the ground on which they stood. It was all covered in the sodden, scrubby brown grass. But beside him Katherine was nodding.

"I see it," she said.

"Tell me what you see," said Spider.

"The shapes of the blades of grass farther out," she said. "They're different than the ones here, fatter."

"What else?"

Katherine sniffed. "It smells different. Wetter perhaps."

Spider smiled. "Not bad," he said. "You might make a guide yet." Katherine looked pleased. "I wonder," Spider went on, "if you would have seen it if I hadn't told you it was there?"

Katherine's face fell. "No," she said.

"Not to worry," said Spider, almost kindly. "You just have a lot to learn; luckily you've a whole lifetime in which to learn it. Now stay close. We don't want any accidents."

They had been walking parallel to the wall for a good two or three hours when Spider stopped and sniffed. "I think we're very near," he said. He prodded the ground all around with his staff. "Katherine? Is our way to the wall safe?"

Katherine looked for a long time. "I think it's safe," she said finally. "The grass looks the same as it does over here."

Spider nodded. "Good. Then let's go."

They were less than seventy-five feet from the base of the wall when Spider stopped again.

"Wait," he cautioned.

"Quicksand?" asked Joe.

"No," replied Spider. "There's a Scraper coming."

"Is it after us?" asked Katherine in a whisper.

"I doubt it," replied Spider. "These machines don't usually search the ground. They prefer their prey up high. Take a look on the wall. Is anyone climbing?"

Katherine and Joe scanned the wall.

"There's someone about three-quarters of the way up," whispered Katherine in a horrified voice.

Joe recognized the boy he had seen on the truck. He and the guide Kilpatrick were climbing the wall. Wisps of cloud passed over them.

"Three-quarters of the way up," mused Spider. "Then they've no chance."

"What do you mean?" asked Joe.

"I mean they won't make it."

"We can help them," whispered Katherine. She pulled the next-to-last distracter from the backpack and quickly set it.

Spider gently took it from her. "We can't," he said. "That would only bring one of the other machines after us."

"But it might work," said Joe desperately. "It might distract the Scraper thing long enough for that boy to get away."

"No," said Spider, putting the box on the ground. "A Scraper's not like a Goliath; it can't be distracted. Once a Scraper has its sights on its quarry it locks on to them."

Spider's voice was drowned out by the roar of the Scraper's engine. Joe stuck his fingers in his ears as a large gray tank crawled through the mud toward the wall. This new machine was a huge, faceless steel box propelled by two whirring tracks. It proceeded at a moderate pace, flinging great clods of mud as it skidded forward. It had no gun, just a flat lid studded with rivets where a gun turret would have been.

High on the wall, the guide and the boy began to climb faster. The clouds cleared for a moment, and Joe could see the top of the wall. It wasn't so far above the climbers. Maybe Spider was wrong. He couldn't see how far up they were.

The Scraper stopped about fifty feet from the wall, and the engine cut out. There was a low mechanical groan as the riveted hatch opened, and a hollow *clonk* as it fell back against the tank. Then came a whirring noise as a pipe as thick as a tree trunk rose out of the hatch. A long, spidery arm telescoped section by section out of the pipe until it stood over seventy feet high. Joe breathed a sigh of relief. The arm was far too short to reach the full height of the wall. But the Scraper hadn't finished yet. Suddenly there was an explosion at the top of the arm and five long, heavy chains shot out into the air and came rattling to the ground.

The arm began to sway back and forth like the arm of a metronome. The chains clanked together as they followed the movement; then, as the arm picked up momentum, the chains began to fly. They whipped across the wall with a horrible grating sound. Joe winced. The chains were certainly long enough to reach the climbers. They would scrape that boy and his guide off the wall like bugs from a windshield.

Joe didn't want to watch, but he couldn't turn away. The guide and the boy disappeared behind the wisps of cloud. The arm lashed forward, then drew back. Joe held his breath. The clouds swirled and parted momentarily. The climbers were still there. The clouds closed together. The whipping arm flashed forward, dragging the chains behind it. Hidden in the clouds, the chains grated and slashed against the stone. The arm flew back, and the next time the clouds cleared, the wall was empty.

The chains crashed to the ground and the telescoping

arm folded in on itself, dragging the chains in after it. The hatch closed and the engine started; then the Scraper retreated across the mud in the direction it had come.

Joe was shaking all over.

"What happens to that boy in his own world?" he stammered in a barely audible whisper.

Neither Spider nor Katherine answered. The silence buzzed like dead air on the radio. Joe stared up at the empty wall and shuddered.

"Who could have built a machine like that?" whispered Joe.

"The Meridians are crueler than you can imagine," said Katherine.

"Perhaps," said Spider.

"How many charges make it over the wall?" asked Joe.

Spider got to his feet and set off. "Hardly any," he answered without looking back.

Joe scrambled after him. "Then it's suicide to try."

"Maybe," Spider replied. "But we're not going over, we're going through."

Katherine's mouth dropped open. "How?" she gasped.

"There used to be a way, built when the war began. It's just a matter of finding it. Now hurry up and be quiet."

Spider reached the wall first. He ran his fingers over

the rusty metal panels, reaching high and crouching low.

"Who put these panels here?" asked Joe.

"The authorities, to stop anyone from passing this way."

"You mean the Meridians," corrected Katherine.

"Hmmm," said Spider.

"Well, it's not likely to be anyone else out here, is it?" protested Katherine.

"Keep quiet. I have to listen for the space behind the wall."

Spider stopped, pressed his ear against the metal and tapped gently, then moved a little farther along the wall and tapped and listened again.

Joe looked at Katherine. Her pale face was even paler now.

"Joe, come here and tell me if there's anything you see in this plate right here."

Joe looked closely where Spider was pointing. There was nothing different about it except . . . "The rust is—" he began to say.

"Darker?" asked Spider. "It's darker than the rest, isn't it?"

"Yes," replied Joe.

Spider rubbed his hands together. "Good," he said, a note of triumph in his voice. "Our way through is right here."

Katherine and Joe stared at the place where Spider was pointing. It was right in the middle of one of the great iron patches.

"Oh" was all Katherine could say.

Spider felt for the edges of the panel. They were not within reach.

"Where's the edge?" he said. "Show me; tap on the edge for me, Joe."

Joe ran to the closest edge of the panel and tapped. It was a good five feet from where Spider stood. Spider's shoulders twitched.

"This is useless," said Katherine.

"Get me the hammer out of the pack," said Spider.

Katherine quickly passed him a claw hammer. Spider shuffled along the panel and began to tap at each rivet along the edge. The iron clanked like a broken bell.

"That's going to bring the machines after us," said Katherine anxiously.

"Can't be helped," replied Spider, tapping louder. "We'll be caught and killed for sure if we try to go back. It's waiting for us to start climbing."

"What is?" asked Joe.

"That one behind us now," said Spider.

Joe turned. The Scraper was about fifty feet away, and its hatch was beginning to open.

Spider tapped the hammer against a rivet.

"If we're lucky," he said, hammering harder, "the rain will have helped us here." Suddenly the rivet's head flew off in a shower of orange dust. "Yes!" exclaimed Spider, moving to the next rivet. "They're rusted through."

He deftly knocked the head off several more, then set the claws of his hammer in the crack between the panel and the wall and began to lever the iron away.

Behind them the Scraper's long arm was fully extended and the barbarous chains clanked together on the ground.

"What now?" asked Katherine, her voice rising.

"Don't panic," said Spider. "We have a little time."

Joe stared at the Scraper. It had started to wave its long arm back and forth, building up speed. Soon the chains would lift off the ground and lash through the air. If any part of that whip caught them, they would be smashed to bits.

"Help me," hissed Spider. He had opened a space big enough for his fingers and was now trying to pry the panel away from the wall with his hands. Joe and Katherine set their hands in the space and pulled as hard as they could.

The Scraper's arm swung faster. The long chains screamed through the air and crashed to the ground less than thirty feet behind them. Joe and Katherine spun around. They watched in horror as the Scraper's telescopic arm lifted the clanking chains behind it. They tilted their heads back as the arm reached its full height. It began to sway. The chains swung through the air behind it. Katherine and Joe couldn't take their eyes off the machine's hypnotizing swing.

"Joe! Katherine!" Spider shouted. "Don't give up now! We've nearly got it!" Katherine and Joe hurried to help him. Pushing the Scraper to the back of his mind, Joe grasped the iron and pulled. More rivet heads sprang off. The iron panel groaned and leaned out from the wall, but each time it sprang back. It was caught in one corner at the bottom.

"Quick, scrape away the sand!" Katherine cried.

Joe dropped to his knees and began to dig like a dog, frantically scooping the sand out of the way. The whipping chains sank into the sand no more than six feet from where the three of them stood. The chains had come so close that time that the wind that followed them had pushed him back against the wall. The Scraper's arm swung away. Next time the chains would find their mark.

"We've got to get it this time!" cried Spider. "One, two, three!" Joe grabbed the bottom of the panel, stuck a foot against the wall, and pulled for all he was worth.

The last of the rusted rivets popped along the top and flew like bottle tops through the air.

"Watch out!" Spider grabbed Joe by the shoulder and yanked him out of the way as the enormous panel fell away from the wall and crashed against the ground.

Behind them the Scraper was lifting its arm.

Spider quickly ran his hands along the wall. "Here it is," he panted. "Quick, inside now."

"Where?" cried Katherine desperately. Joe looked. Spider was crouching by a narrow crack in the wall. It was almost as tall as Joe but wasn't wide enough to poke a stick through.

"It's bigger than it looks!" shouted Spider over the noise of the chains being drawn back. Spider grabbed the backpack off Katherine and thrust it through the narrow gap. "See?" he said. Joe was surprised. The large pack had slipped through easily. *It must be something to do with the angle of the gap,* he thought.

Joe was still thinking about this as Katherine climbed through after the pack. He hardly noticed she'd gone. And he barely saw Spider as the old man crouched low, twisted sideways, and slipped inside the rock. He would still have been standing there if Spider's head hadn't reappeared.

"JOE!" the old man bellowed. "WILL YOU COME ON?"

Joe jumped. He leapt at the rock and was through the gap only a split second before the machine's terrible chains crashed down, sweeping across the ground where Joe had just been standing. The heavy chains hit the iron panel on the ground and smashed it to smithereens.

CHAPTER 14

Inside the Wall

Inside the wall there was barely enough room to stand. The great stones pressed in at Joe's chest and back: he could only move sideways, like a crab. Spider was ahead of him.

"That's it, go on," Spider told Katherine. "You can do it. Feel your way. Joe, stick close; it's only like this for a short while."

Outside, the great chains railed against the stone, drowning out Spider's calm, even voice. Joe looked back out through the opening and saw the Scraper lining up outside the hole. Its mechanical arm swung back, then forward, trailing the lethal chains after it. Smash. They cracked against the wall. Sharp splinters of stone fell off the wall behind him.

But then the Scraper stopped, its chains falling to the ground. It began to retract its telescopic arm. When the arm was a quarter the size it had been, the Scraper swung it rapidly from side to side so the arm repeatedly hit the edges of the hatch—bang, bang, bang.

"What's it doing?" shouted Joe above the din.

"Summoning other machines," said Spider. "Hurry, Katherine. We haven't got all day."

"But I can't see the way ahead!" wailed Katherine.

"Neither can I," replied Spider testily. "Just reach out and feel your way."

As Joe watched, the Scraper retracted its arm. The lid rose up and closed with a clang.

Then came the familiar high-pitched whine of a Goliath's engine.

"It's a dead end!" cried Katherine in exasperation. "There is no way through!"

"There has to be," retorted Spider. "Try higher up."

Silence, then Katherine gasped. "It's here! It's above us!"

"Dead end, my foot," grumbled Spider. "A bit of faith goes a long way."

Joe listened as Katherine scaled the wall and pulled the pack after her. Spider followed, then said, "Come on, Joe, grab my hand. I'll pull you up."

But Joe didn't move. "It's too late," he replied in a low voice, barely moving his mouth. "There's a Goliath . . ."

Joe could see it through the crack. It was standing in front of the Scraper, swiveling its turret from side to side, trying to locate the target. If Joe moved a muscle, it would lock on.

"Don't worry, lad," whispered Spider. "I'll find a way to get you out of this."

Joe barely dared to breathe. The stones of the wall were cold, and the coldness seeped right into his bones. Before long his whole body was aching.

"Spider?" whispered Katherine.

"Quiet," replied Spider.

"But, Spider," Katherine tried again. The turret on the Goliath twitched. It was trying to locate the sound.

"Shhhh!" Spider hissed softly.

"But, Spider!" Katherine repeated in a low, irritated voice. "Use that distracter out there."

Joe's eyes opened wide. She was right. He could just make out the tiny box on the grass behind the Scraper.

Spider and Katherine were being very quiet, but from the faint rustlings Joe could tell they were up to something. Whatever it was, he hoped they would hurry up. The Goliath now stood absolutely still, like a cat waiting for its prey to make a fatal mistake.

A moment later the silence was shattered by the wailing of the little box. The Goliath's turret spun around and a stream of fire spewed from the gun, hitting the wall, the grass, and the Scraper.

Spider grabbed Joe by the back of his collar and tried to drag him up the wall.

Joe did his best to help, but the soles of his old sneakers were wet from the rain. Then he made a terrible mistake. He looked back through the crack. The Goliath had lost interest in the distracter. Its gun was now pointing right at him. In the deepest part of its muzzle there was a tiny orange dot of light.

With one tremendous pull Spider lifted him into the tunnel.

"MOVE!" Spider yelled at Katherine. Katherine scrambled along the tunnel in front of them. Joe hurried after Spider. The ball of fire smacked into the wall Joe had just climbed, filling the tunnel with its deadly heat.

Joe crawled faster than he'd ever crawled before. In the orange light from the fire he could see the worn soles of Spider's hobnailed boots. He kept his mind focused on those and crawled and crawled and crawled.

On he went, through dark, narrow, twisting ways until Spider finally said, "Ease up."

Joe leaned against the wall, the sound of his own heartbeat thudding in his ears. It was pitch-black.

Joe heard Katherine fumbling in the backpack; then a flashlight switched on. Katherine shone it up and down the tunnel. The walls were covered in a pattern of neat little cuts, all running the same way. It was as though whoever had dug these tunnels had taken a great deal of care over them. But it wasn't an unbroken pattern. Close to where Spider was sitting, Joe noticed four lines that had been carved into the wall to form a square. Inside this square was a different set of markings—sharp, jagged little cuts. Joe had seen something like them before, but he couldn't think where. Spider traced the square with his finger, then set his hand over the markings as though to hide them.

"Who made these tunnels?" asked Katherine, reaching up to touch the neater, more regular pattern of adze marks in the wall beside her.

Spider smiled. "The Heathermen, of course."

Katherine snatched her hand away from the wall, as though the marks in the stone had burned her. Spider caught her wrist.

"They weren't traitors," said Spider emphatically. "They wouldn't have hurt Cornell or Elysia or Merid, neither. You'll see that one day."

Katherine pulled free of him.

"Just like those machines out there on the plain weren't a part of their dirty inventors' magic?" she sneered. "Just like Araik Ben didn't murder a defenseless woman and start a war?"

Spider moved so fast Katherine didn't even have time to flinch. He grabbed her by the collar and shook her.

"You know nothing," said Spider. "Nothing! Araik Ben loved . . ." Spider stopped and pushed Katherine away. He wiped his nose on his sleeve. "Enough," he barked. "The man is long dead. Let's say no more about it. The sooner I hand you over to your brother, the better, and good riddance."

"Likewise," retaliated Katherine as she gathered up the pack. "Where now?" she asked, moving forward down the tunnel.

"I'll find out," said Spider. He took out his notebook and felt through the pages until he found the one he wanted. It was full of the punched-out pinpricks. Spider ran his fingers over the marks on the page, making little "hum" and "ah" and "ho" sounds to himself until eventually he shut the book with a snap and put it back in his pocket.

Spider took the lead and they crawled along the tunnels for hours. The beam of Katherine's flashlight was growing yellowish by the time Spider called to them to halt.

"What's that terrible smell?" Joe asked.

Katherine pulled her scarf up over her nose. "I don't

know," she muttered. "But I'll be glad to get out into the fresh air."

"It'll get worse before it gets better," Spider informed them. "But I think you'll find it's worth it in the end. Now move well back."

Spider was struggling with something in the ceiling of the tunnel. Katherine shone the weakening beam of the flashlight on it, and Joe could see that it was a hatch with a heavy ring in the middle. Spider twisted the ring and pulled. With a grating sound the hatch fell open and muddy, brown water gushed through it, splashing onto the tunnel floor.

The smell was everywhere. It was so strong that their eyes watered and they coughed fit to burst. Joe covered his nose with his sleeve and barely noticed the water pooling around his knees.

"Come on," said Spider. "A bit of bad stench won't kill you." He grabbed Katherine and pushed her toward the hatch. "Up you go. That's right, climb up through there. You'll find you can stand up on the next level and might be able to breathe a bit easier. You next, Joe."

Joe followed Katherine through the hatch and found himself in a much wider and higher tunnel. Gray light filtered into the tunnel through a narrow shaft in the arched ceiling. Joe stared at it and saw a tiny square of dull gray sky far above him.

Joe peered along the tunnel. There was a narrow pavement at either side, and in the space between ran a fast-moving, shallow brown stream. Small black shadows scampered in and out of the water.

Rats! thought Joe with a shudder.

"Get to the side," said Spider as he climbed through the hatch. Joe and Katherine waded through the stream and stepped up onto the pavement. Spider knelt in the rank water and pulled the hatch shut behind them. As soon as he'd made sure it was secure, he climbed onto the pavement and led them down the tunnel.

"Where are we?" asked Katherine, pressing her scarf tightly to her nose.

"In the sewers," replied Spider. "Not the sweetest spot for sure, but such a network as will serve us well. Down here we can move from one end of the Long City to the other with little chance of being seen."

Katherine pointed her flashlight at the walls. The rats rushed toward the light.

"Turn it off," warned Spider. "Rats'll always go toward a light. They have terrible eyesight, and they'll think it's an escape hole. Besides, best save the battery while you can; you may need it later. Make do with the light from the street for now; there should be some of that."

Joe looked up as they passed under the next opening.

It's nighttime! he thought. That meant they'd been in the tunnels and the sewers all day or perhaps more than one day.

The way through the sewers seemed to take forever. There were so many tunnels. Spider led the way, turning into this tunnel, then that, like a man who knew exactly where he was going. There were very few shafts of light, and for much of the time they had to feel their way along the wall in total darkness.

"Hold up," said Spider. Joe and Katherine stopped and leaned wearily against the tunnel wall. Spider was feeling the bricks, but by this time neither Joe nor Katherine could be bothered to ask him what he was doing. "Right here, that's it. That's the shaft we need. You first, Joe. Grab hold of the ladder." Spider put his arms around Joe's waist and lifted him up into the darkness. Joe felt cool air blowing onto him from above. He turned his face toward it but couldn't see anything.

Then suddenly there was light. Beyond the grating he saw the same flash of pale light he had seen on previous nights. The ladder on the wall was behind him. He turned and reached for the rungs.

"That's it. Up you go," said Spider. "Wait for me when you get to the top."

Joe grasped the cold iron rungs and began to climb. He climbed as fast as he could, and when he reached the grating he stuck his nose close to it and gulped at the night air. Katherine quickly climbed up beside him, Spider's pack scraping along the rough brick. Spider stood beneath them on the ladder.

Joe wrapped his fingers around the grating above them and tried to shift it, but it didn't budge. It was too heavy.

"What now?" asked Katherine.

Spider didn't answer. Instead he let out three long, low hooting sounds like an owl. Almost instantly the sound of a horse's hooves could be heard on the cobbles over their heads.

A moment later a horse and cart passed over them and stopped above the grating.

"Be ready," whispered Spider.

Suddenly two men were under the cart, lifting and sliding the grating away. They hauled Joe out of the sewer. Katherine was next, then Spider, and in moments the three of them had been loaded onto the cart and covered with empty sacks. With only the faintest noise the grating was replaced. Then the driver clicked his tongue and shook the reins, and the horse resumed clip-clopping slowly up the street.

CHAPTER 15

Mary's Place

Joe pulled the cloth back slightly from his face to try to watch where they were going. He couldn't see much because the sides of the cart were piled high with full sacks and there were no streetlights along the way, but when the gray light bloomed in the sky he could make out buildings, or rather the remains of buildings, on either side of the road. Tall houses leaned over the street, their gables almost touching. Their windows were mostly broken, and much of the wood was charred black. Some of the buildings' facades had caved in. It looked as though they'd been punched by an enormous fist. In some places there were no houses at all, just high piles of rock and rubble and broken furniture. Wood smoke drifted in the air.

Eventually the cart passed beneath a high, dilapidated archway and came to a stop in a dismal courtyard strewn with rubble.

Spider climbed down off the cart, then turned to help Joe and Katherine. While Joe lifted the pack onto Katherine's shoulders, Spider thanked the two men and said goodbye.

The gray light bloomed once more and bathed the courtyard in monochromatic tones. The surrounding buildings were in a terrible state. Two of them had collapsed, leaving only piles of bricks and stones. Spider made his way toward one of these piles and gently tapped his staff along the rubble. He stopped when he found a small column of three or four stones balanced precariously on top of each other. Spider crouched low and ran his fingers up and down the tower of stones one, two, three times, then stood and knocked the pile down with the tip of his staff. As he returned to where Joe and Katherine were waiting, a smile broke over his face.

"I don't know about you," he said, rubbing his hands together, "but I'm famished. Let's see if we can find some grub. Come on, this way." Joe was puzzled by the glee in the old man's voice. What on earth was there to be happy about in this grim place?

Spider led them to a boarded-up window in one of

the remaining housefronts and swung the board out of the way. "Through there, that's it, up you go," said Spider.

The house they entered had no roof and only three full walls. The fourth had been knocked down and lay shattered in the yard beyond. Looking up, Joe could see where the second and third floors of the house would have been because the walls were covered in different wallpapers and there were doors and fireplaces and even windows stuck high up. The doors opened onto nothing at all.

Spider led them through two more broken-down buildings before stopping in front of a charred and blackened door.

He knocked two soft knocks, then three fast, short ones, then two more raps, then one, pause, another, pause, then two last—soft but firm.

They waited. The silvery gray light lit the sky and faded twice more before the door opened and a wrinkled hand beckoned them to enter the dark chamber beyond.

When the door was closed behind them, they stood for a moment in the darkness while their unseen host fastened several well-greased bolts and locks. Then a black shade was lifted off an oil lamp and a soft yellow glow filled the room. An old woman, barely half Spider's height, stood on her tiptoes and hugged him heartily.

"Carey, my love, you read the stones right then, I see?" She stood back and smiled at him.

"I did and was mightily relieved to see you got my message," replied Spider.

"Oh yes, love you, but could you pick a bird with a better temper next time? That crow nearly bit my finger off."

Spider laughed, and the woman hugged him again. An instant later she pulled away.

"Phew!" she cried, batting her hand in front of her nose. "I see you came in by your favorite route." She laughed and shook her head. "I don't mind. Bless you. When I heard you were coming I prayed you would make it across the plain, and here you are."

"Mary," said Spider, running his hand over her cheek, "you're looking as young as ever."

"It's so flattering when a blind man tells you that," she laughed, slapping Spider playfully on the chest. "I'm still younger than you, you old fool." She turned to Joe and smiled at him. "And you must be the boy. Joe, isn't it?" Joe nodded. Mary shook his hand warmly, and Joe smiled. She was the sort of person it was impossible not to like.

Mary turned to Katherine. "And you're Tom's sister, Katherine, are you?" she asked.

Katherine bristled. "What if I am?"

"Oh, don't worry," said Mary. "I'm not here to say anything bad about your brother. I make it a rule never to say anything bad about anybody. Tom has a lot of good points; even Carey here has to admit that."

Spider grunted reluctantly. Mary laughed. "Now," she said, sitting down on an overturned crate and gesturing for the others to do likewise, "I want to hear everything. Don't keep me in the dark this time. What's really happening in Quarain? Is there any progress toward peace?"

"Mary, Mary," said Spider, lowering himself onto the makeshift seat. "I'll gladly tell you everything, but we've been traveling all day and we're hungry."

"Oh my goodness, of course you are!" said Mary, jumping up. "You've probably had nothing but his awful porridge for days. You must be half starved." Mary opened a broken-down cupboard in the corner and brought out a plate of rough bread rolls. She deftly split each in half with a knife and spread a generous dollop of dripping from a pot on all of them.

"So, Carey," she began as she returned to her seat, "Joe here's the one who thinks—"

"Is looking for his sister," Spider said, interrupting her. Mary nodded, then studied Joe's face.

"Do you know where she'll be?" Joe asked. "She's got

blond hair and looks a little like me. It's really important that I find her and take her home. My parents are worried sick."

Mary smiled and shook her head. She reached out and rested her hand on his shoulder. "I'm sorry, lad," she said, giving his shoulder a sympathetic little squeeze. Then she instantly pulled her hand away. "Carey!" she exclaimed. "He's soaked through! Did you not think to give him a coat? He must be freezing. Here, lad, I'll sort you out."

Tutting loudly, Mary turned to a box in the corner and pulled out a large bundle of rags.

"Put this on, Joe," she said, unrolling the bundle. The rags were all stitched together to make a large coat. Joe slipped his arms into the sleeves and pulled the coat on. "There, that will help you dry out," she said, smiling. "Carey! What were you thinking? The poor child's exhausted. You've never kept him going at your pace, have you? And Katherine? It's a wonder they survived."

"I kept it slow and steady to suit them," said Spider.

Joe raised his eyebrows. Spider had been hurrying them ever since they'd started on this crazy journey. Joe wondered how fast Spider's real pace would have been.

"Here," said Mary, proffering the plate of grease-smeared rolls. Joe took one and tried not to wrinkle his nose. The rolls looked even less appetizing than the cold porridge. Mary wasn't offended. "Go ahead, try them. They taste much better than they look, I promise you."

Joe nibbled on his and found that Mary was right. The bread roll, though hard on the outside, was fresh and light inside, and the dripping was as salty and as tasty as freshly fried bacon. Joe gobbled up the roll in seconds and wondered if he could ask for another. But the old woman looked poorer than anyone he'd ever seen, and he decided it was better not to ask.

After they'd eaten, Spider sent Joe and Katherine to a corner to get some sleep. Then he began to talk to Mary in a low voice. She leaned forward and listened intently.

Joe settled against a wall and tried to listen, but he was still hungry, and an empty stomach on top of a day of racing through tunnels and sewers was too much for him. Before long his head dropped forward onto his knees and he began to doze. He was almost asleep when he heard the strange coded knock that Spider had used earlier.

He lifted his head and saw Mary standing by the door. After a little while she opened it and stood back to let the newcomer enter. It was another old woman and an old man. Both beamed when they saw Spider and shook his hand heartily. After a few muttered words with Spider and a brief glance across the room at Joe and Katherine, they left.

Mary saw them out but didn't return to her seat. She waited by the door. Before long the knocking signal came again. This time one old man on his own was admitted. Again there were the handshakes and the low words and the noddings and the smiles and the glance at Joe and Katherine in the corner and then the old man left.

This was only the beginning. From that moment on it seemed as though there was a constant stream of visitors to the cramped, cold room.

Joe looked over and saw that Katherine was eyeing the visitors with extreme distrust.

"Who are they all?" he asked a whisper.

Katherine shrugged. "I don't know," she replied. "Perhaps Spider's trying to sell us to these smelly old crones. I wouldn't put it past him."

Spider's staff whistled through the air and stopped a quarter of an inch in front of Katherine's nose. Katherine froze.

"Keep your mouth shut if you don't have anything nice to say," Spider hissed. "Those that come here are your elders and betters. They know more than you ever will, they've seen more than you'll ever see. You'd be wise to be respectful. They are all that is left of the Heathermen."

"No!" Katherine's face grew even paler. "You're lying."

"Am I?" Spider looked as though he was about to say more, but another coded knock at the door stopped him. Spider nodded at Mary, and she lifted the latch. Another of the old men entered, with shuffling steps. The man and Spider sat together talking quietly while Katherine fumed.

Joe didn't know what to say to her and thought it best to leave her alone. He lay back and closed his eyes. The bullet wound on the back of his hand hurt. He tried not to think about it. After a little while he fell fast asleep and dreamed again of Hannah lying in the hospital bed while his parents kept vigil by her side.

CHAPTER 16

Breaking In

When Joe woke the next morning, Mary was going about her daily tasks. The old woman built a fire in the dusty grate and hung a teakettle over it. Then she stood and took the wooden shutters from a large window. Daylight, or a sort of daylight, filtered in through the filthy panes. The weather looked as grim as it had been on every previous day. There was one difference. The dawn had brought with it a fog. A real pea-souper. Joe watched the mists swirl past the window.

Spider slept without stirring till after midday. No more Heathermen came to the ramshackle room, and Mary spent the whole morning puttering about. She seemed to be constantly tidying, but what there was to tidy, Joe couldn't see.

Beside him, Katherine was silently removing everything from Spider's backpack and taking stock. In the bottom, she found the one remaining distracter box. She lifted it out and laid it gently on the ground. Then she began to unpack the pockets.

"What are you doing?" whispered Joe.

"Looking for anything that might be useful," she said. "If I had the control for this box I'd take it, but he's got it in his poacher's pocket, the big one inside his coat."

"You'd take it?" queried Joe. "Take it where?"

"To get my brother out. I'm tired of waiting."

Spider started to laugh.

Katherine rolled her eyes. "He can't even be trusted to be asleep when he's snoring," she said, stuffing her pockets with the most useful items she could find.

"You wouldn't know one end of the Druckee from the other," Spider said. "You'd be caught and locked up in seconds." He laughed some more.

Katherine looked furious and tried to get up. Spider pulled her back down.

"Settle yourself, miss," said Spider, still chuckling. "I promised to take you to the Druckee, and I will. But we'd be fools to go out there in daylight. Just you hold your horses till nightfall, and we'll be off."

That day was one of the longest and slowest Joe

could remember. It was worse than a rainy winter Saturday at home. At least at home he had his things, his projects, his models. Here there was nothing to do except sit and wait.

When evening finally came, however, Spider sniffed and stood.

"Let's go," he said as he quietly opened the door. "We'll take a look at the old place first, and then I'll have to do some thinking."

Spider stepped out onto the street and beckoned them to follow him. The street was crowded with people, and they all seemed to be heading in the same direction. Horses and carts blocked the road, and crowds of people walked three abreast on the pavements. Joe was stunned. The last time he'd been out, the streets had been deserted.

Joe had never seen a city like this. It must have been incredible before the war. For one thing, there didn't seem to be a straight line anywhere. The buildings that were still standing leaned, swooped, curved, or twisted as they loomed above him. Many had ornate balconies decorated with scrolled railings and flattened swaths of wrought iron. Battered shop signs still hung above some of the doors. Joe could just make out the words "The Monkey Café" on one, and a simian face staring out at him from the peeling paint.

Spider walked swiftly, jabbing his staff on the cobbles and touching his hand to the wall as he went. It was as though he knew the city by the feel of its doorposts and corners. Joe and Katherine had to hurry to keep up.

As they went along, Joe noticed lights in some of the glassless windows, and some doors stood open. Joe could see rooms not dissimilar to Mary's within. One door they passed swung open, and the smells of food and beer and the noise of a full tavern escaped into the night. Joe caught a glimpse of a smoky, crowded room full of raucous laughter and singing before the door swung shut.

They went along with the crowd for some way until they reached a large square. Here the houses were tall and imposing, though like everything else, their walls were blackened from the soot in the air.

Spider steered Joe and Katherine down a dark, narrow alley. He let go of their arms and hurried ahead. For a man who couldn't see where he was going, he moved quickly. At the far end of the alley was a high, brilliantly lit, cream-colored wall with crenellated battlements and a red roof beyond. Spider stopped short of the end and pulled the other two into the shadows against the alley wall. He sniffed.

"That's the Druckee," he whispered. "I could smell it a mile away. You two go look and tell me what you see."

Katherine and Joe hurried to the end of the alley.

Together they peered around the corner and stared up at the massive block of the Druckee.

Joe stared up at the imposing edifice of the prison. The walls were so smooth and the gate was so well guarded that he couldn't imagine how on earth they were going to break in and rescue Katherine's brother. The whole idea of it seemed ridiculous. He tilted his head back and shuddered. Even if it was possible to scale those smooth walls, there were guards with guns positioned all along the battlements. Just then a break in the thick fog revealed an inky black pool of sky beyond the bright lights. At that same moment the silvery gray lightning lit up the blackness. Through the hole in the fog, Joe could see the silhouettes of three impossibly tall towers—towers that seemed to reach forever into the sliver of night sky. The silver light faded and the fog closed in again.

A wide street ran parallel to the prison, with houses on the near side and a low wall along the other. Beyond the wall was a wide moat filled with choppy, dark water. The prison was lit by floodlights that made its cream walls gleam. The lights would make it difficult to slip into that prison unnoticed. There were no comforting shadows in which to hide. The upturned spotlights lit the underside of the low fog. Gray wisps swirled about

the red-roofed watchtowers and broke over the battlements like waves over rocks.

"SHARE IT!" someone shouted out in the street.
Other voices joined in, and the whole crowd began to
chant. "SHARE IT! SHARE IT! SHARE IT OUT
NOW!"

Joe and Katherine looked at each other, then stuck
their heads farther out of the alley. A large crowd had
gathered by the heavily fortified entrance to the prison.
A drawbridge guarded by a wall of sentries lay across
the moat. The crowd kept surging forward, only to be
pushed back by guards on the bridge.

"Let's get a closer look," said Katherine, pulling Joe
out into the street.

Katherine squeezed through the crowd and after
much elbowing found them a position by the low wall.
From here they had a good view of the entrance to the
prison. At the end of the drawbridge was a high archway
lit by glaring electric lights. In the shelter of the archway
a group of guards sat smoking and playing cards. They
took no notice of the unruly crowd at the gate. Above
them the sharp iron spikes of the portcullis protruded
beneath the arch.

In the courtyard beyond the archway Joe could see
Orlemann's sleek black car parked by a long, low building.

To the left of it stood the mercy mission truck. Soldiers were unloading the supplies for the city and carrying them inside the prison. This was what the crowd was after.

A portly officer strode over the drawbridge and held up his hand. When the crowd was quiet the officer lifted a megaphone to his lips and read from a sheet of paper.

"Ambassador Orlemann has instructed me to inform you that he understands that you are all hungry. He assures me that you will all be given your rations tomorrow. Bring your identification papers and your ration books and you will receive food and water for you and your family. Now, unless you want my soldiers to forcibly break up this illegal gathering, I suggest you disperse and go home peacefully. The office will be open at 7:00 a.m. sharp. No lines are permitted to form until 5:30 a.m. Good night."

With an assortment of moans and groans the crowd began to break up and the protesters drifted away.

"We've waited this long for food, what difference will a few hours make?" Joe heard one man say.

The woman beside him sniffed. "A lot of difference to those who are dying. A curse on Elysia and Merid. They've brought this on. Them and their jealous ways."

Elysia *and* Merid? Joe looked at Katherine to see

what she made of this, but she didn't react. Perhaps she hadn't heard.

"Let's go," said Katherine, pulling on Joe's arm. "Spider'll be thinking we've run off."

"I saw the three towers," said Joe as they rejoined Spider in the alley.

"Mary told me the library is still standing," said Spider, turning his face toward the sky. "I'm glad of it. From the top of those towers you can see the whole land—on a clear day, that is. They used to be open to everyone, but since Cornell was . . . since she died, no one's been allowed in. Those towers are probably all that's left of the old university. When the war began and the Long City was besieged, the Druckee was built around the university, like a manacle around a wrist. At the time they said it was to protect the arches and to keep the university and the library safe. Orlemann himself designed the Druckee. He is skilled in those ways. He said that such a fortress would be impossible to penetrate. No one thought of it as a prison then. It's strange how something that was built for a seemingly good purpose became something quite different. When I was there they set me on a rack and stretched my bones to try to get me to tell what I knew, but I never told them anything."

"You were a prisoner in the Druckee?" asked Katherine.

"Indeed I was," replied Spider with a shudder.

Joe snapped his fingers. "I remember now. Back when I first met you, you said that someone had once escaped the Druckee. That was you? Right?"

"All ancient history," said Spider, smiling. "Yes, it was me. That's why I look this way. When I left that place I was nearly half a foot taller than I had been and my hair had turned white. But they did me a favor. No one recognized me." He grew serious. "This is no time for memory lane; to business. How many are at the gate?"

"Ten, maybe eleven," replied Katherine. "Plus the two officially on guard. But there are plenty more up on the battlements. They watch everything that goes on below. I don't think there's any chance of getting to my brother that way."

"Not to worry," Spider said. "While you were gone I was busy listening. I heard your Tom and his friends prattling on, but their voices are faint. They must be many floors down, which will make our work easier."

"Easier?" said Katherine, her voice rising. "Easier? Didn't you hear how many guards are at the gate?"

Spider laughed. "Don't worry," he chuckled. "A garrison like this won't be difficult at all!"

Spider rubbed his hands together and pulled his hat farther down over his face. "Come along then; we don't have all night," he said as he turned and set off in the opposite direction to the prison.

Which way they went now neither Joe nor Katherine would have been able to say. Spider led them up one alley and down another, through squares and courtyards, over piles of rubble, and through empty buildings until finally he brought them to a deserted street. In the middle of the street he stopped and waited. Katherine started to say something, but Spider stopped her. Joe realized the old man was listening.

After a few moments Spider nodded and led them out into the road. He carried his staff in front of him and ran it back and forth lightly across the cobbles. Suddenly it rang out with a different sound, and Joe saw that it had connected with another of the sewer grates.

"Not again," protested Katherine.

"Do you want to get your brother out or not?" asked Spider.

Spider lifted the grate and held it open while Joe and Katherine climbed down the metal ladder in the shaft. Spider followed them through the manhole and gently set the grate back in place before joining them at the bottom of the shaft.

"Katherine," said Spider, taking a few steps along the tunnel, "bring your light over here, but cover the beam before you turn it on."

Katherine did as she was told, and when she switched on the light both she and Joe saw that Spider had taken out his notebook.

"Katherine, give the light to Joe. Now here," he said, handing her the book. Joe slipped his hand through the wrist strap on the flashlight and held it up to the book. "There's a drawing of a butterfly in here," Spider went on. "It's somewhere near the end. Find it. Hurry now."

Joe cupped his hand around the dim beam of light and directed it onto the notebook while Katherine rifled through the book's thick pages until she found the drawing. The butterfly covered half the page, and the patterns on its wings were drawn in painstaking detail.

"Here it is," she said, holding the book open.

"Good," said Spider. "We'll use this to lead us back to the Druckee."

Katherine looked at Joe across the book and shrugged.

Spider tapped the drawing with his finger. "Look closely at the veins on the wings," he said. Katherine held the book up to the light. "There's a map hidden in the drawing," explained Spider. "Your brother deserted me before he had time to prick holes in the drawing for me to read by. You'll have to use your eyes. Look. The veins in the wings show a plan of the tunnels."

Joe wondered if the whole book was full of plans like this. Was that why Wyn wanted it?

Katherine studied the butterfly map. "This way," she said, setting off along the main sewer. Spider walked alongside her, plowing resolutely through the filthy water.

Joe followed them. Something that Spider had just said was bothering him. *Your brother deserted me before he had time to prick holes in the drawing for me to read by.* Something about this tugged at Joe's mind, but he couldn't put his finger on what it was.

The journey back to the Druckee, or rather to the place beneath the Druckee, seemed endless. Katherine gave directions, then Spider led them through the great tunnels and sometimes through the not-so-great tunnels. There were places, Joe later shuddered to remember, where the tunnels were so narrow and the ceilings so low that they had to crawl on their hands and knees through the stinking waters.

"Nearly there," whispered Spider as they emerged from one particularly putrid tunnel. "The walls are thick, but I can hear your brother clearly now," he added. "Listen!"

Katherine and Joe held their breath. The water running through the tunnels drowned out most of the sound, but beneath it Joe began to think he could hear another noise. A low burbling. It could have been men's voices, and if he'd been able to listen longer he would have been almost sure of it, but Spider prodded him.

"Let's get in and out of here sharpish. We need to be long gone before it's discovered they've flown."

They turned down another tunnel. Spider sniffed again. "We should be there," he said. "Joe, shine your light ahead and both of you tell me what you see."

The light struck the first of three formidable iron grilles that barred the way. This first was set with lethal spikes, and Joe could see that the other grilles farther down the tunnel were just as gruesome. In the center of each was a gate that was chained and padlocked shut.

Katherine and Joe carefully described everything they could see to Spider.

"Good," he said when they had finished. "And beyond the grilles?" Joe shone the light through the metal bars. It was barely strong enough to reach into the shadows beyond the third grille, but Joe held his arm as far out as he could and the light fell across a small metal hatch halfway up the wall. Joe told Spider about it and the old man nodded.

"Yes, that's it," he said. "We just have to get to that, and your brother, Katherine, is as good as free."

"But how do we get there?" Katherine asked, grabbing hold of the thick iron bars and trying to shake them.

Joe ran the beam from the flashlight through the bars again. Beyond the last gate he could see that the tunnel twisted to the right and disappeared into the dark shadows. Joe pointed the beam down and the weak light shone over the black water, lighting up the place where the pavements should have been. Something was strange here. The water did not move the way water normally did, and the pavements were not made of the same stone as before but of humped black cobbles. These cobbles seemed to move in the light, seemed to writhe and wriggle and crawl over each other. Joe stared harder, trying to understand how a pavement could move in this sinister way. Then he felt sick.

The water and the pavements at the side of the tunnel were thick with squirming black bodies. The tunnel was full of fat black rats.

"I know how to get through these," said Katherine, still holding the immovable iron bars. "We've that last exploding box in the backpack," she said.

But Spider shook his head. He took the notebook from her, closed it carefully, then put it back in his pocket. "We could use that if you want to bring the whole city after us, not to mention probably dropping the building on our heads. No," he said conspiratorially, "I know a much better way. Joe?"

There was something in the way Spider said his name that made Joe certain that things were about to get extremely unpleasant.

"Yes?" Joe gulped.

"There is a way through each of these metal grilles. Feel beneath the water."

Beneath the water! Joe squirmed inside but gritted his teeth and, reaching down, felt along the bars and soon found a place beneath the water level where the bars had been cut away.

"You're saying—" began Joe.

"—we have to go down there?" said Katherine, finishing his thought.

"If you want your brother out, you do."

Joe and Katherine exchanged a look.

"But what about the rats?" asked Joe.

"Nothing to worry about," said Spider. "Ignore them. Pretend they're not there. They won't bite if you don't struggle. Let them pool around you. They'll soon get bored if they think there's nothing to fear. But be careful about one thing. Narrow your eyes till they're almost closed, or the rats'll want to leap toward the reflected light they see there. Their eyesight is bad, and they'll think the light is a hole."

Joe shuddered. The rats in the sewers beneath the Druckee were as big as cats. And they were everywhere.

They swarmed through the water and along the pavements at the sides of the tunnels. The cold tips of their tails whipped against his legs. They had greasy black fur and sharp yellow teeth. The last thing Joe wanted to do was dip into that putrid sewer water.

"You first," said Katherine, taking the flashlight from him and hanging it on one of the sharp spikes. Joe nodded; then he drew a deep breath, grabbed hold of the railing, and pushed himself down into the water. As he struggled through the gap, he felt the rats crowding around him. His eyes were tightly closed and he held his nose with one hand, but the feeling of the claws that caught against his forehead as the rats swam by made him want to scream and never stop. Then he was through the hole in the grating and leaping out of the water on the other side, gasping for air.

"Shhhh!" cautioned Spider. "Try to keep calm. You'll only get the rats riled up if you behave like that."

Joe tried to calm down, but when Katherine grabbed hold of his leg to pull herself through he lost it and started to scream. Katherine grabbed him by the shoulders and shook him.

"It'll be all right," she said, speaking to him as though he were a little boy. "Calm down! Breathe." Joe took a deep breath.

"All right now?" asked Katherine. Joe nodded. Katherine

took down the flashlight from where Joe had hung it, then waded carefully through the foul water and swimming rats. Joe followed her to the second set of railings. Together they felt along the ironwork for the hole beneath the water level. Katherine found it and, holding her nose, disappeared into the murky depths. Joe took a deep breath, dropped down, and half swam, half crawled through the hole as quickly as he could.

Only one more to go, he thought as he emerged this time more slowly and more carefully through the swimming rodents. Moving stealthily, he joined Katherine by the third railing. Katherine shook the flashlight to try to wring the last ounce of energy out of the failing batteries. The light was growing weaker and weaker. Now it wasn't strong enough to reach Spider back beyond the railings.

"Won't last much longer," she said. Joe waited while she hung it on a spike and ducked under the third grate. It suddenly occurred to him that he was doing all this for Hannah. To find Hannah. To save Hannah. And he wondered meanly if she would ever do anything like this for him. But then he felt guilty. He was sure Hannah hadn't ever wished that he was dead. And if she'd never wished for anything so horrible, she'd never have to do anything like this for him, would she?

"Come on," said Katherine. Joe nodded and ducked down under the water.

Katherine had already climbed onto the narrow pavement and was now standing by the little metal door in the wall. When Joe joined her she was examining it carefully. The door wasn't so much a door as a flat metal panel flush against the wall. And no matter how hard they tried to pry it open with their fingers, it wouldn't budge.

"No use," called Katherine to Spider. "We don't know how to open it."

"It'll open by itself in a minute," said Spider. "Your job is to keep it open when it does. Meanwhile, stand back and watch out for the rats."

Joe looked down at the rats that swarmed about his feet. Why was Spider warning him about them now? he wondered. A moment later there was a horrible gurgling sound from behind the door. The rats started to pull themselves out of the water and swarm onto the narrow pavement. Soon they were three deep around Joe's legs, and still they kept coming. They clambered over one another and clawed at his soaking wet trouser legs. Joe tried to keep as still as he could and not think about them. He tried to think only about the door in the wall.

Suddenly it opened. It was hinged at the top and so

swung open from the bottom, and as it did, a torrent of rotting garbage came spewing out. They'd thought that the stench in the sewer couldn't get any worse. They were wrong. Katherine and Joe jammed their hands over their noses and stepped to the side, breathing only when absolutely necessary.

This was what the rats had been waiting for. They were frantic to get at the stinking, semidecayed food that fell out of the chute. Joe and Katherine tried to kick it into the water so the rats would follow it there.

"Keep the hatch open!" yelled Spider. "If it closes, it will be locked until tomorrow. You don't want to spend twenty-four hours down here, do you?"

Joe didn't. Neither did Katherine. They looked back and saw that the torrent of garbage was almost done and that the hatch was closing. Katherine reached up and tried to stop it. Joe did the same, but it was obviously on some sort of hydraulic system and they would need something stronger than their arms to hold it.

"The flashlight!" Joe cried, and Katherine stuck it in close to the hinge. The force of the hatch's closing killed the light and crushed the metal casing of the flashlight as though it were paper, but it couldn't crush the batteries inside. The mechanism whirred and sputtered trying to close the hatch, but it failed. With a series of loud, protesting clicks it gave up and stopped.

"What now?" asked Katherine. "Do we have to go up there?"

"Shush!" said Spider. "They're coming."

Joe heard a noise—a rattling, swooshing sound. Something was coming down the chute! Joe stepped out of the way. He didn't want to be treated to any more stinking garbage, but just as he was thinking this, something shot through the metal hatch and landed with a splash in the filthy river of rubbish and rats. A second splash followed immediately after. Then a third, and a fourth, and then three more.

"Which way now?" asked a voice in the darkness.

Spider struck a match. "This way," he said. It was so dark in the sewers that the light from a single match was as bright as a beacon.

"It's them," said Katherine. "It's the Skulkers."

Joe looked at the hard faces of the Skulkers in the flickering light. They looked as mean as a month of Mondays, scowling across the darkness at Spider. One man's scowl was the deepest.

"Spider Carey!" he said, spitting out the words. Hatred shone in his eyes. "What treachery are you up to, old man?"

The match in Spider's hand fell to the water and went out.

"I came to get you out," replied Spider, striking

another match. "My companions by the wall will show you the way." In the faint, flickering light seven scowling faces turned toward Joe and Katherine.

Katherine was smiling from ear to ear.

"Tom!" she gasped. "Tom!" And not minding the rats or the men or anything, she leapt into the water and flung her arms around her brother's neck.

CHAPTER 17

Breaking Out

"It's really you!" squealed Katherine, grinning up at her brother. Tom looked embarrassed. Joe recognized the look and knew exactly how Katherine's brother was feeling. It was the way Joe always felt when Hannah made an embarrassing display of sisterly affection.

"Yes, ha-ha, it's me," said Tom as he unclasped his sister's arms from around his neck. "C'mon, men. Let's get out of here," he said, looking around at his comrades. "We want to breathe fresh air before this night's through."

"Yes, sir," said the other Skulkers. Tom looked expectantly at Katherine.

"Oh, right, come on, this way." Still grinning,

Katherine showed them the underwater gaps in the iron grilles.

Katherine came through last. Her brother had already joined the huddle of Skulkers along the wall and was giving them whispered instructions.

"Tom!" she called as Spider yanked her up. "Don't even think about going anywhere without me!"

Tom turned and answered with a grin. "Sorry, Kat, I've got to see my men get back safe. No girls allowed." The other men laughed at this. Tom shrugged and smiled at his sister. "Don't worry, Kat. I'll find you later. I promise!"

Spider lit another match. "Is Brasque with you?" he asked in a clear voice. The Skulkers fell silent. Tom took a step toward Spider. He cleared his throat and spat in the water.

"Would we tell scum like you if he was?" he said coldly.

Spider held the match dangerously close to Tom's face. "No," replied Spider. "But Brasque would."

Suddenly a light appeared in the tunnel. Joe, Katherine, and the Skulkers all froze.

"What is it, Joe?" asked Spider, catching hold of his shoulder.

"A light."

"Where?"

"On the other side of the grilles. Beyond the bend."

Suddenly the light was blindingly bright.

"There they are!" yelled someone from behind the dazzle of three powerful flashlights.

Spider pulled Joe and Katherine into the nearest alcove along the wall.

"SKULKERS, RUN!" cried Tom. "GO! Make for Herdwick's Bairn!"

The Skulkers fled, and the guards opened fire. Bullets ricocheted off the tunnel walls, none of them hitting their mark.

"TOM!" cried Katherine. She would have run after her brother, but Spider caught her arm and pulled her back.

"Let him go," he said. "Skulkers are trained to run like rabbits. You'd never keep up with him. We'll find him later. Right now we have to get out of here."

"Where'd they go?" grumbled one of the guards behind the lights.

"Impossible!" said another. "No one can move that quickly."

The guards shone their lights down the now-empty tunnel.

Spider pulled Joe and Katherine closer into the

alcove, but as Joe moved he stepped on the back of a large rat. The rat squealed and sank its sharp teeth into his leg. Joe slipped, lost his balance, and fell into the water. Quick as a flash, Spider grabbed him and pulled him back, but the damage had been done.

"There's some of 'em still down there!" cried one of the guards.

A bullet grazed the brick edging close to Joe's head. Someone rattled the grilles fiercely.

Then they heard the jangling of keys.

"Is there light enough to read by?" asked Spider as he reached into his pocket and pulled out his notebook.

"Yes," replied Katherine as she took the book from Spider.

"Then find that butterfly, quickly. See if there's a way out of here."

"Hurry up, will you?" grumbled one of the guards.

"Let me have a go," said another. The guard grunted with the strain, then laughed. "Ha!" he cried. "All it needed was a bit of elbow grease, you great clodhopper."

This declaration was followed first by the sound of the heavy chain being slipped off the bars and then by the shrill squeal of the gate. They were through the first gate!

In the light made by the guards' spotlight Katherine

opened the notebook to the butterfly. Joe leaned across Spider so he could see the drawing. He was good with maps and was the first to spot their escape route.

"Look—there's a tunnel running parallel to this one."

Katherine nodded. "Yes, I see it. And there's an opening from this tunnel to that." She sounded excited, but then her voice fell. "But to reach it we'll have to get across this tunnel right under the guards' noses."

Spider nodded. "Don't worry about that. Think about the important stuff. Can you see the opening?"

Katherine looked one way, and Joe the other. Joe was the first to spot the low, dark arch with water pouring through it.

"It's an arch," Joe told Spider. "It's not far."

"Far enough to be killed trying to cross," said Katherine. "But what's the alternative?"

"Exactly," said Spider. "We'll have to take our chances. Are you ready?"

"Yes," said Joe, who didn't want to wait in that alcove to be shot or captured.

"You ready, Miss Apprentice?" he said over the squeal of the second gate being pried open by the guards.

"As I'll ever be," she replied.

"We'll go on the count of three," said Spider. "Joe, you lead. One, two, three."

On three, Joe pulled them across the tunnel.

"Oi!" shouted one of the guards. The spotlights swung up and lit the tunnel bright as day. "Stop or we'll shoot!"

An instant later Joe plunged through the low arch while bullets bounced off the walls around them.

CHAPTER 18

The Skulker's Apprentice

"Are we all in one piece?" spluttered Spider, who had landed on his back in the water. It was pitch-black in this tunnel, and Spider's matches were now sopping wet. Without Katherine's flashlight or the light from the guards' flashlights they couldn't even see the book, never mind read the map on the butterfly's wings.

Joe tried to stand up straight, but as he did, he banged his head hard on the ceiling. They could hear the guards shouting, and then came a low, grinding creak that set Joe's teeth on edge.

"They've got that last gate open," said Spider. "Quick, Katherine, the book. There'll be light in a minute."

Spider was right. Light from the guards' spotlight

suddenly shone through the water. Katherine opened the book and with Joe's help hurriedly checked the next four or five stages of their journey on the map. Once they got away from the guards, they would have to feel their way in the dark for the openings.

"You lead, Joe," said Katherine. "You're better at maps than me."

"This way, then," Joe said as he crouched low and set off at a run. After several turns he saw a change in the darkness ahead. It was a bloom of silver light. *There's got to be an air shaft close by,* he thought.

"Come on!" he called.

An hour later they were standing next to what had once been a building. Somewhere nearby was the Skulkers' hideout. Only the door frame of the building was still standing. Spider ran his hands over it, carefully picking out the carving with his fingertips.

"See the lamb!" he said. Joe and Katherine stepped closer. The carving was worn with age and part of its head was missing, but they could see the image of a lamb's body across the top of the door frame.

"But why a lamb?" asked Katherine.

"Your brother said to meet at the Herdwick Bairn," replied Spider. "*Herdwick* is a breed of sheep and *bairn* means 'baby.' A baby sheep is a . . . ?"

"Lamb," answered Joe.

"Not a very clever code, is it," said Spider. He turned and sniffed the air in all directions. "Ah, this way." He set off over the hill of rubble and climbed until he reached the place where the next-door house was still standing. There he crouched and poked his staff at a narrow crack that ran along the base of the house. The crack was barely as wide as a man's face. Spider leaned toward the house and sniffed.

"They're in here," he whispered. "Follow me quiet as you can." He lay on his belly and, setting his face sideways against the rubble and his shoulders flat on the ground, he wriggled headfirst through the crack. Katherine and Joe followed.

"Watch out," whispered Spider a fraction of a second before he, then Joe, then Katherine slid down a steep slope into what must once have been a cellar. The ceiling was arched and the walls were made of brick. Spider stood and ran his hands over the walls, muttering to himself.

He smiled and stepped back from the wall. Very gently he set his fingertips against one of the bricks and pushed. The brick sank back, and an instant later a narrow section of the wall swung open. Beyond it was a noisy, smoke-filled cellar full of Skulkers.

The Skulkers they had rescued from the Druckee

were so busy telling their comrades of their daring escape and how they had planned it for weeks that no one noticed the wall as it swung silently open.

Joe was almost knocked back by the mixture of smells. The sickly smell of stale beer fought with the delicious aroma of roasting chickens. Beside the chimney a little dog, a Jack Russell, ran on a wooden wheel to keep the spit turning over the fire.

"Then we fought the sewer guards!" shouted one Skulker gleefully. "Hundreds of them there were! Then we broke through the old railings with our bare hands and fled."

A large man with glittering eyes and a full black beard was sitting in a chair close to the fire. He had a cigar stub jammed in a corner of his mouth. The man pulled the cigar from his mouth and pointed it at the men. "And you say no one helped you?" he said.

"Brasque, how can you ask such a thing?" laughed another of the escapees. "Who would have been there to help us? Of course we did it on our own!"

"Really?" asked Brasque. He took a long drag on his cigar and threw the stub into the fire. "Then how did you keep the hatch open? Was it not difficult?"

"Very," announced Tom. "But we had our strength and our wits to guide us."

Katherine was outraged. Spider grabbed her hand to hold her back, but she yanked it away.

"You're a liar, Tom Heany!" she cried.

The instant she spoke, every Skulker leapt to his feet. Pistols were drawn and knives unsheathed.

"Hold your fire!" the bearded man bellowed as he pushed his way through. "What's he lying about?" he asked Katherine, crouching so his face was level with her own.

Katherine looked rattled but stood her ground.

"He's saying they did it on their own," she said, defiantly jutting out her chin. "They didn't. We helped them, and they know it. They'd never have got out if it hadn't been for Joe and me . . . oh, and Spider."

"Well," said the bearded man with another laugh, "I'm inclined to believe you. You certainly smell as though you've been down in the sewers."

Joe caught a flicker of irritation in Tom's eyes. "Brasque . . . I—" began Tom, but the man with the beard shushed him and turned instead to Spider.

"Carey," he said with a wry smile. "I thought you were dead."

"I don't die easy, Brasque," Spider said with a smile. "You of all people should know that. Besides, I heard you were in the Druckee with the others."

"Me?" laughed Brasque. "I'm not an easy fish to catch. Now come in, come in. I'm glad, more than glad, that you have come to join us in our quest."

"Join? Nay, I've not come to join you," answered Spider. "But I'm willing to allow that we both have the same end in sight."

"To find an end to this war?" said Brasque, clapping a hand on Spider's bony shoulder. "Yes, we agree on that at least, but may we not find other ways to serve each other's cause?"

"Not while you see violence as the only way to end the violence," replied Spider.

Brasque's smile only grew wider at this, and his belly shook as he laughed. "After all these years of so-called diplomacy, do you still think this war will end by Orlemann's efforts?"

Spider shook his head. "No, far from it. A different kind of diplomacy is what is needed now. Orlemann? Bah! His kind of diplomacy reeks of something rotten."

"I agree," said Brasque. "I have my own views on that for sure. But as you are here, why not avail yourself of our hospitality? You and your two compadres are soaked and stinking. Let us at least help you to some dry, clean clothes and give you something to eat."

Spider acquiesced to this, and half an hour later the three of them were washed and dressed in a different assortment of rags while their own clothes were washed and pegged out to dry on a line that ran across the cellar. Joe sat by the fire, wearing gray pajamas that were covered all over in a faded football pattern. They reminded him of some he had at home.

Brasque and Spider were deep in conversation. There was no doubt that Brasque was the leader of these men. He was big and strong and looked as though he could command anyone to do anything. Beside him Spider looked puny. The old man could barely support himself without the help of his staff. But the more Joe watched them, the more he understood that he'd got it wrong. Brasque was almost deferential toward Spider. After a while it seemed to Joe that Spider was the real commander in the room.

"Everything went according to plan with the escape, I presume?" Joe heard Brasque ask Spider.

"It did," said Spider. "The timing couldn't have been better, but there was one thing—"

"What was that?"

"In some ways it was all a little too perfect, a little too easy. I can't help but wonder how we all got out of there alive. Surely the Druckee guards aren't such poor marksmen as to miss ten people in a very small tunnel?"

"You're suggesting someone other than ourselves wanted the escape to be successful?"

"Perhaps," said Spider. "Or perhaps I see conspiracies everywhere in my old age. It is a danger in our line of work."

"It is indeed," laughed Brasque. "It is indeed."

They continued talking as Brasque led Spider to a large wingback chair at the far side of the fire. Brasque pulled up a three-legged stool and sat in front of him.

"But can't you see the risk, man?" Spider was saying. "Think of the bloodshed."

Brasque grunted and started to say something. Spider cut him off.

"It's too dangerous. Have you forgotten what happened at Creg Bay? You'd barely got fifteen men landed on the south side before they were annihilated by the machines. The rest of you had to flee for your lives. Are you willing to risk that again?"

"No," replied Brasque testily, "I'm not. And I haven't forgotten, either, but this time it'll be different. I've looked at this from every angle. Where else but over the mountains can they be making those lethal machines? All the evidence points to a base in the north, beyond the Long Lake. You have to understand, the only way to stop this war is to cross the plain and destroy those factories. We leave tonight."

"If those factories are there."

"It's a risk I'm willing to take!"

Spider ran his hands through his scraggly hair. "Say you and your men make it over the north plain to the Long Lake, and say somehow—though I have no idea how—you find a way over the lake, and say you don't get lost in the mountains, and say you find your way to whatever is set up beyond the mountains. Then what? There'll be so few of you alive by that time that you'll have no power with which to strike. Don't you see? You will be severely depleting your forces for what could be nothing more than a wild goose chase."

Brasque shook his head. "But if we are right, Carey, a few men will be able to set enough explosives to destroy even the biggest factories. Imagine—no more Goliaths or Scrapers or Zamramies. No, Carey, there's been enough diplomacy, enough talk. We all want this war to be over. Now's the time to fight back."

Spider shook his head. "Aren't you forgetting something?"

Brasque looked up at Spider. "You mean the charges?"

Spider nodded. "What if they aren't being sent through the arches at all? What if they're being used to build the machines? Did your men find out anything in the Druckee? Did they see the arches?"

Brasque shook his head. "No. The guards were tipped off. My men never even got close to them."

"Couldn't your agent—"

"No," replied Brasque. "A guard must have a level-five security pass to the arches. Not many have that."

"Such sophisticated security," mused Spider. "Orlemann takes good care of the charges, does he not?"

"You've learned something new, Spider?"

"No. I know no more than you, but my suspicions grow each day." Spider paused for a moment; then he said softly, "Don't do it, Brasque. Don't risk your lives or the safety of those charges."

Brasque glared at Spider. "No. The wheels have already been set in motion. We are going tonight."

"Just wait one more day, twelve hours even. Let me send him in and find out for certain what's happening to the charges. If they are safe within the Druckee walls, then I swear I won't try to stop you—in fact, I'll guide you across the northern plain myself."

"We already have a guide. Tom'll take us; he says he learned his guiding from the best."

"Tom? He could guide you back to Quarain well enough, but he doesn't know the lay of the land north of here any better than you do. I know it well. Give me a few hours, Brasque. Let me see what I can find out."

Brasque looked at Spider for a long time, then took a deep breath. "And the boy? Will he do what you ask? It's as great a risk for him, if not greater."

"I know," said Spider. "There's only one way to find out." He turned toward Joe and opened his mouth, but Joe spoke first.

"What exactly do you want me to do?" he asked.

Spider grinned. "I hoped you were listening. Clever boy. Clever boy!"

Half an hour later Joe sat staring into the fire. The chickens that turned above the flames crackled and spat, but he didn't notice them. He was thinking about Spider's request. It was a strange one. He was asking Joe to go willingly to the Druckee, pretend to be one of the charges, and there allow Spider to sell him to the guards so he could get inside and find out what was happening to the charges.

Of course Joe had said yes. What else could he say? He was here to find his sister, and if the charges were taken into the Druckee, then that was where he had to go. But Spider's plan was dangerous, and Joe worried what would happen if, once inside the prison, he was found out and fell into the hands of the secret police.

Spider sat down next to Joe. "We've got someone on the inside who will try to help you," he said.

"Then why can't he—"

"Because they are watching him. One false move and we'll lose him completely. Now, listen up—the arches are far beneath the building. It's even more of a labyrinth down there than it is in the sewers. You'll need this."

Spider took his notebook from his pocket and handed it to Joe.

"There's a drawing of a sycamore leaf about a third of the way in that'll show you the layout of the prison. The three arches are in the very center of the building, three or four floors down." Joe opened the book and found the drawing taped to the page. The arches were in the middle of the leaf. They were disguised as looped veins. Spider leaned forward and closed the book. He stuffed it inside Joe's pajama top.

"Be careful with it," he said. "Don't let it fall into the wrong hands. I expect you to bring it back to me all in one piece."

Just then an argument erupted at the back of the room.

"Are you or are you not going to sign me on?" Katherine yelled.

Joe stood up and saw Katherine waving a sheaf of papers under her brother's nose. Tom looked embarrassed, bemused, and furious all at the same time.

"Look, Kat," said Tom, "I can't sign you on. I'm not a guide anymore. I'm a Skulker, and Skulkers don't have apprentices."

Tom pulled her down onto a seat and tried to look her in the eyes, but she kept her face turned away from him.

"Kat, listen to me," Tom implored. "Please. Forget all this. Go back to Quarain, or better still, go back to fetching. You'll be safer in the trenches than you will here."

"I can't leave Carey," said Katherine ruefully. "I signed myself over to him, believing that you would take me on when I found you. What an idiot I am!"

"But, Kat—"

"No," Katherine said, jumping to her feet. "You don't get to call me Kat anymore."

She turned and hurried to the secret door. A moment later she was gone.

Joe ran over to Spider, who was still by the fire.

"Katherine's gone," he said.

"Then we'd best find her," said Spider, reaching up and pulling their coats down from the rack above the fire.

"Twelve hours, then," Spider said to Brasque. "I'll not tell anyone of your whereabouts."

"You wouldn't leave here alive if I thought you might," laughed Brasque. He shook Spider's hand, then turned to Joe and raised his eyebrows. "And what about you?"

"I won't tell either," replied Joe. "Cross my heart," he added, crossing a finger over his chest.

"Swear it," said Brasque, suddenly serious.

"I swear," said Joe.

Spider draped the heavy, ragged coat around Joe's shoulders.

"Come on, Joe, lead me out of here," he said as they made their way across the room. "We've much work to do tonight, you and I."

CHAPTER 19

The Sale

They found Katherine sitting in a doorway half a block from the Skulkers' hideout. Her eyes were red.

"It was too smoky in there for me," she said. "I had to leave. It made my eyes sting."

"Nothing worse than smoke for the eyes," agreed Spider. "Even dead eyes feel it keenly sometimes." His tone was far gentler than Joe had heard before.

Spider laid his hand gently on Katherine's shoulder. "So you're still my apprentice then?"

With a little wail Katherine dropped her face against her knees.

Spider patted her back. "Tell you what. I'll let you go if you like, but"—he waited till he had her attention—

"if you'll take my advice, you'd be wise to stick with me."

"I know," replied Katherine, wiping her cheeks on her sleeve. "I think, if it's all right, I will stay with you, at least till something better comes up."

For once, Spider didn't argue. He stood up, held out his hand, and helped her to her feet.

"Come on, then," he said. "We've got a busy day ahead."

The three of them started down the street. Katherine trailed a few yards behind, lost in her own thoughts.

"Listen, Joe," said Spider, speaking quietly, "you're going to have to act a bit when we get to the Druckee. After they've been tested the charges are quiet and do whatever they're asked to do. You're going to have to behave like them—be quiet and don't draw attention to yourself. We need them to think that you've already been checked out. Do you understand?"

"I think so," replied Joe.

"And don't react to whatever you hear me say or see me do when we get to the guards, all right? You have to trust me. More lives than yours depend on it."

"Where will I find you when I get out?" Joe asked.

"Don't worry about that," replied Spider. "I'll find *you*. No matter what, I'll find you."

They turned the corner and stopped. Ahead of them

stood the Druckee. The vast bulk of the prison looked even grimmer and more imposing in the gray daylight.

"Katherine," said Spider, "wait here until I return."

"Why? What are you going to do?" she asked.

"There isn't time to explain," replied Spider. "Wait here; I'll be back shortly. Joe, lead me to the wall of the moat."

When they reached the low wall Spider sat down on it. Joe sat beside him. Spider tapped his hand. "There is one thing, Joe, I didn't tell you before," said Spider. "It's about those machines, the ones they use to test the charges. I think I know what they do and why the charges behave differently after they've been tested.

"They say those machines listen for secrets, but not just any secrets. I believe they listen for the secrets of which we are most ashamed, the secrets that make us feel we'd rather die than have them be known. The big secrets, the ones that eat away at your heart like a slow-working poison. Do you know what I mean, Joe?"

"I think so," answered Joe. He knew exactly what Spider meant.

Spider went on. "I believe that the police use these secrets to make the charges behave. I think they tell the charges that if they don't do what they say, they'll tell their secrets to the world." Spider paused. "If they catch you, if they test you, they'll use what they learn to try to make you do what they want. But if you have a clear conscience they can't get at you, Joe. Do you understand?"

"Yes," replied Joe. He didn't like where this conversation was going.

"Everybody has secrets, Joe," said Spider kindly. "Don't carry anything in there with you that can hurt you. If you want to tell me anything, Joe, you can. Once it's told, no one can threaten you with it anymore. Do you want to tell me anything?"

"No. I don't have any secrets," said Joe. He knew Spider was being kind. But his secret was so big, so awful, that even Spider would be horrified by it.

"Very well," said Spider. "Then let's get on with it."

When they reached the drawbridge, Spider grabbed Joe firmly by the arm.

"Here we go," he murmured under his breath. "Remember, be careful in there."

The sentries at the entrance drew their swords and crossed them.

"Where do you think you're going, blind man?" snarled one of them.

"Got a charge here," said Spider in an oily, ingratiating voice. "Thought he must have wandered off; found him sitting on a pile of rubble."

The guards exchanged a look, then uncrossed their swords and returned them to their scabbards. "Take him to the sergeant up yonder," said the one on the right. Spider and Joe set off across the drawbridge toward the main gate.

"NO!" came a loud cry from behind them. Joe turned and saw Katherine tearing across the road toward the drawbridge. The sentries drew their swords.

"Halt!" they shouted. But Katherine ducked under the swords.

"Hell's teeth!" muttered Spider. He squeezed Joe's arm. "Remember, you stay quiet." Then in a loud voice he called back to the sentries, who were already chasing Katherine. "She's with me!" he cried. "My apprentice, my eyes. She's coming to help me." Spider caught Katherine by the back of the neck and pushed her out in front of him. She wriggled like a fish on a hook.

"Get off me!" she wailed. "I knew you'd betray us. You're going to sell him, aren't you? You miserable old—"

Spider shook her hard. "I'm not selling anybody," said Spider under his breath. "Joe's in on it. He's going on the inside. Now lead me across this bridge and don't say anything!"

Katherine turned her furious eyes on Joe. He nodded imperceptibly. "All right," growled Katherine. She pulled her neck free and moved Spider's hand to her shoulder.

In the courtyard three pajamaed charges sat on a bench by a door. Joe looked down at the clothes the Skulkers had given him in exchange for his own—dull gray pajamas just like the charges were wearing.

Ahead of them stood a fat sergeant with his hands on his hips. "What have you got for me then?" he asked, staring hard at Joe.

"Found this un," said Spider. "Must've been brought through the old way, then abandoned. You can see he's already been tested, but he's in good health apart from that. What'll you give me for him?"

The guard looked the three of them over, then cleared his throat and spat on the ground.

"Fifty," said the sergeant.

"Hundred" was Spider's response.

"Fifty-five," said the sergeant.

The haggling went on until a price of seventy was agreed on. "Over here then," said the sergeant, leading Spider to a small office that was built into one side of the vast gateway.

"This is crazy," Katherine whispered to Joe. "My brother—" She stopped and fell quiet. Joe didn't say anything. He knew it was better not to.

When Spider returned, he was counting out several banknotes and a handful of coins. He wore a look of supreme satisfaction on his face. "Not bad for a day's work," he said. He took hold of Joe's arm. "Where do you want him?" he asked. The sergeant looked at Katherine and nodded at the charges in the courtyard.

"That lot's about to be taken inside. Put him over there with them," he said.

Katherine led Spider and Joe up to the charges by the door. Spider shoved Joe toward the group, and as he did, he accidentally dropped one of the coins. Spider fumbled to find it, and in doing so, brought his head level with Joe's.

"Good luck, Joe," he said quietly. "Keep your wits about you."

Spider found the coin and with a loud "ha!" snatched it up greedily. As soon as he was up, he turned and, counting his money as he went, let Katherine lead him back to the drawbridge.

Joe's courage almost failed him. He was about to cry out after Spider when he noticed two secret policemen standing in the corner of the courtyard. One of them held a small brown case at his side. Joe slowly closed his mouth and let his face go blank. Like Spider had said, he'd better keep his wits about him.

CHAPTER 20

The Holding Tank

Joe sat where he'd been left with the other charges on the bench. After what felt like hours, a door at the other side of the courtyard opened and two guards came shambling across the cobbles toward them.

"Come on, you lot!" shouted one of them. "On your feet! You know what we'll do if you don't look sharp!" The charges stood, and Joe followed suit. The guards herded the four of them toward a pair of stout oak doors in the prison building.

The guards led the children through a series of small entry rooms that led into a hall full of pillars.

In the center of the hall the pillars encircled a large table and a wide, high-backed wooden chair. Fat white candles burned in a candelabra on the tabletop and dripped wax onto the wood. Standing in the middle of the table was a model of some sort of machine. It was intricately built, with a fat engine block in the middle and rows of four caterpillar treads lined up along the bottom. On top of the engine block was a crane with pulleys and cables and on the opposite side a hefty counterweight.

Joe faltered in his step. He would have liked to take a closer look at the model, but the guards were hurrying them. They were herded through a set of double doors, along a short corridor, and down a staircase. Here the walls were of bare stone, and the wide steps, which spiraled down into the earth, were worn at the edges. As he went, Joe let his fingers graze against the wall, as though just by touching it he could force himself to remember his way out of the prison. He could already tell that it wouldn't be easy— there were so many twists and turns. Up these three stairs, down this corridor, down twenty stairs, up two, a long walk, then more stairs leading down. At long last they reached an area of the prison where the corridors were lined with doors. One of the doors stood ajar, and inside, Joe saw what looked like a room in a museum where instruments of torture were displayed. He shuddered and looked away.

Joe was busy wondering if he would ever be able to find his way out when the guards stopped by a closed door. The first guard opened the door, and the second steered the charges into the room.

Beyond the door was a large, damp-smelling cell. It was crowded with charges of all ages. There must have been thirty or more. Most of them were sitting on wooden benches, but a few sat on the floor with their backs against the wall. All of them silently turned their dirty faces to the group by the door. *They look scared,* thought Joe. He ventured a small smile at one of the younger ones, but the little boy just turned his eyes to the floor and stared at his feet. Joe stared around the room, searching for one small blond girl, but there was no sign of her.

The guards steered Joe and the other children to an empty section of one of the benches and made them sit down.

"So all this lot in here came in on that last mercy mission, did they?" asked one guard, looking around at the charges.

"That's right," replied the other. "They'll be taken down closer to the arches tonight. I hear the cells down there are much more comfortable. A much better place for them to wait till it's their time. Just look at 'em. Poor little mites. Ah, well, better get 'em fed."

The guards left the cell and a moment later returned. One carried a basket, the other a wooden cask. The first guard handed out bread and cheese while the second ladled water from the cask into small cups that each charge held out. The children obediently took the proffered food and ate and drank quickly. The guards gave Joe and the other newcomers a cup each and filled them with water. Acting like the others, Joe obediently drank. The water tasted like metal.

Once all the charges had been fed, the guards opened the door to leave, but before they left, they turned back to the children.

"Nighty-night, then," said one.

"You are soft," tutted the other as he removed a torch from its bracket by the door. "Time for sleep, you lot. And no funny business or you know what'll happen."

At the guards' command all the charges slid to the floor. They turned, folded their arms on the benches, then settled their heads down on their arms. Joe did the same. As he turned to lay his head down, something pricked his chest. He slid his hand up under his coat. It was the sharp corner of Spider's book. Joe adjusted the book, laid his cheek against the wooden bench, and wondered how on earth he was supposed to get through that heavy cell door.

The guards watched the charges, and when the last one was settled they left, closing the door behind them. Joe waited for the sound of a key turning in the lock, but it never came. All he heard was the sound of the guards' footsteps as they walked away. Then he realized that if Spider had been right, the guards didn't need to lock the cell door. The charges wouldn't try to leave, not while someone threatened to tell their most shameful secrets.

The cold from the stone floor seeped into Joe's bones, but he didn't want to move in case the guards returned. Around him the other charges obediently fell asleep. Slowly Joe sat up. A faint light filtered in through the barred window in the door.

Carefully Joe took out Spider's book and opened it at the drawing of the leaf. He tilted it toward the door and in the dim light tried to understand the map that was hidden in the myriad veins.

It was perhaps an hour later when Joe heard the sound of footsteps coming back toward the cell. He quickly closed Spider's book, stuffed it back inside his pajamas, then settled his head down on the bench and pretended to be fast asleep.

"Wake up, time to go!" cried a loud voice as the door was thrown open. Suddenly the cell was filled with light. "Up you get. On your feet. Look lively!"

Like the other charges, Joe lifted his head and blinked in the light. Some of the children groaned and yawned in protest, but even so, they did as they were told and stood up. Joe got to his feet and found a place in the line. That was when he noticed that with the guards were four secret policemen. One of them was wearing an officer's hat decorated with gold braid.

"Dismissed," he told the two guards.

The guards touched their knuckles to their foreheads, then turned and left. The four secret policemen eyed the charges coldly.

"Let's get them on their way then," said the commander. "Look sharp."

With that, his three subordinates herded the children out of the cell.

They traveled along numerous corridors and down staircases that went deep into the earth. They must have been seven or eight stories down when a shout came from behind them.

"SIR!"

"Halt!" the commander barked. The charges stopped and leaned against the wall. The commander walked to the back of the line, where the other three policemen joined him. Keeping his face low, Joe turned his head as far as he dared so he could see what was going on.

Another secret policeman ran out of the shadows and caught up to his colleagues. It was Radworth! Joe shrank back against the wall. Radworth was talking to the commander in a low voice. Joe tried to hear what he was saying, but he spoke too quietly.

Then the commander raised his voice. "Enough, Mr. Radworth. Return to the upper levels. You have no clearance. You cannot pass through here."

"But, sir, with all due respect, he himself asked me to hurry down and help you."

"I have enough men already," came the gruff reply. "Besides, what's he doing interfering with this? He's never bothered before. He's always left it up to me."

"You know how he is," said Radworth with a laugh. "Especially now with the impending armistice. He wants to control every last detail."

The commander did not laugh back. "Do not get smart with me," he snapped. "Operation Arches is set at security level five. That means that everyone involved in this procedure has been cleared by him personally. Until he summons me and instructs me in person that he wants you to join this team, you, Mr. Radworth, are surplus to requirements. Now go back and find something to do. There're plenty of motorcycles that need cleaning if you're stuck for something."

Radworth looked furious, but he didn't retaliate. "Yes, sir," he said. With a firm salute, he clicked his heels, turned, and marched back into the shadows.

The commander returned to the front of the line and gave the order to move on.

He led the charges to the end of the corridor, then down yet another staircase. This staircase was different from the ones before. It was wide and curving and it looked as though it was made of a different type of stone than the rest of the building.

"Halt!" said the commander when all the charges had reached the bottom of the staircase.

The secret policemen stepped to the front of the line and shone their flashlights into the gloom. As the lights swiveled over the ceiling and walls, Joe saw hints of something that he couldn't quite work out. Then with a loud clunk the commander turned on the lights.

They were in a large, circular room with a domed ceiling. The entire room—the walls, the ceiling, the floor—was decorated with an incredible mosaic. All four of the secret policemen were staring at the mosaic, drinking it in with their eyes. The commander let out a sigh. He seemed, for the moment, to have forgotten about the charges.

On the inside of the dome was a beautiful summer sky with high white clouds, large clear blue patches, and birds—swallows and starlings and finches—soaring above the earth. On the curved wall was a lush forest with woodland birds, deer, foxes, squirrels, rabbits, and mice peeking out from between trees and blades of grass. As the wall curved, the landscape changed to green fields and meadows full of flowers that rolled away toward magnificent snow-covered mountains in the distance. A beautiful purple-tinged plain swept down toward a sea that sparkled in the sunshine. The floor of the room was covered in tiny tiles that formed leaves of grass and multicolored wildflowers. Here and there mushrooms and toadstools stood among the flowers.

The mosaic was breathtaking. But there was one thing in the domed room that seemed entirely out of place. In the middle of the floor stood a low wall. It was perhaps three yards long by one and a half yards high. It was a wall made of gray bricks that looked as though they had been hastily cemented together. This wall spoiled the whole effect of the room. Joe looked away from it and tried to focus on something more appealing, but there was something about this patch that kept drawing his attention back to it. The shape of it intrigued him, the way it was separated into three curves at the top. Then it dawned on him. These were the arches. The bricks were there to block them up. Joe felt an awful rushing in his head. If the arches were bricked up, then how would any of these charges get home? How would Hannah? How, for that matter, would he?

The commander blew his nose noisily. "Can't dawdle

here all day," he said, turning the light off. "Let's get them on that train before the ambassador comes and finds us all here getting weepy." He pressed a metal panel that was set into the wall, and with a mechanical clonk a hidden door in the mosaic swung open. Beyond the door there was another staircase. This one was much narrower and steeper than the ones before. The charges followed the commander down the spiral steps. They traveled in silence, down and down and down in single file. This staircase was taking them far deeper than the sewers. It was stiflingly hot and stuffy.

Eventually the steps opened onto what looked like an underground train station. There was a long platform, and beside it, at a lower level, silver tracks disappeared into a dark tunnel at the far end. Electric lights on the ceiling flickered and buzzed. The secret policemen lined the charges against the wall.

An underground train, thought Joe. The charges weren't going home or anywhere else through the arches; they were being taken to another place. Just as he thought this, a dry, hot wind blew through the tunnel, which was immediately followed by the sound of an approaching train. A single headlight appeared in the distant darkness.

One of the secret policemen walked from the back of the line. Another walked from the front. They met right in front of Joe. Joe lowered his eyes but kept his ears open.

"I thought he'd stopped needing them in the mountains," said one of the policemen.

"Not yet," said the other. "He's stopped building the tunnel now. Apparently it won't be needed once the armistice goes ahead. But he still needs this lot for the mine and the factories, and as long as he needs them, it's over the mountains they go."

The factories? Joe flinched. *The mine?* He felt panic rising inside him. Spider had been right to worry about the Skulkers' plans. If Merid had a mine beyond the mountains, and if the Skulkers discovered it and tried to blow it up, what would happen to the charges?

But there was something niggling at his brain, something one of the men had said. They'd said "his" mine, "his" factories. What did they mean by that? Did the mine not belong to Merid then?

There wasn't any time to wonder about this. Joe had to do something. He had to get back to Spider. If the Skulkers went ahead with their plans, they could risk hurting the charges who were kept there. And Hannah? If Hannah wasn't in this group in the tunnel, then she must already be in this mine beyond the mountains.

The train roared out of the tunnel and stopped with a screech of brakes. There were only two cars. They were brightly lit but had no seats, just long leather straps hanging from the ceiling.

As the policemen led the line of charges to the train, Joe slid back along the wall toward the stairway. The line of charges was his cover—as they moved forward, he moved back. But the line was going to end very soon. The staircase was some way away, and he would certainly be spotted if he made a dash for it.

Joe waited until all the policemen were looking toward the train. Then, quick as a flash, he shot across the narrow platform and dropped down onto the track, landing heavily between the train and the platform wall. From the end of the train to the end of the platform was only twenty yards.

He was halfway there when he saw another train's light approaching from the opposite direction. He flattened himself against the wall.

It was a miracle he wasn't crushed. The steel wheels and pistons passed by less than an inch from his face. Joe's wounded hand knocked against the wall, and he bit down hard on his lip to quash the impulse to cry out. The two trains connected with a loud clang; then Joe heard someone rattle chains and attach the cars together. Now there was hardly any room for him to move. Inch by slow inch he shuffled through the narrow space.

When he made it to the end of the car he could see

that if he could just get up level with the platform, he'd be on the stairs in one quick step. Joe climbed up the back of the train and hung on, waiting for the moment to be right. As he waited, he noticed that this car was different from the others. It was dark, and the outside shone like an expensive car. The windows at the back were made of black glass and he couldn't see anything through them, except every now and then a small red light that winked in the darkness.

Joe peered around the corner and saw the policemen and the last of the charges disappear into the front car. The platform was empty. This was it. He took a deep breath, then leapt off the train and onto the stairs. In less than a second he was running up the narrow staircase. He ran until he could run no more and had to stop and catch his breath. Were they following? He listened hard. He couldn't hear anything above his own heart thumping fit to burst.

After a hard climb up the stairs to the mosaic room and then navigating his way through the prison corridors with Spider's map, Joe at last found himself outside the large wooden doors that led into the great pillared hall.

Slowly he opened the doors, then silently stole inside. He reached the middle of the hall and peered around a pillar toward the table where the candles still burned. The light flickered in the metallic sides of the little model.

He scurried to the table; then, checking that there was no one around, he crouched till the model was at eye level. It was an incredible little machine, similar to the large earthmovers he knew from his magazines. He'd even attempted to build a similar model, but it had been crude and clumsy compared to this. Here, every detail was perfect, from each of the individual rivets in the metal panels of the engine block to the crane with its complex arrangement of cables and pulleys. There was a tiny handle on one side of the engine block, and Joe, forgetting where he was or any danger he might be in, turned the handle and gently opened the little panel. He gasped. This wasn't just an empty shell of carefully constructed metal; it had an engine inside! He peered through the window of the cab and saw a tiny, jewel-like row of levers and switches. Lying on the table beside the model was a small silver key. Joe picked it up and weighed it in his hand. He wondered if it would fit the door to the cab. His hand shook with excitement as he lifted it toward the keyhole.

"Well, look who's come to say hello," said a voice behind him.

CHAPTER 21

The Tower

Joe jumped, and the little key fell to the floor. He spun around. At first he couldn't see who had spoken. Then a figure stepped out of the shadows.

Joe groaned inwardly. It was Wyn. Sweaty, ruddy-faced, foul-smelling Wyn.

"I was wondering when you'd come to see me," said Wyn. The little thief grinned at Joe. Joe noticed that Wyn was better dressed than he had been. Better dressed, but still as filthy. There were food stains down the front of his velvet coat.

"Nice outfit, Wyn," said Joe. "Spying must pay well." Wyn's smile grew broader. Joe took a step back and felt the edge of the table behind him. His hand moved toward the candelabra.

"I'm very glad to see you," smirked Wyn. "My catching you will go down well with my patron. He's very interested in meeting you. Still not been tested then? Nah—you wouldn't be trying to run away if you had."

Wyn took another step forward, his glassy eyes shining greedily.

Joe picked up the candelabra and held it high. "This'll hurt if it hits you," he said with as much confidence as he could muster.

"Put it down," Wyn said. "Don't be daft, Joe. We could help each other. I don't want to brag, but I've a lot of influence with his excellency these days. I can make sure they treat you decent. No testing, that sort of thing. I saw your sister, by the way."

"Hannah? Where?" asked Joe.

Wyn lunged forward, but Joe reacted quickly and threw the candelabra. It caught Wyn on the side of the head. The three burning candles flew out of their holders, flinging hot wax across his cheek. Wyn screamed in pain and backed away, clutching his face.

Joe bolted. He ran blindly through the hall, not knowing if he was headed in the right direction but hoping, praying that there would be a way out. He reached the wall and found a small door. He tugged on the handle. It opened easily, and he flew through it. In the next instant he found himself fleeing along a gloomy corridor. Even as he ran he noticed it seemed strangely different from the ones in the part of the prison he'd been in before. It smelled fusty, a mixture of mildew and damp wool. Far behind him he heard Wyn shouting for the guards.

Joe ran on. He turned a corner and ran up a flight of wide steps, then found himself in another fusty corridor. Here the only light came from the row of arched windows that stretched along the left-hand side. These windows were black with grime and glowed a dirty amber from the prison lights in the courtyard outside. In the dim light Joe noticed a narrow arch on his right. Through it he could see steps spiraling up into the gloom. He paused only a moment and then ran past. To go up those stairs to who knew where would be madness. There was thick dust on the steps, and his pursuers would know instantly where he'd gone.

He hurried down the corridor, praying that there would be some other way out. But he could see no doorways to the outside world. He ran to one of the windows and wiped off the grime with his fist. Through the smear he could see a series of slanted roofs that reached across the courtyard. He guessed that these were the roofs of the great hall. They looked easy enough to climb across if he could just get down there.

He ran his hands around the window frames, searching for a catch, but the dirty windows had been welded shut. Their metal frames were bubbled at the edges, and their latches and handles had been removed. He could go back to the arched doorway and run up the dark stairs, but what if there was no way down? He'd be trapped like a wasp in a bottle.

"There he is!" yelled Wyn. "Get him!"

The guards' feet thundered on the bare boards as they charged down the corridor. Joe fled to the far wall. *Please, let there be a door,* he begged silently as he ran. There was no door, but there was another dark archway in the corner. This, too, had steps leading up. He threw himself away from the wall and bounded up the stairs two at a time.

The stairs spiraled up to a curved landing that bent to the right and led to another flight of stairs. There were narrow, glassless slits for windows on his left, and as he passed, he glanced out. He must have risen quickly, for now he could see nothing but the dense night fog. The stairway grew narrower as he climbed, and he could easily touch both walls at the same time. But the stairs didn't wind in a tight coil. They stretched around in long, lazy circles, as though circling a wide core. Every twenty steps or so there was a door, but though he tried each one and rattled the rusted padlocks on their bolts, none of them opened.

The guards' footsteps echoed up the stairs behind him. Joe hurried on. Through the windows he could see that he had now climbed above the clouds. As he came around the northern side of the tower, he saw the black mountains rising above the fluffy, settled blanket of fog. But there was no sign of stars in the sky, for far above the mountains was another layer of cloud, heavier and darker than the fog itself. Sandwiched between the layers, the silvery gray light blossomed behind the mountains and faded slowly.

Through the windows on the southern side Joe saw the dark shapes of two towers, and suddenly he knew where he was. He was inside one of the three towers that stood inside the Druckee. Spider had said they were part of the old university. Joe ran on and on, up into the sky, pausing only to try the locks on the doors. Soon Wyn would catch him, and he knew what would happen then. He would be taken down and tested. Running was only delaying the inevitable.

Joe turned the last curve in the spiral and found that there were only two doors remaining—one to his right, which, like the others, bore a heavy padlock; and one straight ahead, effectively sealing off the corridor. There was no lock on this one. The bolt was thrown open and the latch hung free.

Joe opened the door. Beyond it was a short flight of

nine or so steps. He would have run up them, but as he set his foot on the first step, he heard voices from above.

"They must be somewhere in this damn city," said one. Joe had heard the voice before, but it was not so cold or steely then. *It's Orlemann!* thought Joe. The ambassador went on. "Even with the fog filter, I can see nothing. We have to flush them out. I don't want any of them about when I make my move, understand? What's all that commotion below?"

Joe realized Orlemann must have heard Wyn and the guards lumbering up the stairs. And it took him only another second to understand that if he didn't find some other way out, he would be caught between the two.

He looked back the way he had come. The guards would turn the corner at any moment. Joe darted back toward the last door he had passed and grabbed the padlock. Like the others it was not only locked but also rusted solid. No amount of tugging would open it. He doubted it could even be opened with a key, it was so ancient.

Joe turned around and pressed himself against the door, willing himself to melt through it. He closed his eyes. One of the two parties would reach him soon enough; the only question was who would get there first—Orlemann or Wyn. Joe pressed harder against the wood as the sounds of his pursuers grew ever louder.

Then, miraculously, the door at his back swung open, and he fell into the room behind. He landed with a jolt on his backside.

He stared in amazement as the door closed against the light, or rather, part of the door. Joe could see that most of the door had remained solidly in place, while just a narrow panel had opened to let him through.

"Keep quiet," whispered a voice in the darkness. "Keep still till they think they missed you. Then we'll light a lamp and talk."

Joe stayed still and listened to the confusion outside in the passageway.

"What's all this?" Orlemann demanded in a soft, menacing tone. "No one is allowed in the towers. Why are you here?"

Wyn's voice was unctuous. "Apologies, Your Worship-fulness, one of the charges escaped and we followed him up here."

"A charge? Escaped? What sort of charge has the sense to escape?"

"A chatty one that hasn't been tested yet," groveled Wyn. "It's the one I told you about, remember? The one I found at Quarain. He slipped in here somehow. I caught him nosing about your desk, fiddling with one of your models. We followed him up—"

"Quiet!" snapped Orlemann, cutting him off. "You say he was studying one of my machines?"

"He was, sir. He was looking at your new model most intently."

"Very well. Find him and bring him to me."

"Excuse me, sir, the way I see it the only place he could have gone was in one of these storerooms up here."

Joe heard a rattle at the padlock, and then on Joe's side of the door something, some creature, flew against the wood. It scraped and scratched and let out a blood-curdling cry that started as a scream, then settled into a hideous, stifled rattling, like the demented chatter of a wild beast. Joe silently scurried from his place close to the door and huddled against the farthest wall.

Three-quarters of the way up the door a small, square hatch was thrown open and gray light filtered in from outside. Now Joe could see the silhouette of a woman's face. She looked as wizened as an old apple. The long, curled-over fingernails on her bony hands scratched like talons at the opening in the door. Orlemann's face appeared at the hatch. The woman backed down, whimpering.

"Shall I have them take your toys away?" asked the ambassador in a cold, matter-of-fact voice.

"No!" the woman begged, slapping her palms against

the thick wooden door. Like her scream, her voice sounded more animal than human, and Joe shivered. What would such a creature do to him when the others left? Perhaps he'd be better off letting Orlemann and Wyn find him now, but some instinct held him where he was.

"Pardon me, sir," said Wyn. Joe listened. "Let's not bother with her now. We've got to find that boy, don't we?"

This was immediately followed by the sound of a sharp slap.

"Ow!" Wyn whined.

Joe heard a click. Then the beam of a flashlight suddenly pierced the gloom. Joe pushed himself even farther back behind the stack of what he now saw were fat, dusty, leather-bound books. The leather was wrinkled like old elephant skin, and the edges of the books, once gilded, were now mottled with damp.

The beam of light slid around the back of the room, revealing that the walls were more than damp—they almost were running with water. Water dripped through the ceiling into buckets that were already full to the brim. The room was crowded with rotting junk. More books lay moldering on a stout-legged table, and even more were crammed any old way along the dilapidated shelves that ran along the damp walls. One side of the strange room was piled high with massive tangles of bent and corroded metal and twisted skeins of wire. The floor was made of broken mosaic tiles. Deep puddles had formed in the cracks.

"Enough," said the ambassador. The hatch in the door was slammed shut. Orlemann's voice was muffled through the wood. "There's no one but her in there," he said. "This door hasn't been opened in twenty years. You must have missed the boy on the stairs. Hurry back and sound the alarm. Check every door along the way. I want him found."

"Yes, sir," said Wyn. Then he barked at the guards, as though losing Joe had been their fault. "All right, you lot. You heard his excellency. About-face. Get down them stairs now!"

Joe could hardly breathe; the musty smell of the books was unbearable. He covered his nose with his hands and listened as the sound of several pairs of feet tramping down the stairs faded into a velvety silence.

"Where—" began Joe in a whisper. But the creature scuttled across the darkness and clamped a thin, ice-cold hand over his mouth.

"Shhhhh," the creature whispered in his ear.

Joe kept still and listened. He heard the soft grate of metal against metal. It sounded as though the padlock was being lifted up and twisted. Someone was still on the other side of the door. Joe held his breath for what felt like an eternity. Then he heard a soft harrumph, and he knew it was Orlemann. Next came the sound of the padlock being softly laid back against the wood. This was followed by a rustling, then a footstep and then another, as the ambassador padded quietly away down the stairs.

The cold hand pulled away from his mouth. Joe's lips felt numb from the pressure. He opened and closed his mouth to bring back the feeling. He sat still in the darkness for some minutes, too terrified to make a break for it. The creature moved away from him across the darkened room and disappeared into the farthest corner.

After a while a candle was lit and held aloft. The light moved nearer, but the woman who carried it held it so far out in front of her that it was impossible to see anything beyond the bright flame, only mysterious dark shapes and shadows. The candle came closer and closer and closer. Joe could hear the candle wax spit and crackle on the newly lit wick.

It came so close that he could feel the heat from the flame. He pressed himself back against the damp books and threw a hand over his eyes. A drop of hot wax hit his fingers. Joe squealed in pain. The light instantly drew back, and cold fingers reached out to brush away the scalding wax. Joe looked up and saw his captor. A strange bedraggled woman in a tattered silver dress stood there gazing down at him. Joe gasped.

The woman drew back and held the candle high. Joe stared up at her owl-eyed, and the woman stared back. Her face was cold and twisted and so white that she reminded Joe of those creatures that live in the deepest part of the ocean and have no need of color. Her pale yellow hair was wild and matted into thick clumps. Two dead rats dangled from her belt, and a third was draped over her shoulder. Her fingernails were impossibly long and dirty and looked as though they could tear your face off with one swipe, but it was her eyes that frightened Joe the most. They burned like white-hot coals in her face.

Her satiny dress shimmered like a mermaid's tail. It was as long as a ball gown, but it was disheveled and hung about her narrow frame in torn strips and tatters. The mottled, fraying rosebuds that were sewn onto it shone a grisly yellow in the candlelight.

Joe looked down at the woman's feet. She was barefoot and stood ankle-deep in a murky puddle without seeming to notice. All her attention was fixed on Joe.

She scanned his face with her desperate eyes and shifted her jaw, grating her teeth with a stomach-churning sound. Then without warning she lashed out and grasped his hand in one of hers. She dug her filthy fingernails into his skin.

"Ow!" squealed Joe. The woman let go of his hand.

"So you are real," she said. She smiled, and the madness in her eyes faded. "I'd begun to think I really had gone mad." She reached out and gently touched Joe's face with the back of her forefinger.

"Where did you come from?" she whispered, softly stroking his cheek with her ice-cold fingers. "You poor little angel. You look worn out. Lie down and sleep now. We'll decide what's to be done in the morning."

Joe's eyes opened wide. No one had ever called him an angel before.

The woman took his wrist in her talon-like hand and pulled him up from the ground. The back of his pajamas was wet from the puddle, and he was shivering with cold. The woman led him to a raised bunk in the corner. It was piled high with rat skins that had been sewn into a blanket. It was the least inviting bed that Joe had ever seen, and tired though he was, he hesitated. The woman gave him a little shove and made him sit on the edge. Then she lifted his legs by the ankles and swung them onto the bed. She covered him with the quilt of skins. Joe didn't mind the furry rat skins once he was lying there. It just felt so good to lie down. Besides, the skins were surprisingly soft and comfy and didn't smell nearly as bad as he'd expected them to. Joe rolled his head against the velvety pillow and settled down to sleep.

The woman stroked his cheek, then padded barefoot to the other side of the room and set the candle on the corner of a desk that was littered with papers and books. Once there she seemed to become possessed. She frantically searched through this file or that book, never, it seemed, finding what she wanted. And all through her searching she muttered softly to herself, as though she were having a conversation with somebody else. She moved with quick, jerky bursts of energy, flying from one part of the room to another like an angry dancer.

Joe watched her through his lashes and wondered how he would escape this time, but he was too tired to think about that now. He would worry about it in the morning.

His dreams were the usual kaleidoscope of disturbing images; he saw again his mother's face as the ambulance doors closed, and then as always the feeling of rushing up to Hannah in the hospital bed but never getting close enough to tell her he was sorry, never ever getting close enough to see her face, only seeing her hand on the cover. This time Joe took hold of her hand and curled his fingers around her cold, small ones, but then he surfaced from the dream and realized he really was holding

someone's hand. The fingers were cold and scratchy. He
started and pulled away with a jerk. His hand was throb-
bing. It was still bruised and bloody from the gunshot
wound in the trenches, and it hadn't helped that he'd
scratched the scab off when he'd knocked it on the wall
by the train.

The wild-haired woman stood beside his bed, staring
down at him with her intense, birdlike stare. She leaned
forward and smiled a terrifying smile. Joe wondered how
long she'd been standing there.

"Who are you?" he asked in a whisper. "What do you
want with me?"

At this the woman put a finger to her lips and turned
her face to the door. Then she suddenly darted across the
room and pressed her ear against the hatch, listening to
the outside world.

With her face still pressed against the door, the
woman looked at Joe. From the way she watched him
Joe wondered if she had forgotten how he had come
there the night before.

The woman darted back across the room toward
him, her feet slapping through the puddles. She moved
so fast that Joe thought she was going to attack him. He
sprang off the bed and ran into the far corner by the
worktable.

"It's all right," she said, twisting her fingers nervously.

"I won't hurt you. I promise. My name is Cornell. I've been a prisoner here for as long as I can remember."

"Cornell?" replied Joe. "The third sister?" Cornell nodded violently. "But everyone thinks you're dead. That your sister had you killed."

Cornell smiled a bitter little smile. "Yes. Everyone thinks I'm dead." Then she crossed the room, all the while muttering to herself. "He told them I was dead, told each of my sisters I was killed by the other." Cornell was pacing back and forth now, and her eyes shone once more with the crazed light. "But I'm not dead, am I. He wouldn't have dared to kill me. That would have been going too far. I may still be valuable. He's kept me prisoner here, though in the beginning he said it was for my own protection. He said he was protecting me from my sisters. Ha!"

Cornell flew to the table and began to rifle through the mess of papers. "I'm not killed," she muttered over and over.

Joe looked at the papers on the table and noticed that they were plans and notebooks, the pages of which were covered with drawings and diagrams. In the middle of the table sat Spider's book. Joe scowled. She must have taken it from him while he slept.

"That's mine," he said. Joe snatched the book up, and as he did so the folded piece of parchment fell out from between the pages. Cornell swooped down and picked it up.

Her eyes were on fire as she opened it up. "Where did you get this?" she asked ferociously. "Where?"

"Nowhere," replied Joe, taken aback. "It was in the book when I got it."

Cornell grabbed the notebook and quickly leafed through its pages. "Then this *is* his book," she said. "I thought it must be. Do you see? This means he knows I'm alive. Look." Cornell reached to the top bookshelf and took down a large volume. Hugging it to her chest, she crossed the room to the wall opposite the door. She ran her fingers over a narrow arch on the wall that was made of small bricks. "This used to be my window before Orlemann had it blocked up. When I was first imprisoned, I was desperate to let someone know where I was. I did something so terrible that if anyone who knew me found this they would realize how desperate my situation had become. I, Cornell, chief librarian of this ancient university, tore a page from one of our most valuable treasures. Then carefully, oh so very carefully, I folded it into the neatest paper dart you could imagine. It had to travel beyond the walls of the Druckee, so it had to be perfect. I had only one chance. I would not risk another treasure. Once I had made my dart I threw it out of that sliver of a window and watched it fly through the rain, watched it fly far beyond the walls of this prison, watched it and watched it until it had gone so far I could no longer see it at all. But now I see it got where I wanted it to go. I hoped against hope that it would find its way to my friend, and I see now that it did. You have brought such hope with you today. If Araik Ben knows I am alive, I will be saved."

"But . . . ," Joe began. Cornell looked so wild with glee that he wasn't sure how she would take the news he was about to give her. "I'm sorry, but . . ." Cornell stopped hopping about and stared at Joe expectantly. He just had to say it. "Araik Ben is dead." Cornell didn't move. She just stared at him. Then slowly she began to shake her head. "No, really," Joe tried again. "He died at the beginning of the war. He was hung for being a Heatherman. They said he killed you. They said he started the war."

Cornell was silent for a few more moments. Her eyes searched the floor; then all of a sudden she began to laugh hysterically. Tears ran down her cheeks. "He's not dead. He sent you to me."

Joe shook his head. "Nobody sent me up this tower. I ended up here by accident. I was just trying to get away."

"Then how did you get Araik Ben's book?"

"It's not his."

"If it wasn't his, it wouldn't have these markings in it. I know his writing. I know his name. Look." She opened the first page, and Joe saw that it was covered with the markings he had seen on the walls of the tunnel into the city. They were the same as the ones he'd seen on Spider's bandaged staff and on the back of the page that Cornell said she had thrown out of the window. "Look—don't you see? That's Araik's way of writing his name. There. Araik Ben."

"It's just scribble."

Cornell shook her head. "No, it's overwriting. The Heathermen were experts in it, and they used it as their code for everything. Look—turn the page around and around. See? His name is written once that way, then once on top of it the other, then vertically one way, then the other. If you know what you are looking for, it isn't so hard to decipher. That book belongs to Araik Ben, or I don't know how to read."

"No," protested Joe. "It's Spider's; he gave it to me. Spider's a guide, an amazing guide. He's blind, but he brought me across the plain."

Cornell laughed again and danced gleefully around the room. "Spider? Ha! So, Araik, you call yourself Spider, do you? Clever man. You stayed alive. You always told me you wouldn't die easy."

Joe stopped dead still when he heard that. Spider had

said that often. He remembered the way Spider could change in an instant—how one minute he seemed feeble, the next strong. The way he was so secretive. The way that that night at Mary's shelter so many of the old Heathermen had come to see him. And the way he'd been with Brasque in the cellar by the Lamb—then Spider had seemed filled with quiet power.

If Cornell was right, if Spider was Araik Ben, the leader of the Heathermen, Joe didn't want to think what Katherine would say if she knew that.

Suddenly Cornell stopped dancing. "Blind?" she asked, slumping against the table. "You said he was blind?" Joe nodded. "So that accounts for the pinholes in the pages. Oh, the poor man."

Cornell took Spider's book from Joe and ran her hands over the pictures that were covered in tiny pinpricks. "Who did this for him?" she asked.

"His apprentice Tom," said Joe. "He was the one who left Spider to die on the plain." Joe hesitated. Something about that didn't feel right.

"Left to die by an apprentice?" Cornell ran her hand over Spider's book. "Poor Araik. You never had much luck with apprentices, did you?"

Cornell opened Spider's book to the back page; then, taking a pin from her matted hair, she rapidly stabbed a pattern of small holes into the paper. When she had finished she gently closed the book and held it against her heart. Her bony fingers trembled as she touched the tattered spine. Then she thrust the book toward Joe.

"Take it," she said. "Take it back to him when you go."

Joe took the book and slid it into the pocket of his coat. *But how exactly am I going to get it to Spider?* he wondered. He had to escape from the Druckee first.

Cornell moved to the shelves and lovingly touched the books that stood there.

"These"—her voice cracked as she spoke—"these are the records of the Heathermen's finest works. It's a crime how they are left to rot and molder with me in the towers. A crime." She pulled out one of the books and handed it to Joe. "Go careful with the pages," she said, "but look. This was where the miracles began, in the minds of the Heathermen, the minds of the inventors—look."

Joe carefully opened the sodden pages of the book and saw that they were filled with strange and wonderful drawings. It was like looking at the plans for the world's most amazing fair. Colored diagrams of fantastic flying machines, bizarre methods of transport, even fair rides. There were other drawings, too, diagrams of inventions. There were racing crab-legged vehicles designed to scurry sideways, and some that looked like giant caterpillars that could hold six or more passengers. There were wooden horses and cars that could go underwater, even tunnel underground. For a moment Joe forgot where he was. He just stared and stared at the book, wanting to hurry on to the next page and at the same time wanting to linger and stare forever at the one in front of him. He had never seen inventions or machines like these. They were mad and brilliant and beautiful.

"Araik Ben began the society of Heathermen," laughed Cornell. "He was one of the finest inventors we ever knew. If it hadn't been for the war, most of his students would have gone on to greatness. One was particularly brilliant. You've seen him. His name is Orlemann."

"Orlemann was an inventor, too?" asked Joe.

Cornell nodded. "He was indeed. He was Araik Ben's apprentice, but in the end he . . . well, he wasn't perhaps made of quite the right stuff." Cornell sat quietly for a moment and gnawed at her lower lip. Then she slapped her knees with her hands and stood up.

"This library," she said, "was the Heathermen's sanctuary and their workshop. Now these towers are nothing but rooms full of decaying books and papers.

"Oh, but you should have seen the way it was." Cornell's face became bright with the memory. She smiled a faraway smile. "Every year, at midsummer, they

held the great fair at Quarain. It was there that the
Heathermen and women displayed and demonstrated
all they had invented in that year. It was lovely then. The
fair lasted for two wonderful weeks. There was no rain,
like there is now, and the days were sunny and bright.
And the machines they built—oh, you never saw anything like them. And, of course, everyone had a lovely
time, especially the children. Especially the children."

Cornell gently took the book from Joe and lifted it
back onto the shelf. She turned and shrugged, causing
the rats that dangled at her waist to judder and swing.
Then she crouched down on the floor and poked at a
puddle.

Joe waited in silence. He had the feeling she was
about to say something, but she was quiet for so long
that he started to think she had forgotten he was even
there. At long last she spoke.

"Once I lived like a queen; now I live on scraps. I live
well enough. Rats are not the most digestible of foods,
but one can get used to anything if one wants to survive.
I play the lunatic when the guards drop by, but that is so
seldom these days that I do not bother with it much.
They have no idea how well these books have fed my
mind. I have read each one a hundred times and confess
I am the better for it. Without these volumes I would

have gone much madder than I am." With that she covered her face with her hands.

"If," Joe asked, "you have been in here all the time, how do you know about the war?"

Cornell's head shot up and her eyes burned bright. "I have eyes in my head, do I not?"

"Yes, but . . ." Joe looked at the blocked-up window. Cornell laughed and jumped to her feet, pulling him up with her.

"Come, I'll show you. I have my ways to get about. The door took me two years to fix the way you saw it when I pulled you through, but it is useful."

She led him to the door and, after listening for a minute with her ear against the wood, dug her nails into a deep crack that ran up one side of the door. Then she pulled. The right side of the door swung back into the room, leaving the padlock and chain in place. Cold air rushed in from the corridor. Cornell slipped out, then beckoned for Joe to follow.

"Come," she said, closing the panel in the door behind her. "I'll show you why I am visited at all. He has to pass my door to get to where he's going." Her bare feet padded along the corridor toward the closed door at the end. Joe followed, occasionally glancing out of the narrow windows and reminding himself, as his stomach flipped over at the sight, of just how high the towers were.

When they reached the door, Cornell lifted her hand to her head and drew from the ratty bird's nest of her hair a barbarous-looking hat pin. Joe shrank back.

Cornell laughed, and with a sweeping gesture rammed the hat pin into the keyhole of the padlock on the door. She bit her lip as she rattled the pin around, twisting it this way and that, until the lock sprang open with a satisfying click.

Cornell opened the door and led Joe up the even narrower staircase within.

"We're going on to the very top of the tower," said Cornell. "I hope you have a good head for heights."

A sharp wind blew down the stairs toward them, and Cornell's hair and tattered skirt whipped about.

At the top of the stairs Cornell struggled with the bolt on a small door. With Joe's help she shot it back, and the door, snatched by the violent wind, flew open.

"Fresh air!" cried Cornell as she stepped out onto a narrow parapet. Joe leaned out from the shelter of the doorway and saw some fifty yards away the top of one of the other towers poking through the fog. To the north he could see the craggy mountain peaks. The daylight was grim and unchanging. Far above the towers the higher, thicker layer of clouds smothered the sky like a blanket of felt.

The parapet that Joe would have to walk around was less than two feet wide, and the wall on the outer edge of it, Joe could see, would come up only as high as his knees. It gave him a sick feeling in his stomach. If he stumbled or tripped, or was blown away by the wind, he would fall hundreds of yards through the fog and not stop till he hit the cobbles in the courtyard far below.

The parapet ran around a little tower that was only three or four yards high and, except for the fact that it had no windows, was similar to the top part of a lighthouse. There was a small door near the top, and about halfway round, a short ladder reached up to it.

"That's where they take those poor children," said Cornell, pointing to the mountains. Cornell sighed. "They used to find so much happiness here, but now they find nothing but hard, grim work beyond the mountains, toiling day and night in the shadow of his mechanical dragon. His Amadragon." Cornell turned and spat with the wind. Then, suddenly reaching out and taking a firm hold of Joe's collar, she pulled him onto the parapet. Joe thought he was going to die. The wind tore at him like a thousand ice-tipped nails.

"Now I'll show you how Orlemann watches his war."

"*His* war?" asked Joe.

But Cornell didn't answer. She was already climbing up the ladder to the little door.

Joe watched her climb and forgot his own fear as he worried about her. She was so light the winds could easily snatch her off the ladder.

But Cornell reached the door without mishap. She opened it, then beckoned to Joe. He swallowed hard and, trying to ignore the way his knees were shaking, started up the ladder. The wind seemed to blow even more fiercely as he clawed his way up each rung. He glanced over at the sharp-ridged mountains. What was Hannah going through over there? It was a sobering thought. He gritted his teeth and climbed.

Cornell helped him through the door, then closed it behind him. The room at the top of the tower was pitch-black.

"Isn't there any light?" he asked.

"Shush, wait and watch," replied Cornell.

As Joe's eyes adjusted, he realized there was light in the room after all, but it was not the sort of light he expected it to be. There was a large, shallow dish upon a table in the middle of the room. The dish was as big as a tractor wheel, and it glowed white in the darkness. Joe inched forward and gazed down. A gray image was swirling over the dish—a darker shadow upon a lighter one. Joe knew what this was. It was a camera obscura, an amusement he'd seen in an old-fashioned arcade a long time ago. He remembered how he'd been able to watch the outside world from the inside of a dark room. His father had said there was some sort of lens on the roof that brought the image down to the dish inside. He'd been fascinated by it and would have stayed there all day, but Hannah had grown bored within moments and insisted on opening and closing the door to the outside. Letting in daylight had made the image in the dish disappear.

Joe suppressed the memory and concentrated instead on the dish in front of him. He couldn't see anything but the gray circle; then he realized what he was looking at.

"This is just showing us the fog," he said. "We can't see through that."

"Shush," said Cornell. "Put these on." She handed him a pair of goggles, then took hold of the pulleys that operated the lens. "They'll help you see through the fog. It takes a bit to get used to them, but stay with it. You'll see soon enough."

Joe pulled the goggles over his eyes and stared down into the dish. At first he could see even less. The goggles were made of thick glass that was cut like a crystal, with so many facets that all he could see were several blurry images of the same things—the dish, his own hand, and

Cornell's pale face in the dim glow. But soon he began to see other things as faraway images broke through the uniform gray of the fog.

Now he could see the layout of the Druckee far below him so clearly that he could even see the tiny, antlike guards scurrying along the walls and around the gate. It was amazing. He could see the cars in the court-yard and the many undulations of the roof of the great hall.

"Let's look a little farther afield, shall we?" Cornell adjusted the levers, and the image of the Druckee shrank a little. Now he could see the city streets around the prison, the guards on the drawbridge, and the rooftops of the buildings. He could see the bomb sites and the crowds on the streets. Cornell adjusted the lever again, and the image seemed to swing across the dish. When it was still, Joe could see the edge of the city, and the city wall, and beyond this the plain he had crossed with Spider and Katherine. He could make out the derelict machines and even the moving form of a Goliath and a Scraper. The Goliath was firing its jet of flame at some-thing. Joe shuddered as he remembered how close he'd come to getting burned alive. To the far east he could make out the trenches and the crowded hump of Camp Quarain and the roads full of trucks and buses—the roads he had traveled along with Spider and Katherine.

Beyond Quarain there was the gray strip of the sea, and beyond that, nothing but the dull, rain-clouded sky.

"Now, let's have a look to the west." Cornell swung the lever again, and the image in the dish swirled madly. The plain and the city passed in a blur, but when Cornell stopped it again, Joe thought she must have reversed the controls. There was the plain again beyond the city wall. And on the plain were the trenches and the derelicts. Two Goliaths chased someone this time, and even though they were so far away, both Joe and Cornell hid their eyes as a Zamrami turned on its powerful, blinding light. Beyond the plain he could see trenches, and beyond these, roads that appeared to be crowded with buses and trucks. In the far distance there was a town or an encampment close to the edge of the land. A strange feeling crept over him. It looked just like Quarain, but he knew with all certainty that he was looking at another place.

Joe's head was swimming.

"You see, they don't know," said Cornell. "Over there"—she pointed to the collection of ramshackle houses and motley tents—"they think they must bring the charges to the city to be safe and that the machines on the plain are from Elysia. While over here"—she swung the levers and the image swirled madly to Quarain—"they think the machines that stop them getting to the city belong to Merid. But the charges aren't safe here. No one sees the truth through the fog."

Joe shook his head. He didn't understand. "If what you say is true, then whose soldiers occupy the city—Elysia's or Merid's?" he asked.

"Whose insignia do they wear?" asked Cornell.

Joe thought. He couldn't remember the guards in the Druckee or the soldiers he'd seen on the street wearing any. "I don't know," he said.

"It's neither!" she said quietly. "The people in the city believe that my sisters joined together and killed me, and since then both of their armies have laid siege to us. Orlemann has turned us all against each other."

"But he's Elysia's ambassador," said Joe.

Cornell nodded. "And Merid's, too. And in the city I expect he says he's mine or working on behalf of my poor dead soul. What better way to engineer a war where no one wins but him?" Cornell sighed and rubbed her temples. "But I can't fathom how he has kept this deception going for so long."

Joe knew. He quickly told Cornell about all the form-filling and confusing paperwork; about all the rules and the clerks at the big house in Quarain. He told her about the spies and the counterspies and the secret police. Cornell listened in silence, then nodded.

"And at the center of everything sits Orlemann like a big, fat spider in the middle of his intricate web."

"Then it's Orlemann who is running the war," Joe said almost to himself. "It's Orlemann who is using the charges to build the machines, not Merid. Orlemann is behind everything."

Cornell was busy turning the levers of the dish once more and swinging them over to the south. Here a spit of land jutted out into the sea past the area he recognized as no-man's-land, where Katherine had first brought him through. The trenches had been pushed back, almost to the edges of the land.

Cornell's eyes glittered as she studied the picture in the dish intently. "Look, something is happening here at the Point," she muttered in a low voice. "Roads being built. Pathways from both directions. How long will it be? I wonder."

Joe's head ached. He didn't know the answers. It wasn't his job to figure out this war, was it? No; his job was the same as it had always been—to find his sister and take her home. Then he had an idea. He pushed himself away from the edge of the dish and took the lever from Cornell's hand. The image of the spit of land quickly slipped away; then the mountains came in view.

The image in the dish skimmed the lake Spider had

told him of, the Long Lake; then it crossed over a range of immense ragged mountain peaks. Joe had just the briefest glimpse of a wide valley on the other side, of blackened sheds and buildings, when suddenly the door flew open and the dull gray daylight made the picture in the dish disappear. A large, bull-headed man was silhouetted in the doorway. Cornell ducked behind the table, but Joe couldn't move. The man had caught him by the ankle and was pulling him toward the door.

"Gotcha!" Joe instantly recognized Radworth's gruff voice.

Joe glanced down and through the distorted filter of the goggles saw her pale face staring up at him.

"Tell Araik I'll be waiting for him," she whispered, then sank back into the gloom.

"Come on!" Radworth growled above the wind. "Let's be having you!"

Radworth swiftly pulled Joe to the door and manhandled him down the ladder. A moment later, still wearing the strange goggles, Joe was standing on the parapet. Radworth handed him over to two guards. One twisted Joe's arm behind his back and pushed him along the narrow walkway toward the stairs. Joe couldn't see where he was going. He pulled the goggles off his face, but he didn't try to get away. There was nowhere to go. He couldn't run across thin air.

When they reached the steps the guard threw him down them. The other guard laughed as Joe fell sprawling to the flagstones.

Joe lay there, winded. When eventually he ventured to raise his head, the first thing he saw was a pair of very shiny boots. He lifted his head and saw that the boots belonged to Orlemann. The ambassador frowned at him as though he were some strange new species of animal. Orlemann nodded briefly at one of the guards, and in the next instant Joe was hauled to his feet.

"So you're the clever lad," said Orlemann. It was a statement, not a question. Joe's eyes flickered to Cornell's door behind Orlemann. It was still intact. At least they didn't know who had helped him. He didn't want Cornell to get hurt. Orlemann took Joe's chin in his hand and observed him with a mixture of approval and displeasure. "Clever enough to vanish into thin air, get past us. Where did you learn that trick? I wonder."

Orlemann let go of Joe's chin. "Take him downstairs to the great hall, and you can test him," he instructed Radworth. "I have some business to attend to, but don't start the fun without me. This one interests me. He may prove useful."

CHAPTER 22

More Secrets

Radworth kept a tight grip on Joe's arm as he marched him down to the bottom of the tower.

When they reached the great hall Radworth led Joe to the center of the room and stopped in front of the table with the model on it. Another table had been set up close by. It was covered in a long white sheet and had rails at the sides and wheels underneath. It was like an operating table or gurney. There was a stool beside it.

Radworth lifted Joe onto the table and made him lie down. He tied a long strap like a safety belt over Joe's stomach, then he sat on the stool and pulled a trolley toward him. On it was his brown suitcase. Joe felt sick.

He stared at the clamps and wires and dials housed inside the little box.

Just then Wyn emerged from the shadows. He crossed to the table where Joe lay and looked over Radworth's shoulder. The little man's greasy face shone in the candlelight, and his eyes twinkled keenly as he watched Radworth at work.

"Wyn, help me," begged Joe. "Please, don't let him test me. Make him stop, and I'll give you whatever you want. I have Spider's book. It's here in my pocket."

"Oh, have you? Can I have it? Really?" Wyn intoned sarcastically. He smiled and plucked Spider's book from Joe's pocket. Then Wyn brought his greasy face so close to Joe's that his pockmarked nose touched Joe's cheek.

"Thank you very much," he sneered. "Mind you, I can't do anything to help you now. You should have listened to me when you had the chance." Wyn turned away, walked to Orlemann's desk where the candles still burned, and held the book to the light. He scowled as he flipped through the pages; then his face cleared and he grinned from ear to ear. "Oh yes!" he muttered to himself. "Oh, this is wonderful. Wonderful!"

Joe groaned and turned his attention back to Radworth, who was now sorting out the dials in the case. Joe gazed at the ugly scar that ran from Radworth's eye to beneath his chin. He studied the way the skin was shiny and twisted and the way the scar pulled the muscles of his cheek and lip into a permanent grin. Radworth must have felt Joe looking at him. He glanced up, and for a moment their eyes met. Radworth's eyes were icily cold. He looked away and felt along the underside of Joe's arm, pinching the flesh as though to see where the best place to fix the clip would be.

The doors to the hall flew open. Orlemann entered and marched smartly to the desk in the center of the room. Carefully he moved the silver model to one side. Then he put some papers down in front of him and took his seat.

"Very well, Mr. Radworth, one moment and then you may proceed," he said. Wyn scurried forward, clutching Spider's book.

"Your Excellency—" he burbled, but Orlemann held up his hand.

"Not now," he snapped. "I have more important things to see to. Now where's . . . there he is. Come forward. What have you to tell me?"

Joe twisted his head back to see who Orlemann was talking to and saw a man standing at Orlemann's desk. His back was turned toward Joe.

"I know where they are," he said. Joe was sure he recognized the man's voice, but he couldn't place him. "They're all hunkered down in a cellar below the ruins of the old Lamb on Barnsley Street."

Joe realized that the man was talking about the Skulkers' secret hideout. But how did he know about the Lamb?

"Marvelous," said Orlemann, clapping his hands and rubbing his palms together. "Those traitors will be swinging from the gallows before dawn. Excellent work. You may have been with me for only a few months, but I am promoting you to full security clearance. You have indeed proved yourself an asset to my organization, Mr. Heany."

Joe recoiled in horror as the informant turned his face toward the light. It was Katherine's brother, Tom!

Surely this wasn't happening. Tom, working for Orlemann? But then Joe remembered Spider saying how the escape had been a little too easy. He remembered how Spider had been betrayed, had been set up by Tom before. But it still didn't make sense. Why would Tom betray the Skulkers? Why would he betray Brasque? There had to be another explanation. Then it hit him. Tom was the insider Spider and Brasque had spoken of. That had to be it. Tom was the Skulkers' agent in the Druckee. Relief flooded Joe's mind. Tom was here undercover. He was here to help the

Skulkers. Of course—that made more sense. Joe had to find a way to let Tom know what he'd discovered about the charges.

"Ambassador Orlemann!" Joe tried to sound tough, but his voice trembled as he spoke. "I know that it was you who started this war."

Orlemann got to his feet. "Oh, really?" he asked, sounding bemused. He walked to the front of the desk.

Wyn held Spider's book up. "Your Excellency, if you've got a moment, I think this might be—"

"Not now," Orlemann said fiercely. He turned to Joe. "What else do you think you know?"

Joe went on. "I know you've had the arches blocked up so no one can pass through, and I know that you take the children over the mountains and force them to build those terrible machines that roam the plain. And I know that you take them there by an underground train. I've seen the train. I know how you get them to do what you want. You blackmail them. You blackmail little children."

Joe stopped. He was out of breath, but he'd said what he had to say. At least now Tom would pass this information on to Brasque. At least now the Skulkers wouldn't blow up the mine, not when they knew Spider was right about the charges.

Wyn hovered behind Orlemann. "Your Excellency, if I might have just a—"

Orlemann spun round. "NOT NOW!"

"Very good, sir." Wyn gulped when he saw the fierce expression on Orlemann's face. "I'll just be over here when you . . . need me."

Orlemann turned back to Joe.

"Have you quite finished with your little speech?" Orlemann asked Joe. Joe nodded. "Good. You are indeed a chatty one. I'll be very interested to see what sort of secrets a boy like you hides in his heart. You may continue with the testing if you please, Mr. Radworth." Orlemann returned to his desk and began to look through some papers.

Joe winced in pain as Radworth fitted the cold clip to the underside of his arm. Radworth leaned over to adjust it, and as he did, he whispered so only Joe could hear.

"When I turn the dial, start to scream like murder. Put on a good show. You won't feel a thing. I haven't connected the wires. We'll talk later."

Joe stared in astonishment. Radworth was helping him! Was Radworth Brasque's ally? But if Radworth was their agent on the inside, what was Tom doing there?

Radworth poked Joe in the ribs to make him pay

attention. Joe watched carefully as Radworth turned the dial. When the pointer reached number two Joe began to wail, at three he started to scream, and at four he screamed like his life was ending. And as he screamed, Radworth pretended to listen to Joe's secrets through his headphones and made notes in a small book on the table.

But both of them were so caught up in their performance, Joe screaming with his eyes closed and Radworth with his head bent over his book, that neither noticed Wyn approach. Neither saw him edge closer to the table.

Suddenly Wyn slapped Joe across the face. The shock made Joe stop screaming. He opened his eyes. Wyn was holding the unconnected wires in his hand.

Radworth went for his knife, but Wyn was ready for him. Before Joe knew what was happening, Wyn had stabbed Radworth in the ribs. The policeman fell forward, his own knife clattering to the floor and skidding away.

"I think I've found our traitor, Your Excellency," gloated Wyn.

"Well spotted, Wyn," said Orlemann. "He's been very careful up till now, but we won't have to worry about him anymore, will we?"

"No, sir," said Wyn. "Now, sir, if you've got a moment I'd like to—"

"One thing at a time! First we need to deal with this boy. Take over the investigation, please."

Wyn smiled, snatched the headphones off Radworth's ears, and put them on. He straddled the stool and sat down, then quickly connected the wires to the box and turned the dial to two.

This time Joe screamed for real. He screamed and he screamed and he screamed. It was worse than the time he'd had a tooth filled without anesthetic. Worse than the time he'd broken his leg in two places. There was no area of his body that was free from pain. It felt as though someone were sucking all the life out of him, and just when he thought it was as bad as it could be, Wyn turned the dial around farther, and the pain got so much worse.

Suddenly all Joe's thoughts, all his memories, all his fears, and all his secrets were being ripped out of his body. He was dimly aware of Wyn beside him. He wanted to beg him to stop, but he couldn't find the words. All he could do was scream and scream and scream while the tears ran down his face.

Finally Wyn turned the machine off and Joe lost consciousness. He must have been out for only a few seconds, because when he came to, Wyn was still standing by the table.

"What a lovely thing to wish for," he said when he saw that Joe was conscious. "Aren't you such a considerate brother."

"Did you get something?" asked Orlemann.

"Oh, yes, sir!" said Wyn. "He's got a lovely guilty secret. He wished that his sister would die."

"Did he now?" said Orlemann.

"Yes, sir, and from what I can gather, it looks like she might." Wyn hooked his hand under Joe's elbow and pulled him upright. Joe felt dazed and sick. He saw Tom watching him coldly from across the hall. Any thought that Katherine's brother was working for Brasque had vanished.

"Get that out of here," said Orlemann, pointing to Radworth's body sprawled on the floor.

Wyn lifted Joe down from the wheeled table and leaned him against the nearest pillar. Joe slid to the floor. He wasn't capable of standing. Tom summoned two guards, who lifted Radworth's body, laid it on the gurney, and wheeled the table out of the hall. Tom left with them. Wyn lingered.

"Your Excellency?" he said smarmily. "Would now be a good time?"

Orlemann groaned. "Very well, tell me what you have to tell me and then get out of my sight."

Wyn hopped up to the table and laid Spider's book in front of the ambassador.

"And?" asked Orlemann.

"It's this book, sir. . . . I thought I saw . . . in the market . . . in Quarain? It's his, sir, I'm sure of it."

Orlemann snatched the book off the desk and opened it, turning it to the light and quickly looking through the pages. Wyn hopped from foot to foot, barely able to contain his excitement. "Why didn't you show this to me sooner?" asked Orlemann.

"Sir, I tried—"

"No matter," snapped Orlemann, looking through the pages. "Where did you find it?"

"A guide had it, sir. Spider Carey. An old rogue. A blind man. He's tall, gangly, with white hair."

"And you didn't think to bring this news to me immediately?"

"I wanted to be sure, sir. I didn't want to waste your time."

"And where is this guide now? Do you know?" Orlemann stood, and his face was almost purple with rage. Wyn shook his head and shuddered. "You imbecile!" hissed Orlemann. "Don't you see? Araik Ben would never have been without this book. This Spider Carey must be Araik Ben! And now we don't know where he is."

"But, sir," said Wyn, pointing at Joe, "I bet he does."

"Does he?" Orlemann said, glaring at Joe. Orlemann glanced at his pocket watch. "There isn't time now. But soon, after the armistice, then I will go after Araik Ben. I swear as long as there is breath in my body I will hunt him down and finish him for good."

CHAPTER 23

The Journey North

"**I** could make the boy tell us where he is, sir," Wyn suggested, moving to where Joe sat slumped at the bottom of the pillar.

"No," snapped Orlemann. "Just go. Leave us alone."

"Very good, sir," said Wyn, who looked deeply disappointed to be excluded from whatever was going to happen next. "I could—"

"You've done enough. Now get out!" commanded Orlemann.

When Wyn had finally gone and the hall door was closed behind him, Orlemann crouched down beside Joe and lifted him to his feet.

"Come with me," he said, leading Joe to the table. Now Orlemann's voice was as smooth as oil. "I'm sorry for the testing. I know it's not pleasant, but it is necessary, I'm afraid. Don't worry, I'm not going to hurt you. I want to show you something." Joe waited by the side of the table.

"It's all right," said Orlemann. "I won't bite. I heard about you when you first came through. A talkative charge, they said."

Joe lifted his eyes. "It's because I'm not a charge," he said, struggling with the words. "I came to find my sister and take her home."

"Ah, yes, your sister. The one you wished would die, is that her?"

"I never meant it!" said Joe defensively. "I was just angry."

"I understand," purred Orlemann. He guided Joe to the table. "I heard that you were looking at this model. It is quite beautiful, isn't it?"

Joe nodded silently.

Orlemann's eyes shone as he ran his fingers over the delicate machinery.

"Look at the detail, the craftsmanship, such perfect scale."

"Does it move?" asked Joe, who was interested despite himself. He loved models and he had to agree that this one was spectacular.

"Oh, yes," said Orlemann. "It moves beautifully. Do

you build models, Joe?" Joe nodded. "And you probably don't like anyone to mess with them when you've spent so much time on them, do you?" Joe shook his head. "Is that what your sister did, Joe? Is that why you were so angry with her? Did she break something of yours?" Joe said nothing. He just stared at Orlemann's model. "I want you to know that I understand how you felt. I don't blame you for what you said to your sister," he added softly. "I couldn't bear it if anyone damaged one of my models."

Orlemann turned to his model, and picking up a soft cloth, he carefully polished the little door at the side. "It is lovely, isn't it?"

Joe nodded. Orlemann smiled. "Don't worry, Joe. I won't tell anyone your nasty little secret, not unless I have to, and I'll only have to if you don't do what I say. Do you understand?" Joe nodded again. "Good."

"Do you know something, Joe? You remind me of myself when I was young. You're bright, I can see that, but it's your imagination that I value. When I first heard about you I wanted to meet you. I wanted to meet this boy who knew of us from his dreams, the boy who had come to find his sister. You've been a slippery fish to catch, perhaps because, as I now learn, it seems you were traveling with an even slipperier one." A spark of anger flashed through Orlemann's eyes. He recovered quickly.

"Now that I have met you," he said smoothly, "I find I am not disappointed. I can see that you appreciate fine craftsmanship. I've never yet met anyone who would treat my models as well as I treat them myself, but I think you would."

"Is my sister in the mine?" asked Joe. Orlemann raised his eyebrows.

"Your sister? Yes, yes, probably," he said, his voice betraying a little impatience. He paused and put the smile back on his face. "Come, Joe; forget about your sister for now. She can wait. You're coming with me. I've been looking for someone like you for a long, long time. I've got a very special project for you. Something, I think, that will interest you very much." Orlemann stood and put an arm around Joe's shoulders. "Come, we must go. The train is waiting."

For the second time Joe found himself being led down through the maze of the Druckee. Orlemann walked quickly, his heels clicking against the stone steps. Joe hurried beside him. When they reached the mosaic room, Orlemann didn't stop to admire the scenery but quickly opened the door in the wall and began to hurry down the spiral steps.

When they reached the station platform deep under the ground, the train was still waiting.

Farther down the platform, Tom was inspecting the

train. When he saw Orlemann he saluted smartly. Joe stared at Tom, and their eyes met briefly. If Tom recognized Joe, he gave no sign. Joe felt very sorry for Katherine.

"Mr. Heany," said Orlemann, addressing Tom, "the signing of the armistice is to take place at the Point at noon tomorrow. I expect you to meet me there."

"Very good, Your Excellency," replied Tom with a curt bow.

Joe looked past Tom. He could see the charges who were packed into the front two cars. He was shocked to see them still there. It meant that they had been waiting there all the time he had been in the tower and the hall.

Joe followed Orlemann into the shiny black car at the back of the train. Wyn, who had been waiting for them on the platform, held the train door open, then tried to follow them inside. Orlemann stopped him at the door. "You'll be up front with the others," he said. Wyn shot Joe a filthy look and grumbled to himself as he stomped along the platform.

"Take a seat," said Orlemann, ushering Joe to one of the luxurious red velvet armchairs in the car. Orlemann sat down behind a large, leather-topped desk that gleamed in the dim light. Meticulously neat piles of paper were arranged on it, and a stand with two gold inkwells and a penholder stood in the center.

Somewhere outside a whistle blew, loud and shrill. Then with a giant lurch the train set off.

Orlemann lifted his head. "The train will take us half of the way. I would have continued the line all the way beyond the mountains, but now there is no need. If you'll excuse me, there is work to do. I have a peace treaty and an abdication agreement to compose." Orlemann smiled to himself and, taking the pen from its stand, dipped it in one of the gold inkwells and began to write.

Joe sank into the comfortable seat and looked around. The car was extraordinary. Three small crystal chandeliers hung from the ceiling and threw their dancing light across the dark, silk-covered walls. The paneled ceiling was made of burnished mahogany. Turkish rugs covered the floor, and the darkened windows were surrounded by gleaming mahogany frames. The window fastenings and all the hardware were made of shiny brass, and at the windows hung great swaths of heavy velvet curtains tied back with thick silk cords. Along the back wall behind Orlemann's desk was a grand fireplace with a gray-veined marble mantel and surround. A wood fire burned in a grate held by two fancy brass andirons. Above the mantel was a large, gold-framed mirror. It was tilted forward slightly, which enabled Joe to see the reflections of the back of Orlemann's head and most of the car. Four of the plush velvet armchairs were arranged around a low oval table in the center.

Joe sat back and rested his head against the wing of the armchair. The car was so luxurious that he was afraid to touch anything. His hands were filthy and his clothes were worse.

Joe listened to the distant rumbling of the engine and felt like a ghost rushing through a dark, silent, lonely world.

He turned to the window and pressed his forehead against the cool glass. With Radworth dead, the Skulkers would never know that the charges were in the mine. They would go ahead with their plan to blow it up. He closed his eyes. He musn't give up hope. He had to find Hannah before it was too late.

The train's wheels screeched, and sparks flew back along the tracks as they came to a stop.

"Here we are," said Orlemann, packing a few of the papers into a briefcase and getting back into his coat. "Come along; we don't have all day."

Joe followed Orlemann off the train and found himself standing on an unfinished platform. In front of the train Joe could see signs of abandoned construction work. It looked as though the workers had downed tools and never returned. The stairs up were unfinished also. They were open to the sky, and rain dripped into the tunnel.

"Not as far to go as at the other end," said Orlemann, leading the way. Joe looked back at the charges, who were being led off the train by the secret policemen who had traveled with them. "Don't worry about them," said Orlemann, hurrying Joe along. "You just wait; you're going to see such marvelous things. You won't believe your eyes." Orlemann laughed and trotted up the stairs. The steps were made of metal and they clanged loudly with every step.

Joe and Orlemann emerged onto the plain. Behind them was the wall of the Long City, and some distance ahead lay the lake and beyond that the mountains. Two buses, four motorcycles, and a long black limousine stood waiting. Orlemann set off toward the car. A liveried chauffeur opened the door.

Joe was about to get into the car when he stopped. The sound of the charges coming up the metal stairs reminded him that they were on the plain.

"What about the machines?" he asked nervously.

Orlemann turned back. "They are my machines, Joe. I'm not going to let them hurt me or any of my friends. Come, I'll show you." He disappeared inside the limousine. Joe ducked his head and climbed in after.

Like Orlemann's car on the train, everything inside this limousine shone with an expensive luster. It even smelled expensive. The seats were of the darkest, softest leather, and the windows were framed in a glossy walnut veneer. The glass in the windows was tinted, and it turned the gray sky purple.

Orlemann sat on the backseat and motioned for Joe to sit beside him. Joe sank into the soft cushions. It was warm in the car and comfortable, but he felt stifled.

"Watch this, Joe," said Orlemann as he pressed a silver button on the window ledge beside him. With the subtle whir of well-engineered machinery, a small, walnut-veneered panel to his right swung open and came out of the wall on an extendable arm. The panel stopped in front of Orlemann and in one smooth motion flipped itself over to display a long line of ivory-tipped silver switches. There were ten switches, and they were all flicked up.

"Have you ever seen a remote-controlled car?" he asked. Joe nodded. "This is similar, though perhaps a little more advanced. This little device enables me to send all the machines a signal that warns them to keep away. Those machines really are brilliant inventions, even if I do say so myself." Orlemann pressed the button on the window again, and the panel secreted itself away. "I can assure you our convoy won't be attacked."

"So that's how you kept them away when you were on the mercy missions?"

"Exactly," said Orlemann with a smile. "Except, of course, when it was useful to have one side think the other was breaking the rules. Then I'd let the machines fire on us if need be."

There was a tap at the window. Orlemann pressed a button and the glass slid down. One of the secret policemen stood there.

"All ready to leave, sir," he said.

"Thank you," replied Orlemann. The glass slid up, and Orlemann spoke to the driver on the intercom. "Go ahead," he said. The engine purred into life. Ahead of them two secret policemen mounted their motorcycles; behind them, the buses revved their engines. The signal was given, and the convoy set off. Joe fell back in his seat as the limousine shot forward across the plain.

CHAPTER 24

The Dragon in the Mountain

Joe watched through the window. Every so often they sped past a burned-out war machine. Upturned tanks were strewn across this part of the plain, too. Some, Joe noticed, were sunk up to their axles in the quicksand. He began to wonder how Orlemann's car, the buses, and the motorcycles could be taking such an easy, straight route across the plain.

Joe craned his neck to try to see the way ahead more clearly. Orlemann noticed Joe's curiosity.

"One of my early inventions," he said, pointing toward the front of the car. "I call it the invisible road. Very useful when you want to move across this sort of terrain. The fibers are made of an immensely strong steel and glass compound that is not only transparent but also absorbs the color of the land around it and allows grass and shrubs to grow through it, thus ensuring its near invisibility." Joe narrowed his eyes and tried to see what Orlemann meant, but he couldn't. Orlemann smiled.

It was then that Joe saw a Goliath barreling toward them. Its sensors must have detected the motion of the cavalcade. It was soon within twenty yards of the limousine, easily within firing range. Joe shuddered as its turret swiveled, turning the gun toward Orlemann's car. One blast would have been enough to destroy the limousine, but the Goliath didn't fire. It held its position for a minute or so, then abruptly spun its gun in the other direction and slowed down.

Joe looked back and watched the Goliath slow to a stop. He glanced over at Orlemann, at his immaculate clothes and manicured hands. Then he looked down at his own filthy nails. He looked as though he'd been scrabbling in the dirt for years. Something was bothering him. What had Orlemann meant when he said that Joe reminded him of himself when he was young? What could they possibly have in common besides an interest in machines?

"Why did you start the war?" asked Joe.

Orlemann smiled and patted Joe's knee. "You'll understand when I tell you, but this isn't the time. I promise I will explain everything once we get to my house, but now I must ask you to be quiet. This is my favorite part of my journey. I think you'll enjoy it."

Orlemann settled back in his seat and gazed out of the window. Joe stared at the mountains ahead and could see nothing that would make this anyone's favorite part of any journey. The sky was growing darker. Night was falling, and Joe reckoned by the time they reached the mountains it would be fully dark. He stared up ahead and soon saw something that caught his attention.

A thin strip of dark land butted up close to the foot of the mountains. As they drew closer, the strip appeared to grow wider. It was amazingly flat and strangely colorful. Then Joe realized that it wasn't land at all. It was water. It was the lake that Spider had spoken of—the Long Lake. A shallow lake full of brightly colored toxic waters, made so by the chemicals that leached out of the black mountains. Spider had said it was impossible to cross this lake because the poisons in the water were so powerful they could corrode anything, even the strongest materials. Even boats clad with iron would disintegrate in seconds.

Joe watched as Orlemann's cavalcade headed straight for the lake at top speed. He clutched the edge of his seat and slid down till he could only just see out of the windshield. Neither the car nor the motorcycles slowed. If anything, they seemed to go faster.

Then suddenly they began to climb, and then, to Joe's astonishment, they sped out over the lake.

Joe sat up, pressed his face against his window, and looked down. The toxic waters raced past at least three or four yards beneath the wheels of the car. What was happening? Were they flying? It didn't feel like flying. The car still seemed to bump slightly on the road. He looked out of the windshield at the two motorcycles in front. They were riding above the water, too. Joe turned and looked behind. The buses, their headlights blindingly bright, were following the same path.

The sky was almost dark. Every few minutes the silvery light that Joe had seen on the plain and in the city bloomed behind the mountains. Now it was much more intense, as strong as the light from a full moon. Joe stared through the window. He wanted to understand how they could be doing this seemingly impossible thing. Then the light came, and Joe saw the magnificent, shimmering, single-span bridge that crossed from one side of the lake to the other.

"It's made from the same material as the road," said Joe out loud.

"Clever boy. That's exactly right," said Orlemann, sounding pleased. "You have to know it's there to find it. When we get to my house I will show you a model. It's easier to see than the real thing."

Now that Joe knew what he was looking for, it was easy to make out the bridge every time there was enough light to see it by. It was an incredible structure. As the watery reflections from the multicolored lake bounced against it, it seemed to ripple and vanish, then reappear. Joe was full of questions. How did Orlemann build such a thing? How did he come up with the idea? How strong was the structure?

Orlemann was more than happy to answer all of Joe's questions. He told Joe the building was easy. And that the idea came to him one day. And that the structure was as strong as, if not stronger than, any steel bridge ever built.

Soon Joe felt the bridge slope down, and then with one final bump they pulled off it and drove onto more visible ground. Now in the light from the headlights he could see the mountains directly in front of them, and to his horror he saw that they were speeding straight toward what appeared to be an immense wall of jet-black rock. Joe expected the cavalcade to turn left or right, but the driver did neither. Instead he accelerated. Joe gripped his seat, convinced that in a few moments he would be mangled in the wreckage of Orlemann's limousine.

Then, just as they were yards from the rock face, the silver light bloomed in the sky, and Joe saw that there was a road in front of them after all. It appeared to have been cut through the mountain. The road surface was the same jet-black rock as the mountain walls, which meant that it was impossible to see unless you were up close. From a distance the mountain had appeared to be impenetrable, but now they were careening over the smooth road. High black cliffs rose on either side of them. Joe felt he was entering a fortress.

"Well, Joe, you saw my invisible bridge," chuckled Orlemann, "and now you are traveling along my hidden road. Are you not impressed?"

"Yes." Joe nodded. "But why couldn't I see it before?"

"A clever illusion, a trick, no more," Orlemann said with a smile. "The mountains are formed of such wonderful black rock that the black road, though plainly visible when you know it's there, simply appears to melt into the rock surrounding it and thus disappear. I believe, Joe, that if you can imagine something, no matter how wild or crazy it may seem, you can somehow make it happen."

"Yes, I've heard that," said Joe.

"Have you now?" Orlemann scowled at him, then looked away. "This is the only road through the mountains," he said, continuing his lesson. "None but those who have sworn loyalty to me know it is here.

Consequently no one has ever attempted to travel upon it. And the way over the mountains is a fool's path."

"Because the rock is magnetic?" asked Joe, remembering what Spider had told him. "And your compass wouldn't work, so you'd get lost?"

Orlemann nodded. "And not just lost. So lost that you know you'd never get out. They say the madness comes upon the unlucky within a few brief hours of getting lost among those peaks." Orlemann shook his head. "I am well protected here. If the lake with its corroding poisons doesn't deter would-be trespassers, the mountains will."

The light bloomed again, making everything around them as bright as day.

"Where does that light come from?" asked Joe.

"From my dragon," answered Orlemann.

Joe's eyes grew round. Then there really was a dragon? The cavalcade slowed.

Now the wide road twisted around and began to slope down. Joe clung to the little ledge at the bottom of the car window, hoping to see everything sooner; then they came around the last broad bend in the black rock canyon.

"The mine!" he exclaimed.

The silver light flashed, and Joe saw the vast saucer

of the open-cast mine spreading out before him. He
blinked. It was so huge he couldn't take it all in at once.
The very size made his head spin. It looked as though
someone had pulled an entire mountain out by its roots
and left an enormous, flat-bottomed hole where the
foothills and the very core of the mountain itself would
once have stood.

Joe narrowed his eyes and tried to work out the scale
of the place. It was difficult without any reference points.
Then he spotted a clutch of buildings off toward the far
side of the saucer. They looked like miniatures. Could
they really be full-size buildings? On the other side of
the mine he saw trucks that looked like tiny toys
trundling up and down the rough valley roads. The light
faded, and the limousine plowed through the darkness,
swerving as the road curved.

"My dragon," said Orlemann, tapping Joe gently on
the shoulder and pointing.

Joe turned and looked out of Orlemann's window.

"Oh," he gasped.

Two enormous malevolent yellow eyes stared out
across the blackness. Joe had never really believed in
dragons, but there it was. He shrank back in his seat.
Suddenly a great shower of silver sparks shot into the sky
behind the yellow eyes. They were as bright as a hundred
thousand flashbulbs. This was the source of the intermit-

tent light he had seen from as far away as the trenches at the front. As the sparks hung prettily in the sky they lit the whole valley as bright as day and revealed the dragon's true identity.

Joe laughed nervously. The dragon wasn't a monster. It was a machine, an enormous earthmover like the kind he'd read about in his magazines.

"It's a bucket-wheel excavator," gasped Joe. "But it's twice, maybe three times as big as any I've ever read or heard about." Joe leaned forward to get a better view. It wasn't easy to gauge how big it was, but he guessed that the "dragon" stood at least five hundred feet high, and it was perhaps nine hundred feet long from end to end.

Joe could see how someone might think it was a dragon. The yellow spotlights for eyes, the great wailing roar it made when the bucket wheel spun, the fiery sparks that shot out of it, and the plumes of smoke that emanated from it, creating the heavy fog and clouds that filled the brooding sky.

The gigantic digging wheel, fifty yards in diameter, could be mistaken for the head of a beast, he supposed. The series of enormous steel-toothed shovels arranged around it, each one big enough to scoop up Joe's entire house, were sharply pointed, like the spikes that ran in a line over a dragon's skull.

Behind the head stretched a long neck of steel girders

that crisscrossed over each other, forming a boom. The dragon's body was the great steel box of the engine housing and gantry, grooved with blackened vents along the side. Instead of scales, the body was covered in skeletal metal walkways and ladders. Girders formed three stout towers that stood one behind the other on the dragon's back like a dinosaur's spikes. They were so high that their tops vanished in the clouds. Garlands of steel cables ran in loops from one to another among gigantic wheels and pulleys. Then at the back of the entire machine a great tail, another series of crisscrossed steel girders, ladders, and cables, stretched out behind it.

This was the dragon, the machine that had eaten through a mountain. Joe knew exactly how it had done it. He'd read enough books and magazine articles about them to know how they worked. When the wheel, the dragon's head, was held against the ground and set in motion, the shovels gouged great holes in the earth. Then as the buckets rose up and over, they deposited the ore onto a conveyor belt, which carried it along the neck of the beast and all the way to the end of the tail. At the tail's end a giant truck would be waiting to carry it away.

The convoy pulled round the last hairpin bend, then bumped down onto the valley floor. It sped up as it set off across the mine toward the distant clump of buildings. Joe jumped to his own window and stared up at the gigantic earthmoving machine as they passed beneath it. It towered over them. He gazed upon the machine in amazement, for to him, Orlemann's dragon was perfect. The entire machine was mounted on twenty huge crawlers arranged in two sets of ten—ten at the front and ten at the back. These crawlers were three, maybe four times higher than Orlemann's car, and each one was at least fifteen feet wide and a hundred and fifty feet long.

The light faded. By the time it returned, the car was almost at the dragon's tail. Joe pressed his cheek against the window and craned his neck back to get a better view, instinctively searching for some sort of identifying name or code. There they were—three tall black letters painted along the back of the gantry. It looked as though there would have been more, but a great smear of soot obscured whatever else was there. Only three letters were showing: A M A. Joe read them as one word: AMA.

"The Amadragon," he whispered to himself, wondering why the name sounded so familiar.

"What did you say?" asked Orlemann.

"Nothing," said Joe, turning around swiftly and staring out of the rear window to get a last look, for they were now nearly past the dragon. He couldn't bear for one moment to take his eyes off it. Orlemann chuckled.

"I'm pleased that you like my dragon, Joe," he said. "It was one of my very early efforts, a machine born out of necessity. But I fear it will soon outgrow that usefulness. I'll have no need for a mine at all very soon." He tapped Joe on the arm and gestured toward the front of the limousine. "Over the years I have been perfecting my designs. Wait till you see them. I think my collection of models will interest a boy like you very much."

Joe didn't want to show Orlemann how interested he was, so he kept quiet and stared out of the windshield. Really he was dying to know, dying to see whatever machines Orlemann was willing to show him.

The buildings ahead of them looked like a series of mine and factory buildings, tottering masses of corrugated metal and pipes. The road ran like a broad corridor through them.

Orlemann pressed the intercom button.

"Take the long way round," he said. The driver nodded. Orlemann switched the intercom off and turned to Joe. "There's something here I think you'll find interesting." The limousine abruptly took a turn to the left. They rumbled up a puddle-filled alley and finally emerged onto the level space behind the buildings.

Orlemann was right. Here were acres of brandnew automatons all lined up in neat rows, like cars in a factory parking lot.

There were hundreds of new Goliaths. Different models, different designs. Joe saw Scrapers and other machines he didn't recognize, all of which bore various mind-boggling and in some cases intimidating amounts of artillery. And there were machines he did recognize because he'd seen them tipped over and burned out in the middle of the plain.

They came to one row full of the same type of machine. It was one he did recognize, though he'd never actually seen it before. He knew it instantly and shuddered. This machine had no guns, just a large spotlight mounted on top of it. It was a Zamrami. The unlit light on its back was the weapon that had deprived Spider of his sight.

"All these are products of my early work," said Orlemann, gazing out across the acres of vehicles. "These"—he pointed to a row of squat automatons that had a wide section of what appeared to be a road on top of them—"are my transportable bridges," said Orlemann. "Very useful when one finds a trench in one's way." He chuckled, then touched Joe on the knee. "With the end of the war in sight, I suppose all these will be surplus to requirements. While the war continued I had to keep up a decent supply. Both sides had to keep believing . . ." Orlemann stopped, then paused and wiped his lips on a soft white handkerchief. "I could, of course, simply dispose of these machines, but I abhor waste. No, I think I shall keep them just in case. Of course, I do have a record of each design, if only for the history books. But you will see, you will see."

Eventually they came to the end of the rows of vehicles, and Orlemann's limousine swept up to the steps of a large, imposing building that gleamed in the light from the Amadragon's shooting sparks. The driver opened the limousine door. Orlemann stepped out, then waited for Joe.

"I call this my house in the country," said Orlemann, gesturing for Joe to ascend the impressive flight of wide steps that led to an ornate portico. Joe hesitated and looked around.

It appeared that some sort of move was under way. Men in overalls were carrying boxes and pieces of furniture and loading them into trucks that were parked to the left of the building. Orlemann watched them with a keen eye. The men became aware of his interest and endeavored to carry their loads with more care.

The building didn't look much like a house to Joe. It looked like a town hall or a museum. He shivered. Even on the outside the house seemed deathly cold, not cold like brick or stone, but cold like metal. He was sure he could feel a chill coming off it. Joe set his foot on the first step, and it rang with a hollow sound that made his teeth jar. That was why it felt cold, he realized. The building, the walls, the doors, and even the steps were made of iron.

"Come along, Joe," said Orlemann. "There's much to see." He was waiting at the top of the steps.

Joe climbed up a little way, then stopped. Something was bothering him. The buses full of children had not followed the limousine to the house, and Joe wondered where they had gone. He turned and stared across the valley. Then he saw the buses parked beside the foundry buildings. The children were being unloaded. Of course—if Orlemann used the children to build his machines, then that was where the charges would be. That was where he would find Hannah. He promised himself that he would go and look for her just as soon as Orlemann had shown him his designs.

The light bloomed, and somewhere on the other side of the valley a siren began to wail, then a few seconds later stopped, and Joe saw rocks flying up from the far hillside. A split second later an almighty boom shook the air and echoed across the valley. Then a great section of the hillside collapsed and slid into the bottom of the mine.

"Instruct the men to lay the final explosives," Joe heard Orlemann say to a clerk who had come out of the building to greet him. "I want it all to come down at once—let's say three hours after we leave?" The man nodded, then hurried down the steps, passing Joe, who was making his way up.

Wyn had reappeared and was now struggling behind Joe and carrying Orlemann's bags. He was grumbling about it as much as he used to grumble about his position with Cloves the fortune-teller. Joe wondered briefly if Wyn was carrying a chop in his sock for Orlemann's supper. Somehow he didn't think so.

Joe followed Orlemann into the house. It was colder inside this mausoleum of a building than it was outside. Joe's breath came out in great white plumes, and he was soon stamping his feet on the polished metal floor to bring the feeling back into his toes.

Orlemann took no notice of his discomfort but, stopping for only a moment to dispatch orders to a servant, hurried off down a dark, gleaming corridor, beckoning for Joe to follow. Orlemann led him into a room where a fire blazed in a large grate. Wyn followed them in, but once he'd put down Orlemann's bag, Orlemann dismissed him.

"I'll call if I need you," he said.

As the doors shut, Joe caught Wyn's scathing look. Joe had the feeling that later Wyn would make him pay for Orlemann's slight.

"I think," said Orlemann as he led Joe to an armchair, "that now is the time for us to have a little chat. Sit here by the fire."

Joe sat down and rubbed his hands together in front of the flames. For such a roaring fire it gave off surprisingly little heat. Joe looked around the room. It was a large chamber, and the steel walls were hung with dark tapestries and velvets. Apart from the chair by the fire and a large desk where Orlemann stood, there was little else in the way of furniture. It was a gloomy room, and the atmosphere made Joe feel heavy and tired. The firelight dancing up the walls was not cheery and comforting and in truth only added to the gloomy effect.

Orlemann didn't say anything for the longest time. He was busy sorting through a pile of books and papers. Some he put carefully in a packing box; others he tossed on a growing pile in the middle of the floor. Joe looked round at the tumultuous sound of a dozen books hitting the floor and wondered what Orlemann was doing. Orlemann smiled.

"I'm moving out of here, and there are only so many things I need to take with me. Books I have read and will never read again take up too much space. The long-awaited meeting between the sisters is scheduled for noon tomorrow, and once they have both signed the peace treaty and abdicated their power, I will not be returning here. The war shall be over and I shall have no more need of this place. In approximately"—Orlemann consulted his pocket watch—"six hours and twenty-two minutes the mine and everything in it will be destroyed. A terrible waste, I know," he sighed, glancing around the plushly decorated but gloomy room. "Even so, I don't want anyone else to have access to my things. You can understand that, can't you, Joe? An enemy could use my machines, my foundries and factories, my house, my mine, even my dragon against me. And then where would I be? In a most vulnerable position, that's where. And there is no one so susceptible to vulnerability as a new ruler. It is essential that I make my position, once assumed, as strong as it can be."

"You'll be the ruler?" said Joe, leaning forward in his seat.

Orlemann stopped sorting through the books for a moment and smiled at Joe. Joe noticed that the book in his hand was Spider's notebook. Orlemann laid it on the table next to the box. "Ruler, emperor, president, king, or some such. I haven't decided on my official title as yet, but it will be along those lines."

Orlemann's smile broadened. "The sisters have had very little to do with running this island since the war began. They didn't realize, of course. How could they? Each was as eager as the other to believe whatever I told them. In such times it is essential to have a diplomat you can trust." He smiled like a crocodile. "Unfortunately for the sisters, they all trusted me and each thought I was loyal only to them." Orlemann paused and gazed for a moment into the fire. "When the two eldest meet tomorrow, it is for each of them to sign not only the peace treaty I have engineered, but also to hand over their power to an interim peacekeeping government headed by—"

"By you," said Joe.

Orlemann smiled again. "Yes, by me. Don't worry, I will be a most benevolent leader. I will be generous and fair, though, it goes without saying, firm. I will have this place back together again in no time. They will never have known such peace. The plain will be cleared of all the troublesome machines. The city will be rebuilt. Of course, there will be rules. Rules will govern what inventions are made; it will not be a free-for-all, as it was so often in the past, when the sisters let the Heathermen run riot with their thinking and inventing whatever they pleased no matter how dangerous or frivolous or just plain silly. And under my rule, no crime, no matter how small, will go unpunished. And the charges who come to stay will be given useful tasks to keep them occupied; they will no longer be allowed to fritter their time away on wasteful amusements. They will all work for the good of the island."

"Why are you telling me all this?" Joe asked.

Orlemann looked straight at Joe. His eyes burned black. "Don't you see, Joe? We should have no secrets from each other."

"What do you mean?" stammered Joe.

"We're very alike, you and I. I understand you. We want the same things. We appreciate the same things. We treasure the same things. I want you to be my student, my heir, my closest ally. There is no reason to create an empire if there is no one to share it with. Think of the machines we could create!" Orlemann sat opposite Joe and lowered his voice. "If you agree to this, Joe, no one will ever dare challenge you or take anything away from you ever again. Think of it. You can have everything you ever wanted. It's all possible."

Joe opened his mouth to speak, but Orlemann held up his hand.

"Don't give me your answer now. First I want to show you something. Come." Orlemann picked up Spider's book, strode across the room, and opened the door. He frowned when he saw that Wyn was waiting there, and Wyn, obeying the unspoken order, disappeared quickly.

Orlemann looped his arm cozily through Joe's and propelled him along the corridor.

"I want you to see my toys before they're removed for safekeeping."

"What about my sister?" asked Joe. "When will I get to see her?"

"Soon enough, soon enough," said Orlemann, stopping at a pair of double doors. With his free hand he opened one door and ushered Joe inside.

Beyond the door the room was pitch-black. Orlemann flicked a light switch, and the bulbs in a hundred glass-fronted cabinets came on. Some of the cabinets were empty, and large, taped-up packing cases stamped "FRAGILE" stood beside them, but it was the sight of the cabinets that still held their treasures that made Joe's jaw drop.

Unbelievable! he thought as he gazed around the room. The cabinets held hundreds upon hundreds of little models, perfect in every detail. Orlemann, too, collected models. It was a collection very similar to Joe's, and yet it was so much grander, so much bigger, so much more complete that it made Joe want to cry. Orlemann's was exactly the sort of collection he wished he had.

Joe didn't wait for Orlemann's invitation. The models drew him like a magnet draws a nail. One minute he was at the door, the next he was gazing down at the model of a tank—quite an early one, guessing from the design. Its proportions were perfect. Each rivet in its armor plating was exactly to scale. Tearing himself away, he moved to the next. Here was an amphibious vehicle, a car that became a boat. It was only a quarter of a yard long, but it was perfect in every detail, including a paddle attached to its side in case of emergencies. Next was a low-riding flatbed truck with a cargo of heavy guns, and beside this was an early submarine.

"Not all of these were built to full size," said Orlemann as he stood beside Joe, "but many were." There were models of all the mine vehicles, including one of the Amadragon that stood alone in a large cabinet. Joe would have gazed at this all day, but after a few minutes Orlemann led him to another cabinet. At first glance this one looked empty, but Orlemann instructed Joe to move his head up and down, and then, as the light caught the structure, Joe saw the model for the invisible bridge and was amazed by it.

"That one was quite a trial to make," said Orlemann, basking in Joe's undisguised admiration of the collection. He held up a pair of goggles similar to the ones Joe had worn to see through the fog in the camera obscura.

"You can see it more clearly through these." Joe took the goggles and put them over his eyes. The almost invisible model of the bridge jumped out at him in stark relief. It was a remarkable structure, elegant and strong. He'd wondered how it could cross the lake without disintegrating in the toxic waters, but now he saw that no part of the bridge touched the water. It was an incredible single span that stretched from one side to the other.

Next Orlemann led him to a cabinet containing models of Goliaths and Scrapers and Zamramies.

"Take this for a moment, please," said Orlemann, handing Joe Spider's notebook, which he had been holding this whole time. Orlemann put on a pair of white cotton gloves, then took out a key and opened one of the cabinet doors. With great care he lifted out a perfect scale model of an early Goliath. Carrying it as tenderly as any mother would her baby, Orlemann led Joe to a velvet-covered table in the middle of the room. At the edge of the table was a padded rail, three and a half or four inches high, forming a little wall around it. Orlemann set the gleaming model down in the middle of the table, then switched on two more lights and angled them so the model's flanks flashed brightly. Joe reached out to touch it, but Orlemann slapped his hand away.

"Be careful. These are not just toys," he said. "These

are working models. You see," he said, leaning in close to examine something on the model's surface, then blowing whatever it was away, "I always make my inventions in miniature before building them at their full size. It is much easier to control the process that way." He gently opened a panel in the side of the machine, then reached into the opening and carefully pressed a small ignition button inside. He stepped back and pulled Joe out of the way.

Orlemann waved his hand, and the Goliath sprang to life. It behaved in exactly the same way that the ones on the plains had behaved. In an instant the little model tracked the movement, took aim, and spewed a forceful jet of fire toward them. Orlemann laughed. He had been careful enough to stand out of harm's way. But the sight of the flamethrower shook Joe. He nearly jumped out of his skin, and as he did, the tiny Goliath swung around to face him. It rolled forward with such purpose that it would have fallen off the table had it not been for the padded rail at the table's edge. The Goliath stopped, carefully took aim, and was about to fire when Orlemann, still laughing, deftly reached in and disabled the mechanism.

"Are you pleased with my collection, Joe?" he asked.

Joe nodded, speechless.

There was a knock at the door.

"Come in!" called Orlemann. A servant entered. Behind him Joe could see Wyn hovering in the corridor.

"The explosives are all in place, sir," the servant said. "May I respectfully suggest that we think about moving your collection out, sir."

"Very good," replied Orlemann. The servant bowed, then turned to the doors and clapped his hands. The doors opened and twenty or so men in white coats flooded in, pushing crates on wheels in front of them. They headed toward the cabinets.

"One moment," said Orlemann. The men stopped and looked at him expectantly. Orlemann slowly lifted a bunch of tiny keys high above his head and shook them so they tinkled.

"If even the smallest"—he eyed each workman with stern disgust—"if even the tiniest, the minutest amount of damage should befall any of these models I will personally see to it not only that the man responsible is ruined forever, but that his wife, his children, his mother, his father, his grandchildren, his grandparents, and even his dog suffer the consequences. Is that understood?" The men nodded. "Well then, get to work and look sharp," said Orlemann as he handed the keys to the servant.

The men worked carefully and quickly, wrapping each model in soft white velvet blankets, then carefully,

carefully laying them inside the packing crates. The crates were specially built for each model and were lined with a thick padding of goose down. Orlemann was even more careful of his possessions than Joe was of his.

Wyn sidled up to Orlemann. "Got anything for me to do, sir?" he asked.

Orlemann didn't even look at him. "Think you can lift a crate as well as any of these men?" he asked.

"Lift?" Wyn looked crestfallen. "Well, I suppose I could," he said. "But I was thinking of something more in the way of a bit of interrogation. I could do something with this boy here, if he's bothering you."

"Just help with the crates," said Orlemann, whose voice had gone as cold as steel. "And don't break anything or I'll break you, understood?"

Wyn grumbled and shuffled off to be useful.

Orlemann was preoccupied now. The packing and removal of the collection went smoothly. The men worked quickly and efficiently. Orlemann watched the procedure like a hawk, ready to swoop down on anyone whose hand trembled or faltered when he lifted any of the precious cargo.

Joe watched the men wrapping the models for a while, but he soon grew bored. He glanced around the room and noticed that the cabinet door beside him still stood open.

Joe inched closer to the open cabinet door. He wanted to take a quick peek at the workings of the Goliath.

Joe stuffed Spider's notebook in the waistband of his pants, then reached out and flicked open the little panel on the side of the Goliath. He bent down to peer inside. What he saw amazed him. There was a minute row of buttons and levers, each one a different color, and one large blue button at the near end that Joe guessed would start the engine. Wires and cables were coiled around a small panel. One of the wires hung down slightly, blocking his view of the entire innards. Very, very carefully he reached inside with his pinkie finger and pushed the wire out of the way, but as he pulled his finger out, his nail accidentally grazed against the blue ignition button, setting the Goliath on alert.

Joe jumped back as the Goliath's gun turret whirred into action. Orlemann turned and, rushing over, caught a jet of flame right in the belly. It set his silk coat on fire. Though he quickly took the coat off and stamped on it, the room instantly filled with the smell of singed silk. Orlemann's face was flushed with anger.

Then something terrible happened. The model Goliath in the display cabinet was still bent on destruction. It swiveled its turret to locate its prey. Orlemann was now out of range, so the machine raced forward. There was no velvet-covered rail at the edge of the cabinet. Joe saw what would happen, but it was too late to do anything to stop it. He could only watch in horror as the Goliath shot forward, overran the edge, plunged out of the cabinet, and smashed against the cold, polished steel floor. Joe caught Wyn's eye and saw a thin, self-satisfied smile spread across his greasy face. Joe dropped his eyes to the floor where the Goliath lay in pieces, its innards still clicking and whirring. Then all at once it stopped.

Nobody moved. The whole room had grown silent, and the air was as cold as icicles.

"I'm sorry," Joe began lamely. "I only wanted to look at it. . . . I only—"

Orlemann's eyes were full of hate. No one had ever looked at him that way before. Joe instantly felt small and dirty and stupid and worthless. He would rather Orlemann bawl at him, yell at him, shout and call him every name under the sun, than look at him in that witheringly cold and callous way.

"I'm—" Joe tried to say again.

"Say nothing," whispered Orlemann in a quiet but truly terrifying voice, "or I swear I will find a way to let your parents know that their daughter, their favorite child, is ill because of you! Take him away." Two men grabbed Joe under the arms and began to drag him toward the door.

"What about my sister?" cried Joe as he was hauled out of the room. "What about Hannah?"

"Go see if you can find her in the factories, why don't you!" yelled Wyn from the back of the room.

Orlemann's frown melted away and he laughed, but it wasn't a pleasant sound. "That's right," he said. "Have a good, long look for your sister at the factories."

Joe didn't see what was so funny about it at all.

CHAPTER 25

The Factories

The two men dragged Joe down the steps of the steel house and shoved him into the back of a car. The car was a wreck—an old army-style vehicle that had been devoured by rust. There were holes as big as dinner plates in the roof that let the rain in.

The guards climbed into the front seats and set off erratically across the plain toward the clump of factory buildings. The driver braked hard to let a moving van go by, and Joe rolled off the backseat. His face hit the floor, where a pool of rust-colored water slopped between the seats. His mouth was filled with the taste of metal.

"Where are we supposed to take him?" asked the driver. "Which factory did the guv'nor say?"

"Does it matter?" asked the other one. "Let's just dump him in the first one we come to and get back. We don't want to get left behind when the mine blows, do we?"

"No, we don't," said the driver. Then he swung the wheel over to the left and hit the brake hard. Joe groaned as he was thrown back and forth in the narrow space between the seats.

The driver and his mate got out and opened the back door. They pulled Joe out of the car and marched over to one of the factories. The driver opened the door, and the other man threw him in. Joe landed facedown in a sprawl on the floor.

The door banged shut behind them, and Joe found himself alone in the cold, coal-smelling dark.

Slowly and painfully he pulled himself to his knees. "Hello?" he called, but nobody answered. His voice echoed against the high metal ceiling. The floor was littered; tools and pieces of metal were strewn about. Joe got to his feet and slowly made his way to the door, but just as he reached it, a rustling sound made him stop and turn around.

"Hello?" he called again. There was no reply.

Joe stared into the shadows at the back of the vast room. Then beyond the sheets of metal that were stacked against the wall, beyond the mound of tires and caterpillar treads, beyond the tool boards and the skeins of twisted metal, he thought he saw someone, something, move. He swallowed hard. It had looked like a child. A little blond girl. Hope gripped Joe's heart.

"Hannah?" he called into the darkness. He found a flashlight on the floor. He picked it up, switched it on, and pointed its broad beam into the shadows. He almost dropped it when he saw what was hidden there.

Hundreds of children—charges—were crammed in the space at the back of the factory. Their faces were soot-smeared, and their clothes, mostly pajamas and nightdresses, were in tatters and rags. Some of the children were asleep, but those who were not stared at him with baleful, uncomprehending eyes.

As Joe stood there gawking, a siren sounded and the children moved as one into the main area of the factory. They flowed around Joe like a river flows around a rock. Occasionally one would glance at him, but they never looked for long. Each child went to a place on the floor, picked up a tool, and began to hammer or to bend or to beat sheets of metal. Some unraveled twists of sharp wire and set them in straight lines on the floor, while others cut through broad sheets of steel with evil-looking metal cutters.

Joe recognized one little boy who was struggling beneath the weight of two buckets full of ore. He'd seen him that first night in the Druckee. This boy had sat beside him in the cell. Joe grabbed the boy's arm.

"Have you seen my sister?" Joe asked. "She's got blond hair and looks like me. Her name's Hannah."

The boy shook his head and tried to pull away from Joe. He looked scared.

"If they catch me talking to you," he whispered, "they'll tell my mom and dad what I did. They'll tell on me."

Joe let him go and grabbed a little girl by the elbow. "Have you seen—" he began, but the girl looked petrified. She pulled away and went on with her work. Joe ran from one end of the vast building to the other, but he couldn't find his sister anywhere.

When he was certain Hannah wasn't in that factory, Joe ran out into the road. He stared down the long strip of the foundry sheds, and when the light from the Amadragon bloomed across the sky, he counted them. There were thirty-two buildings, sixteen on either side of the road. Hannah could be in any of them.

Just as he reached the door to the next building, Joe heard a roaring noise. He looked back and in the darkness saw a long snake of hundreds of headlights advancing quickly along the road toward him. Orlemann's evacuation was under way. Joe darted behind a Dumpster and waited for the fast-moving procession to pass.

First came the motorcycles and then Orlemann's limousine. These were followed by a seemingly endless line of jeeps and trucks that were packed with soldiers and boxes. Joe shrank back into the shadows when he saw Wyn at the rear of one of the trucks. Behind these came Orlemann's automatons.

As Joe watched the procession wind its way through the mine, he wondered what Orlemann intended to do about all the charges still in the foundry buildings. There were open trucks at the end of the long line that were empty. He was certain they would stop and pick up the charges. But the trucks didn't even slow as they passed.

Joe watched in horror as the last truck's red taillights receded into the distance. He turned back toward the first building in the row. Someone had to get the children out of the mine before it blew up, and if no one else was going to, he'd have to do it himself.

He ran back to the first factory and flung open the door. No one took any notice of him. Joe leapt on top of a large crate by the door.

"Listen!" he yelled above the noise. "Please, you've got to listen to me!" But none of them did. They just kept on working.

How was he going to get them out of harm's way if
they wouldn't listen to him? Then he saw the siren
beside the door. It was one of those old-fashioned ones
that was operated by turning a handle round and round.
Joe ran over to it and set it whirring. The high-pitched
sound rose above the clattering and hammering. The
children laid down their tools and turned toward him.

At last he was getting somewhere. Joe climbed back
on the crate. "Good," he said. "Now listen, there isn't
much time. We have to get out of here as quickly as we
can. I want all of you to file through the door, and once
you are out there, wait for me." Joe waved his arms
toward the door, but nothing happened. The children
just blinked at him, then went back to their work.

"No!" shouted Joe. "You have to come with me." But
none of them was listening.

There was so little time for them to get to the safety
of the mountains. How was he going to get the charges
to do what he wanted? The siren had at least gotten their
attention. Joe jumped down from the crate and turned
the siren's handle again. The wail sang out over the factory. Again the children stopped what they were doing
and turned to Joe.

He didn't have a clue what he was going to do, but as
he stood there, an idea came to him. He climbed back
on the crate. Orlemann got the charges to work for him

by listening to their secrets and threatening to tell if the children didn't do what he wanted.

Joe didn't know any of the children's secrets, but they wouldn't know that he didn't know. It wasn't a very nice way to get someone to do what you wanted, but it was for their own good. He had to give it a shot.

Joe took a deep breath and began.

"You horrible lot," he sneered. The children shrank back, and their eyes grew large and round. Joe felt awful, but he steeled himself. "I've been listening to the tapes of all your nasty little secrets and I know everything. And do you know what I'm going to do if you don't do exactly what I say right now?" The children all grimaced and slowly nodded their heads. "That's right," growled Joe. "I'm going to tell everyone—your moms, your dads, your friends, your teachers, even your grandparents, all your nasty little secrets. Now all of you get through that doorway and wait for me outside. Go on! Get out!"

It worked like a charm. The children dropped their tools and silently and quickly filed through the factory doorway. When the last one had gone, Joe jumped down from the crate and ran out into the street.

Joe glanced at all the factory buildings and realized he would need help to get them all evacuated in time.

He picked out ten of the oldest-looking charges and drew them to the front of the crowd.

"You lot are now my deputies," he said. "Don't mess this up or you know what I'll do." The ten nodded gravely, then listened as Joe gave them their instructions. He told them to each go into one of the factory buildings, sound the alarm, and get all the charges to come out into the road. He told them that if the charges didn't listen, they had to threaten them. They had to say that he would tell all their secrets, too, because he knew everything about everyone in those factories, and he wasn't someone to be messed with. The older charges nodded again; then each ran off to a different building.

Joe instructed the younger ones to go to the far end of the buildings and wait for him there, then he ran ahead and found another building to evacuate. By the time he reached it, children were pouring out of the factory buildings on either side of the road. There were so many of them. Somewhere in this vast crowd was his sister. When he had time he would find her.

Soon every factory and every foundry was deserted, and a crowd of two thousand, maybe three thousand children stood silently at the end of the broad road. Joe stood in front of them and stared out across the vast valley of the mine.

On the far side of the mine the last of Orlemann's trucks was winding its way up the steep road that led through the mountains. It was so far away, it seemed hopeless. But he knew they had to try.

"Come on, then, you horrible lot!" Joe shouted. He gave the signal, and the vast crowd set off behind him. Joe felt like the Pied Piper.

They had walked for what felt like hours and they hadn't even reached the Amadragon when Joe called a halt. Some of the little ones sank to the ground. They were exhausted. Joe picked up the smallest child closest to him and hitched her onto his back. The far side of the valley was still an impossibly long way away.

"What's the use?" he asked himself out loud.

"You're not giving up now, are you?" replied a voice in the darkness.

Joe jumped and stared blindly in the direction of the voice. "Spider?" he asked.

The sparks that shot up from the Amadragon were so bright that Joe had to shield his eyes. When the brilliance had faded Joe lowered his hand and saw Spider standing a few yards in front of him, leaning heavily on his bandaged staff. Katherine stood a little to his left, and all around them were Brasque and the men he'd met as Skulkers.

"How?" was all that Joe could manage to ask.

"I told you I'd find you, didn't I?" Spider said with a smile. "You showed us the way, Joe. It was from you we learned that the children were in the mountains. We came to find them and set them free."

Joe was confused. "But I didn't tell you anything," he said.

"No, you told me," said Tom. "Remember when Radworth was going to test you? You told me then."

"But . . . ," cried Joe. "You . . . you're . . . Spider, I saw him with Orlemann. He told Orlemann where the Skulkers were hiding. I heard him say it. I heard him!"

"It's all right, Joe," said Spider. "Tom's on our side. We had to pretend that he wasn't. We've been pretending for a very long time. Not even Katherine knew."

"I had no idea!" cried Katherine. "You wouldn't believe how angry I was when I found out, Joe."

"Well, at least you let me call you Kat again," laughed Tom. "Kat Kat Katty Kat Kat!"

"Watch it, mister. You're still on probation," she said.

"But, Spider," said Joe, still confused, "you mean he never left you on the plain to die?"

Spider shook his head. "Those were all stories, Joe. Tom and I made them up so we could move about more freely. Tom was working for me the whole time. He's a good lad, one of the bravest and the best."

Joe remembered something that Spider had told Katherine in the sewers: "Your brother deserted me before he had time to prick holes in the drawings." Now Joe knew why that had bothered him at the time. If, as Spider claimed, Tom had left him on the plain after he'd been blinded, Tom wouldn't have been around to prick the holes for Spider.

"Then Tom helped you after you'd been blinded?" Joe asked.

"Yes, indeed," said Spider. "Tom saved my life and nursed me back to health. Without him I would never have made it off the plain."

"But Tom . . . he . . ." Joe's voice broke and sank to a whisper. "He just stood there and watched when they tested me."

Tom came over and knelt in front of Joe. "I'm truly sorry about that," he said. "I had no choice. If I'd shown you any sympathy or tried to help you, they would have found me out. You saw what happened to Radworth. They would have done the same to me."

"And if that had happened," said Brasque, "we'd never have found out what Orlemann was doing with the charges. Spider was right to have faith in you. You did well."

"But how did you get here?" asked Joe. "How did you get across the plains, over the lake, how?"

"We followed you," said Spider. "After Tom 'gave us away,' Orlemann's men caught us in the cellar of the Lamb. But once we were inside the Druckee, Tom let us out of the cells and led us down through the prison to the underground train tracks. We came through the tunnel."

"Then on the plain," said Katherine, "we thought we would have to dodge the machines, but we kept to that road of Orlemann's and never saw one. It was as though all the automatons had disappeared."

"Then Spider discovered the bridge across the lake," said Tom.

"No, no," Spider interjected. "That was all of us."

"But you can't deny you were the one who got us through the mountains," insisted Katherine. "We'd never have found that road without you."

Spider shrugged and shook his head. "A blind man can't be tricked by his eyes. I kept thinking that Orlemann had to have made some way through. Anyhow, I had to find Joe, didn't I? I couldn't break my promise to him."

"It's been a good day's work," declared Brasque. "Now all we have to do is find a way to get ourselves and all these children to the Point before the armistice is signed. Merid and Elysia have to be told what's really been going on."

"Oh no!" cried Joe.

"What is it?" asked Spider.

"We don't have much time before the mine explodes," Joe gasped.

"Joe, calm down," said Spider. "It's all right, remember? The Skulkers haven't set any explosives."

"No!" cried Joe desperately.

"Orlemann did. He said the mine would blow up three hours after they left!"

"Hell's teeth!" exclaimed Spider. "How long have we got?"

"An hour, maybe two," Joe said. "I can't be sure how much time has passed since I heard Orlemann talking about it."

"We'll have to act quickly," said Brasque, looking first toward the road through the mountains, then back at the multitude of children. "None of them looks fit enough to walk very far, let alone run," he said.

"We could carry some of them," said one man. "Some of us could take two, even three on our backs or in our arms."

Spider shook his head. "We'd still be leaving too many."

The light from the Amadragon faded and everyone fell silent.

"The only solution that I can see," began Brasque, "is

for those young enough and strong enough to carry who they can and run to the mountains as fast as they can. Every second counts now. It's every man for himself."

But Joe wasn't going to stand for that. "No, it isn't," he said. "You wouldn't leave them here to die, would you? My sister is somewhere in that crowd, but even if she wasn't, I wouldn't leave without the rest of them."

Spider ruffled Joe's hair with his hand. "Good for you, lad," he said quietly. "Good for you. Well," he said in a suddenly cheery voice. He rubbed his hands together. "Now that we've come up with all the obvious answers to our problem, it's time to come up with some truly ridiculous ones."

"Ridiculous?" asked Brasque.

"Yes, ridiculous. Think of something impossible, improbable, or downright ridiculous and go from there."

"Like we all flap our arms and fly out of here," said Katherine.

"Exactly!" said Spider.

"How about we form a long line all the way to the mountains and pass the charges along it?" said Brasque.

"Excellent," said Spider. "Keep them coming."

"What if we each carry one charge, run back, carry another, and so on?" said Tom, getting into the swing of things.

"Lovely!" laughed Spider. "Now we're cooking."

The shower of sparks shot out of the top of the Amadragon. Joe shielded his eyes with his hand.

"Yeah, and we could all climb on the Amadragon and ride out of here," he said.

"What was that, Joe?" said Spider, suddenly dropping the jokey manner. "What's the Amadragon?"

Katherine's eyes glittered. "He means that," she said, pointing at the excavator. Everyone except Spider turned and looked. "He's talking about that gigantic machine, the one that keeps shooting sparks into the air."

Spider cocked his ear and listened to the rumble of the Amadragon's engine. "So Orlemann built the dragon, did he?" he said. "I'd been wondering what that noise was. If they built it to the original specifications, it should get us out of here within the hour. Let's pray that will give us enough time!"

CHAPTER
26

To the Point

At about ten o'clock the next morning, Joe was sitting on a metal beam halfway up the forward tower of the Amadragon and staring across the barren plain. It had been a long night, and Joe had climbed up into this makeshift crow's nest to hide from Spider, who had ordered him to at least try to get some rest before they got to the Point.

Below him, the children they had rescued covered every inch of available space on the Amadragon's wide boom. It was quite a crowd. And besides those still out in the rain, there were children crammed into every room and cupboard in the gantry, too. Joe knew this because he'd searched the entire rig at least two, maybe three times, looking for his sister. He hadn't found her.

Yet, he told himself. *I haven't found Hannah YET!* He still had faith that he would. Sooner or later he knew he would.

It had taken the Skulkers over twenty-five minutes to hurry all the children aboard the giant machine. When Spider had figured out how to operate the Amadragon, Brasque had taken the controls and, cigar jammed into the corner of his mouth, driven the cumbersome machine at its top speed through craters and potholes, laughing all the way.

It was a good thing that Brasque had driven so recklessly. They had only just made it into the pass that led out of the mine in time. Any slower and they would certainly have been buried in rubble when Orlemann's explosives detonated, sending the sides of the great open-cast mine cascading down to the valley floor.

Once through the mountains Brasque had managed, with guidance from people on the ground, to drive the huge rig across Orlemann's bridge over the Long Lake. It had been a crazy balancing act, with the Amadragon's middle treads resting on the bridge and the outer ones hanging over the side.

No matter how nerve-racking crossing the lake had been, rescuing Cornell had been worse. Joe had returned Spider's notebook to him and told him all about his experience in the Druckee, including finding Cornell. When Spider learned Cornell was still alive, he'd laughed and cried for joy.

Instead of heading straight to the Point, they had taken a detour to the Long City. Brasque had skillfully steered the Amadragon right to the city's wall. It had been Joe's job to climb into one of the machine's huge buckets as Brasque raised the boom toward the top of the city's highest tower.

Cornell had been standing on the parapet, waiting for him, matted hair dancing wildly in the wind and her tattered dress flapping about her. Joe had wondered how she'd known they were on their way. Then he'd remembered. *Of course,* he'd thought, *she'd have been watching for us on the camera obscura.*

The wheel had still been some twenty feet below the top of the tower when the boom abruptly stopped. Cornell had stared down at him and for an instant looked even crazier than Joe remembered. Then all of a sudden she'd leapt off the tower. She had held out her arms, her dress billowing around her, and to Joe's amazement had glided gracefully down. She'd landed almost elegantly in the puddle at the bottom of the bucket.

"You came back for me," she had said. "Thank you. I knew you would."

Spider had been waiting on the conveyor belt.

"Araik!" Cornell had said, rushing up to Spider. "The children?"

"As soon as you've warmed up, I'll take you," he had said in a kind, courteous voice.

"All right, Araik," Cornell had said, smiling. Joe noticed the way she barely took her eyes off Spider.

In the cab, Brasque had not been happy. He'd noticed that the fuel was low.

"What if we run out?" he'd asked.

"Then we'll have to find some other means of transport," replied Spider. "And, Joe? You'd best get some sleep before we reach the Point, or you'll be no use to anyone."

So Joe had climbed up into the Amadragon's forward tower, but he'd not been able to fall asleep.

Now it was daylight, and Joe clung to the iron girder beside him and stared out across the plain. He could see the sea in the distance. With luck they still might make it before the armistice was signed.

CHAPTER 27

The Point

Joe looked down at the children huddled on the Amadragon's walkways. *Where is Hannah?* he wondered for the umpteenth time. He knew she was among those children; he'd just not yet managed to find her, that was all.

He looked up. Through the steady rain he could see the sea. They were getting closer every minute. Joe wondered what Orlemann would say when he saw his dragon approaching. He wondered what the Elysians and the Meridians gathered at the Point would say.

To his left, lines of coiled barbed wire stretched far into the distance. Similar lines could be seen on the right. On one side were Elysia's lands; on the other,

Merid's. He realized they must be crossing no-man's-land, where he had first entered this world.

Straight ahead he could see the gentle hills that blocked the Point from the rest of the land. The ceremony was taking place on the other side of those hills. In front of them Joe spied a shadow that ran from one side of the spit to the other. He narrowed his eyes and tried to make out what this could be.

"Hey, Joe," called Katherine. Joe looked down and saw her climbing up the tower. A moment later she was sitting next to him on the beam. She smiled, but she didn't say anything. Joe had the feeling that she wanted to tell him something.

"Joe," she finally began, "your sister—"

Joe pulled a face. "No, I haven't found her yet," he said. "I was just about to go and have another look. This rig is so huge, I could easily have missed her."

"No, Joe." Katherine shifted nervously on the beam, not looking at Joe. "I came to tell you that . . . I mean, I don't think—"

But Katherine didn't get the chance to say what she wanted to say, because Joe suddenly realized what made the dark shadow in front of the hills.

"It's Orlemann's machines," he cried. "We've got to tell Spider and the others."

Brasque and Spider were already aware of the machines, and were trying to come up with a way to get past them when Joe and Katherine burst into the cab.

"That's why we haven't seen any while we were crossing the plain," said Brasque. "He has them all here. I daresay no one inside those hills knows they've got such company."

"He probably operates them with those switches in his car," said Joe. "It's the same way he was able to stop them from attacking his convoy."

"That makes sense," mused Spider. "Let's hope he's too busy with what he's doing to notice us arriving."

The Amadragon drove on across the plain. When they arrived at the dike that separated no-man's-land and the Point from the plain, Joe saw that Orlemann had used his transportable bridges to get his machines across. What worked for Orlemann worked for them. The Amadragon moved smoothly over the temporary bridges.

The great bucket wheel at the front of the rig gave Joe an idea.

"I think," he said, "that if you can get right up behind the machines, the boom might just reach the top of that hill in the middle. Then we could use it as a bridge and cross to the Point."

Brasque and Spider were speechless for a moment.

"Talk about clever!" exclaimed Spider. "Will it work, Brasque?"

Brasque blew out a long, whistling breath. "It might," he said.

"There's only one problem," said Katherine, pointing down to the plain. "Orlemann knows we're coming. Look, the machines are moving."

Everyone looked down. The ranks of automatons were scattering like cockroaches, making space so they could maneuver freely. A dozen Goliaths were circling the Amadragon's crawlers, shooting jets of flame at the caterpillar treads and the lower part of the Amadragon's car.

"Keep her going, Brasque," commanded Spider. "They can't do us too much harm. We'll be all right up here, unless, of course, any Scrapers come along."

"I really wish you hadn't said that," said Tom, who had just entered the cab. He pointed to the window, and everyone looked down and saw, far below the Amadragon, three Scrapers opening their hatches; their telescopic arms were beginning to emerge.

"They might be able to hit the charges with those chains!" said Katherine. "What are we going to do?"

"First, we are not going to panic," said Spider sternly.

"We have to get the children out of harm's way. Is that possible?"

"We could try to get them inside the gantry," said Katherine, "but the rooms are pretty packed already."

"If we could get the older ones to climb up the Amadragon's towers," suggested Joe, "they'd be well out of reach up there. They're fairly easy to climb, and there're lots of places to sit."

"Right! That's what we'll do," said Brasque. "Tom, get the men onto it right away."

Tom nodded and swiftly left the cab.

"And find Cornell!" Spider called after him. "She'll keep the children calm."

Just then the Amadragon lurched forward and a violent shudder passed along its entire length.

"What was that?" Joe cried.

"I'm not a hundred percent certain," Brasque said, desperately turning knobs, checking gauges, and pulling levers, "but I've got a horrible feeling we're about to run out of fuel."

CHAPTER 28

Armistice and Abdication

Brasque was not wrong. Moments later, the Amadragon gave another almighty shudder and then simply shut down. The giant rig coasted to a stop a mere fifty yards short of the hills.

"The boom will still reach, I think," said Brasque, peering out the cab window.

"Only thing is," said Spider, "do we have any power to lower it?"

"There's only one way to find out," replied Brasque. "Here goes." Slowly he moved the boom-lowering lever.

Nothing happened. Brasque tried again. Nothing. Then he pulled on the lever so hard that it broke off in his hand.

Joe looked out of the cab window at the Scrapers on the ground below. All three of them had their telescopic arms fully extended, and they were waving their chains menacingly from side to side. Joe didn't doubt that those chains could reach the forward boom.

Joe went outside, ran along the boom, and leaned over the rail. It was a twenty-yard drop to the hillside below. He'd break his neck if he tried to jump down.

How were they going to get to the hillside? He studied the boom, searching for an answer. That was when he noticed the steel cables that held the whole thing in place. Still, how long would it take to cut through them? They were as thick as his forearms.

Below him the Scrapers' chains whipped through the air. Back and forth, back and forth. The mechanical arms were building up speed. It wouldn't be long before they would be able to reach as high as the boom, perhaps higher.

Joe stopped in midthought. Of course. That just might work.

He ran back into the cab.

"I need this!" he said, grabbing Spider's staff and running back out. As he ran back along the boom, he unraveled the grubby bandages until they fanned from the top of the staff like streamers.

"Joe?" called Katherine, running after him. "What are you doing?"

Joe pointed to the Scrapers below. "I'm betting those Scraper chains will be strong enough to break the boom cables. I just need to get the Scrapers to hit them."

Katherine's face turned white. "That's insane, Joe," she said. "What if those chains hit any of the children? What if they hit you?"

"Can you think of a better plan?"

Katherine shook her head. "Be careful!" she shouted.

Joe ran to the end of the boom, lifted Spider's staff above his head, and began to wave it from side to side. "Come on!" he yelled at the top of his lungs.

The Scrapers responded instantaneously, aiming their flying chains right at Joe. It was terrifying to see the chains from one of them fly through the air toward him, but Joe stood his ground. The chains landed with a horrendous crash on the booms above. The booms rocked so violently that Joe was thrown against the rail. He would have fallen through if he hadn't instinctively reached out and grabbed the rail. The pain in his hand rang out as he swung himself back onto the conveyor belt.

Far beneath him, the Scraper pulled back its swinging arm. The chains slid noisily off the boom and crashed back down to the ground. The cables it had hit reverberated with an ear-splitting twang, but to Joe's dismay they remained intact.

A second Scraper now launched its chains. Again they struck the booms above Joe's head, but this time they hit with such force that some of the main struts crumpled as easily as aluminum foil. Joe ducked and held his arms over his head. When this Scraper pulled back its chains, the boom suddenly dropped a yard or two, bouncing violently. When it settled, it was listing at an angle. Joe looked up. One of the cables had been severed. But five more still held the boom in place.

Joe turned and saw Brasque and a group of his Skulkers hurrying up the boom. "We've come to join in the fun!" shouted Brasque.

Joe and Brasque and the other Skulkers leaned over the rail and began to taunt the automatons far below. In a flash three sets of chains wrapped themselves around the boom like whips.

"Hang on!" yelled Brasque, grabbing hold of the rail and Joe's collar at the same time. The chains pulled back, and the boom jolted down another teeth-rattling few yards.

Before long the Scrapers had severed all but one of the cables. Far below, the machines were preparing to strike again.

"This is going to be the biggest jolt," warned Brasque. "Hold fast when the cable goes."

The chains flew toward them in unison. They screamed through the air. Joe gripped the rail as tight as he could. While he was prepared for the shock of the chains hitting the booms, he wasn't ready for the sudden plunge of the booms, nor the violent bang that sent intense vibrations through his entire body when the bucket wheel landed on the top of the ridge.

The air was full of a terrible screeching, whirring noise. It was a hundred times worse than a dentist's drill.

"Would you look at that?" Brasque laughed above the noise. Joe looked where Brasque was pointing and saw a peculiar sight. The Scrapers' chains were tangled over the girders. On the ground below, the three machines were straining to set themselves free. Suddenly the Scrapers' telescopic arms were torn out of their sockets, and the bodies of the three Scrapers shot backward into the rows of other automatons, rolling over and over in a shower of sparks.

"Good work, Joe," Spider called as he strode along the boom. "Can we move the children across now?"

"I think so," Joe replied. "But we'd better be quick."

Joe handed Spider back his staff. Spider pulled the remainders of the tattered bandages off it and threw them on the ground. Then he beckoned Cornell, who was waiting by the gantry. "We'll take the children with us. They won't be safe here. Orlemann will send more machines once he sees what you've done to these."

Spider was right. They could already see more Scrapers moving toward the Amadragon. They had to get the children off the rig as soon as possible.

Cornell quickly brought them along the boom and helped them over the twisted metal, taking special care as they climbed over the tangle of the Scraper chains. Joe was amazed to see how Cornell was with the charges. She seemed to be able to get them to do what she wanted just by asking. Joe noticed that some of the children looked happier when Cornell talked to them. It made him feel guilty that he'd had to use the same methods as Orlemann to get the charges to do what he'd wanted.

On the hill the Skulkers helped the children down to the ground. Joe and Katherine were the last to leave the rig. Katherine started down the ladder, but Joe remained on the boom.

"I'll catch up with you down there," he said. "I didn't see Hannah leave, and I—"

"Don't, Joe," Katherine said desperately. "There are more Scrapers coming. Don't risk it."

"I'm just going to take a last look!" he shouted.

"But, Joe!" hollered Katherine.

Joe turned to see a Scraper's chains crash down in front of him. The force of the blow severed the boom in two. Joe leapt for the ladder on the side of the wheel and clung to it.

With the boom gone, the giant bucket wheel began to teeter on the edge of the ridge.

A horde of Goliaths were straining to climb the steep hill. Brasque hurried to the teetering bucket wheel and set his shoulder against it.

"Jump down, you two!" he shouted. "I need this wheel!"

Joe and Katherine closed their eyes and threw themselves off the ladder. They landed on the ground winded but unhurt.

"Come on!" Brasque commanded his men. "Give a man a hand! One, two, three. Now!" The giant bucket wheel paused for a moment on the edge of the hill. Everyone held their breath. All at once it rolled down the hill toward the wreckage of the rig, gathering speed and leaving a swath of crushed automatons in its wake.

Brasque, Joe, and Katherine joined Spider, Cornell, and all the children on the top of the hill. The natural amphitheater on the Point was full of people who had come to witness the armistice. But just then none of them looked all that interested in the signing of a piece of paper. They were all staring openmouthed at the ragged collection of men and the army of children on the hill.

"I think we'd best get down there and explain ourselves," said Spider. "Come along." Then using his staff to guide him, the blind man led them down the hill.

CHAPTER 29

The Way to End a War

As Spider and his motley entourage made their way down the hill, the huge crowd parted to let them pass. Everyone was staring. Joe felt extremely uncomfortable. He supposed these people who had come to witness the signing of the armistice were both Meridian and Elysian. He looked around at the staring faces. Joe wondered which were which. He would have been hard pressed to tell.

Spider bent down and whispered in Joe's ear, "Am I heading in the right direction?"

"I think so," replied Joe. He quickly described what he saw.

At the center of the arena was a low platform covered

by a white awning. On the platform stood a long table. Two women sat behind it. Joe recognized one of them as Elysia and assumed that the redheaded woman on the right was her sister Merid. Between them stood Orlemann. The table was covered with documents. All three stared in silence at the approaching group. Joe saw that Elysia's eyes were red.

Orlemann's face was like thunder.

Good, thought Joe. *It's time someone spoiled his plans.*

One woman in the crowd suddenly called out, "The rain's stopped!"

The crowd lifted their faces to the sky. Joe did the same. The woman was right.

"The first time in twenty years," someone said.

Spider reached the platform and bowed. Elysia and Merid stared at him.

A clerk was carefully gathering up the papers on the table. He arranged them into a neat pile, then handed them to Orlemann. Orlemann looked them over, nodded, then put them in a leather notecase. He smiled and began putting on his gloves.

"You'd be a terrible ruler, Orlemann," said Spider in a voice that carried all the way across the Point.

Orlemann looked bemused. "The abdication ceremony is complete," he said. "The sisters have willingly passed their power to me. Terrible or not, I am now their ruler. You've come too late, Araik Ben."

Merid gasped. "What is this?" she asked, narrowing her eyes and carefully studying Spider's face.

"Araik Ben!" said Elysia. "Then it *was* you who sent this boy to procure passes that night in Quarain. I had hoped. I am glad you are alive. I never believed you killed Cornell."

"Liar!" spat Merid, spinning around. Her face was livid. "Araik Ben was carrying out your orders when he murdered Cornell!"

Elysia retaliated with equal ferocity. "When would I have ever issued an order to kill my best-loved sister? You were the one who started this war. You were the one who had my sister killed."

Merid opened her mouth to speak, but before she could, a voice rang out from the crowd. "NOBODY KILLED HER! SHE IS NOT DEAD!"

The two sisters stared at Spider.

"Who said that?" asked Merid breathlessly. "Cornell . . . ?"

"Can it be true?" gasped Elysia. "Is she alive?"

"YES, I AM!" cried Cornell as, with a group of charges in her wake, she hurried past Joe and Spider and ran to the platform, rats swinging from her belt.

Elysia looked as though she was trying to speak, but her lips were shaking too much to form the words. Merid fared no better. They staggered around to Cornell's side of the table and stared intently at her face.

"Is it you?" stammered Elysia.

"Really?" croaked Merid.

Cornell threw her arms around her sisters and all three of them burst into great, racking sobs.

"I'm so happy," blubbed Elysia.

"Me too," wailed Merid. "I'm so sorry, Elysia."

"So am I. I'm sorry, too."

"It's all right now," sobbed Cornell, pulling away to look at her sisters, then immediately hugging them close again. "Hush, shush, everything's going to be all right now."

The entire crowd erupted into shouts and cheers and loud whoops of joy. Elysians hugged Meridians, soldiers hugged clerks, while the old women hugged everyone and anyone they could. The clerks threw reams of paper and printed forms high into the air. The charges were picked up gently and kissed and hugged. Everyone was talking all at once, and the noise was so loud that they all had to shout to be heard.

Then suddenly CRACK! A single gunshot rang out above the crowd. Everyone fell silent and looked at

Orlemann, who was standing by the table with the signed papers in his left hand and a pistol pointed at the sky in his right. He smiled.

"There's just one thing that everyone has forgotten," he began. "We have all just witnessed the abdication of power. The documents are all here." He shook the papers at the crowd. "This cannot be undone."

"Mr. Orlemann," said Elysia, "we signed those documents under false pretenses. That, I believe, will make them null and void."

"Not, ma'am, when they have been signed and witnessed in triplicate."

"It occurs to me," said Merid, "that as my ambassador, every shred of information I received during this entire unfortunate war must have passed through your hands."

Orlemann bowed and spread his hands apart.

"But he was *my* ambassador," protested Elysia.

"He was her ambassador and yours," Joe said. "He's been playing you against each other, don't you see?"

"Careful, lad," warned Orlemann. "Remember what you're risking if you speak. I've seen what horrors you harbor in your heart."

Joe took a deep breath and continued. "Orlemann was the one who started the war," he told the sisters. "He wanted to keep the war going until you were ready to hand your power over to him."

"Don't listen to him," said Orlemann. "This is a boy who told his own sister to go away and die. He wanted her to *die!*"

"No, I never wanted that!" Joe said. "I only shouted at her because I was angry. I never meant it. I'm not like you, not in any way." Quickly he started telling everything he knew, everything he'd discovered on his journey. He told the sisters and the crowd how it was Orlemann who built and controlled the machines on the plain, how Orlemann had taken the charges and used them in his mines and factories to build the war machines.

The crowd began to turn ugly. Even the clerks were shouting and demanding justice.

"None of this matters," growled Orlemann. "I am by law your new ruler. I am officially in charge of this land. You will do what I say!"

"Oh, will we now?" shouted Brasque as he and his men quickly surrounded the platform. Four Skulkers took hold of Orlemann and held him fast.

The crowd cheered. But Joe was watching Orlemann and saw him give a meaningful look to someone in the crowd. Joe followed Orlemann's gaze and caught sight of

Wyn. The little thief sank back into the crowd and disappeared.

Joe started after him. It was soon clear that Wyn was heading for Orlemann's limousine, which was parked some way behind the platform. It was while Joe was skimming around the edge of the crowd that Orlemann spoke.

"I think you'll find," he was saying, "that the war is far from over."

All at once there was a roar of engines and a hundred Zamramies appeared on the crest of the ridge, spotlights pointing down toward the crowd.

"You'd better let go of me," he told the Skulkers. They released him and he turned to the sisters.

"Did you really think I needed your permission to take over?" he asked. "That was a mere formality, a courtesy. I rule this land by the authority of these machines, machines that obey my every command."

Orlemann laughed, reached into his pocket, and pulled out a pair of dark goggles. He put them over his eyes.

"This is my land now," he said. "If anyone tries to interfere with me on my way to my car, I will light my Zamramies." Orlemann pointed to Spider. "If anyone doubts the power of these machines, my old teacher's affliction is proof of their potency. Wouldn't you say so, Araik Ben?"

"All right, Orlemann," said Spider, "you've shown how clever you are. Call them off."

"But I rather like the idea of ruling the land of the blind," said Orlemann nastily. "They'd be much easier to control if they were all crippled like you, don't you think?"

Orlemann grabbed Spider's staff and deftly twisted it out of Spider's grasp. He smirked as he ran his hand over the carvings in the polished wood. "Thank you for this souvenir," he said. "Whenever I see it, it will remind me of how I executed you."

Meanwhile, Joe had crept to the rear door of Orlemann's limousine. The tinted window was rolled down, and he could see inside. Wyn had the control panel out in front of him and was busily adjusting several of the knobs.

On the platform, Orlemann was still talking.

"I could, you understand, save myself a lot of trouble and burn you all to cinders." As he said this, a hundred Goliaths appeared along the ridge and aimed their fire-spouting nozzles at the crowd. Orlemann laughed and picked up his hat from the table. He set the hat on his head. "However, if you behave and acknowledge me as your president or emperor or whatever you want to call me, then I will happily spare you. It's your choice." He turned and trotted down the platform steps. The crowd parted to let him pass.

Joe crouched by the side of the car and watched Wyn twiddle knobs on the control panel.

He had to do something and do it quickly. He glanced up and saw Orlemann heading toward the limousine. Orlemann was halfway to the car when he stopped and turned back. He smiled benevolently at the sisters and the crowd around them.

"I can see that you're all wishing for something a little more spectacular. Oh, very well."

He clapped his hands, and a hundred Scrapers drove noisily over the ridge and took their places by the other machines. Each Scraper opened its hatch and began to unfurl its lethal chains.

Orlemann bowed to the crowd, then turned smartly. The chauffeur stepped forward and opened the back door of the limousine.

The car door opening made Wyn jump, and this was all Joe needed. He yanked the other door open and punched Wyn as hard as he could. It was the shock of the blow rather than the power of the punch that sent Wyn reeling across the backseat.

Orlemann was just at that moment lowering himself into the car and his descending backside landed heavily, squishing Wyn's face. Joe leapt in and lunged for the control panel. He gritted his teeth and, hoping that he was remembering the panel correctly, threw a series of switches and held them in place.

The automatons responded instantly as Joe threw them into reverse. The sky shook with the terrible noise. Orlemann screamed as all at once every machine raced backward down the far slope of the hills. A second later his screams were drowned out by a tremendous crash and a series of fiery explosions.

The Skulkers rushed to the limousine. They seized Orlemann and Wyn and dragged them out.

Spider was right behind the Skulkers. "You had so much talent," he said, taking back his staff. "You could have been the greatest inventor of us all, but you were a malicious, greedy fool. You forgot what I always told you. You forgot that people matter more than things, didn't you, Orlemann?"

Orlemann said nothing.

Spider shook his head in disgust. "Take him away," he said.

As the Skulkers began to drag him away, Orlemann caught sight of Joe.

"People matter more than things, do they, Carey?" he shouted. "How hypocritical of you! Does Joe know how you used him to get what you wanted?"

"What's he talking about?" Joe asked Katherine. She didn't answer. She wouldn't even look at him.

"What's he talking about?" asked Joe, starting to feel frightened now. "Katherine?"

"I tried to tell you . . . ," she began. "I didn't know how. I tried . . ."

Orlemann was grinning. "They lied to you, Joe," he laughed. "They pretended to help you look for your sister, but they knew all the time that she wasn't here."

"What do you mean?" Joe said. His voice trembled as he spoke.

"Your sister isn't here!" Orlemann was shouting now. "She isn't the one who is sick. She isn't close to death, Joe. You are!"

Joe felt as though someone had hit him. He sank to the ground. His injured hand suddenly throbbed, and he nursed it in the crook of his arm. He looked at the bruises and the pinprick-size bloody scabs, then closed his eyes and saw again the images from his dream. He saw the hospital bed, his mother sitting on one side, his father on the other. As before, he looked down at the figure lying so still beneath the blanket. He saw the hand, the hand with the tubes and needles attached to it, and suddenly he knew it was not his sister's hand. It was too big, and the needle marks and the bruises matched those on the back of his own hand.

Joe felt cold all over. He steeled himself and did what he'd never dared to do before. He lifted his eyes to the hospital pillow.

And then he knew for sure.

CHAPTER 30

After the War

It was said that the rain stopped at the same moment the Amadragon ran out of fuel. Its endless plume of smoke had made the clouds and the fog that blanketed the land. Once their source was taken away, the clouds and the fog began to disperse. Now the war was over, the sun came out, and almost everyone was happier for it.

Everyone except Joe.

After he learned the truth, he hid himself in the crowd of charges. Katherine had chased after him, but Joe just shrugged off her attempts to explain why they had kept him in the dark. It didn't matter, he told himself. But it did. He felt like a fool. He'd been blaming himself all along for what had happened to Hannah. But nothing had happened to Hannah. It had all happened to him.

Joe stayed among the charges, but he found no comfort there. The charges were happier now because they were well looked after and there was no one to shout at them or force them to work. No one threatened to tell the world their most shameful secrets.

Orlemann was banished beyond the mountains, and his crystal bridge was destroyed. Wyn and the secret police who remained loyal to Orlemann were sent there also. Orlemann's collection of working models was dismantled by the Heathermen, and their innovative components adapted to make toys of a joyous and creative nature.

The restoration of the city began with the reopening of the arches. Now the children could leave the island when their time came.

Joe kept his head down and tried to stay out of sight. In the end it was Cornell who found him and tried to make him understand. He was out by the city wall, watching a group of workers on one of the many building sites that had sprung up all over the city. Even in his miserable state Joe couldn't help but marvel at the changes. Every morning the sight of the sun hitting the towers and making their bricks gleam like gold made him smile. The sky was now a brilliant blue all day long. It hadn't rained for weeks.

Three of the workers were digging a deep trench for the foundations of the new building when Joe sensed someone standing beside him. He stiffened as Cornell put her arm around him and gave him a squeeze.

"You can't go on like this," she said. "You have to look at things another way. Try to see it from another point of view."

Joe squirmed inside, hating it when adults told him that. He waited for her to go on, but Cornell didn't say any more. He turned to look at her, but she'd gone, and Katherine stood in her place.

"I'm sorry we didn't tell you," she said. She cleared her throat. "To begin with, it was only a little lie to get you to come with me, when you were being so obstinate. But then later, I couldn't tell you." Katherine sighed. "If it's any consolation, Spider said we'd never have ended the war without you, Joe. You gave us hope. Without you I would never have known what the sky looks like when the rain stops. You stopped it, Joe. You stopped the rain, you stopped Orlemann, you stopped the war."

Joe shrugged.

Then Katherine lost her temper. "Would you rather it was your sister who was sick instead of you?" she asked.

Joe turned and looked Katherine in the eye. "Of course I'm glad that Hannah's all right. It's just that—"

"It's just that you're angry we didn't tell you," said Spider as he stepped into the sunlight. "Perhaps we should have," he mused. "Perhaps that would have been the better thing to do. But at the time we thought we were acting for the best."

Joe looked at them then and remembered that they had risked just as much as he had. And they had suffered more.

"How long will I be here?" asked Joe after a long silence. "Tell me the truth this time."

Spider shrugged and smiled. "I don't know, Joe. No one does. One day you're here, one day you'll go." Spider leaned his back against the low wall and turned his face up to the sun. "But I will tell you this—you'll be home much sooner if you stop moping about like a wet blanket. I hear you're putting the other charges off their supper."

"What do you suggest I do?" grumbled Joe. "Keep busy?"

"It would be a start," said Spider. "Joe!" he shouted. "Look around you! We're rebuilding the finest city ever built. We need someone with bright ideas. Will you help?"

"What can I do?"

"Anything you like," said Spider. "Anything you've ever wanted to build or make or invent. Any machine or entertainment or gadget you can think of. If you can think of it, we'll find a way to build it, and build it well, too. Katherine will help, and Cornell and all the Heathermen. I promised Brasque I'd design him a car. Surely you'd have some ideas about that."

Joe couldn't help but be interested. He didn't resist when Spider, still chattering on about all the things they would build, took his arm and began to lead him back through the winding roads of the city.

CHAPTER 31

Home

Joe no longer dreamed. Every night when he tumbled into bed he was too exhausted. He worked hard every day, touring the city with Spider and Katherine, coming up with ideas for parks and fairs and firework shows, helping Cornell reorganize the library, and even pitching in on some of the building sites with the ex-Skulkers, who were all natural builders. His first major project was to plan the rebuilding of the Amadragon, only this time it was made exactly to Spider's original specifications as a fully operational, portable fair. It was going to be wonderful.

One night, though, Joe did dream. It was the strangest dream of all, and it was the last dream he dreamed in that land. And this dream was the only thing he remembered when all other memories had faded away.

He'd stayed up late that night. Supper had been full of laughs. Spider had been there, and Katherine and Tom and Brasque and Cornell and a handful of Skulkers. Everyone had told stories of the days before the war, or of the daft things they'd heard Joe say. They all laughed and ate and drank a great deal, and it had been a jolly, joy-filled evening.

Joe had gone to bed with their voices ringing in his ears, and he'd fallen asleep with a smile on his face. It never crossed his mind that that was the last time he would ever see his friends.

In his dream he was back on the plain trying to get past the automatons. He was alone, and he was frightened. It was raining again, and everything felt so real that for a moment he was sure he'd just dreamed that the war was over. His head hurt, too, like it had the night that Hannah—no, the night that *he*—had fallen ill. In his dream he ducked down under an old derelict out of sight of a Goliath.

When he looked to see if the coast was clear, she was there. Hannah. She was standing a few yards in front of the derelict, and she was smiling at him.

"Hannah," he said. "Hannah, get down."

He knew she heard him, but she didn't move. Her

eyes were shining. There was something strange about her. She was there and yet not there. The rain was falling right through her. It was as though she were a ghost.

"Joe," she said, "it's all right, Joe. You can come home now."

Hannah held out her hand, and as Joe took hold of it the rain and the plain and the derelict all disappeared and he found himself standing beside his sister in the circular room with the beautiful mosaic on the walls and the floor and the ceiling. And there in front of him were the three arches, no longer blocked, but open and waiting for him to pass through.

Joe took a step forward, then hesitated. Beyond each arch was only darkness. There was no way of telling where they would lead.

Hannah squeezed his hand. "Go on," she said, giving him a little smile. "It's okay."

Joe smiled back at her. Then he let go of his sister's hand, ducked his head, and stepped through the arch on his left.

At first he thought he'd made a terrible mistake. Everything went black, and he felt as though he were falling from a great height at a million miles an hour.

"Hannah?" he tried to say, but he couldn't move his mouth. His lips felt dry and stiff, and his hand hurt more than ever. It felt as though someone had hammered a hundred nails into the back of it. Joe desperately wanted to pull the nails out. He tried to lift his other hand so he could reach across, but he found he could barely move his fingers. They felt as heavy as lead.

Suddenly the silence was full of sound. Someone was shouting in a harsh foreign language. Joe winced. The voices boomed and echoed in his ears. He wanted to tell whoever was shouting to shut up and leave him alone. None of the sounds was familiar. Everything echoed. He breathed in and smelled the sharp, lemony smell of disinfectant.

Then someone pulled his eyelid open and shone a light in. Joe screamed and screamed and suddenly found that his right hand was free. He reached over and quickly started to pull at the needles that were sticking in his left hand. Other hands tried to stop him.

"Joe, sweetheart! Leave them in, they're doing you good, darling."

Joe opened his eyes. His mother's face was there, right in front of him. Tears were running down her cheeks, but she was laughing.

"Where's Hannah?" he whispered.

"Shush, lie still, darling," said his mother.

But Joe wanted to see his sister. He wanted to make sure she was all right. He tried to turn his head to see if she was in the hospital room. His father was there, and a nurse, but there was no sign of Hannah. The effort exhausted him. Joe closed his eyes and fell back into the darkness.

When he woke, his mother was still beside him, and Dr. Ben, his pediatrician, was taking his pulse.

"How are you feeling, Joe?" asked Dr. Ben.

"Hannah?" asked Joe, trying to lift his head off the pillow.

"She'll be here soon," said his mom. "Your dad's gone to fetch her from Gran's. Hannah'll be so pleased to see you. She's been coming here every day with the same present for you."

Joe sank back against the pillow. He didn't know why he was so desperate to see his sister. He had the feeling that he had been a long way away, as though he'd been on a journey, but he couldn't remember where.

"Joe!"

Joe opened his eyes and saw his little sister standing by the door. She was grinning from ear to ear. Joe grinned back at her as best he could. Hannah rushed up to the bed. "Look, Joe!" she said, slapping a flat plastic bag down on his chest. "Look what me and Granny got for you. Granny paid, but I picked it. It's a present. Look, look."

Not waiting for Joe to open the bag, Hannah tipped it upside down, and a brand-new copy of *Monster*

Machine magazine slid out onto the blanket. Hannah held it up, not noticing that she was crumpling up the corners with her hands.

Joe didn't care. He looked at his sister and smiled.

"Do you like it, Joe?"

"It's brilliant, Hannah," he said. "Thank you. It's exactly what I've always wanted."

Orlemann's
Iron House

Foundries

Amadragon

Long Lake

Merid's Lands

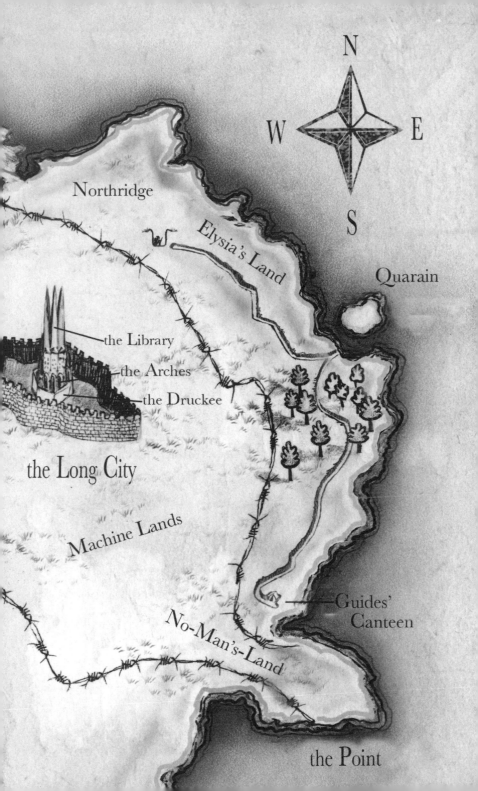

Marcy Malloy

Carol Hughes grew up in England, in a seaside town where her parents kept a small hotel. When she got older, she went to art school to study painting. But instead of drawings, she filled her sketchbooks with notes and stories. Not long afterward she moved to the United States and began writing. She now lives in Los Angeles with her husband and two daughters.

For more information, please visit Carol's Web site at www.carol-hughes.com.